THE
QUARTERS

Mari Bell

ISBN: 069245344X
ISBN 13: 9780692453445

I dedicate this novel to the most influential, loving, supportive, and funny women in my life, my momma, Pearline C. Scrutchins and my grandma, Louise Scott.
I would also like to thank the wonderful community of Bell Quarters.

1

Louise

Momma didn't give me no middle name. She said that's showing off; middle names ain't for folks like us. So, I'm just Louise. Me and my sistah Honey is only a few years part, two to be exact. I'm fifteen, the oldest, and the one in charge since Momma died. She passed on from what they call Turberlis or something like that. I can't say it right, so I'll just call it the TB. Sides, that's what I heard the other folks say it was.

It started with her coughing a little here and a little there. Then she couldn't eat or keep nothing down. Was always bent over and reaching for something to vomit in. She stayed mighty pitiful for a long time. That TB messed up her breathing and, from what it seem, everything else. Standing, sitting, even laying down was troublesome for her. She fought for every breath she took. The end was real hard for her and us too, seeing her go like that. Finally, with his mercy, the good Lawd took her on with him. Momma's funeral was the first and last time I seen my Daddy cry. Granny Rose cried too, but just a little. I heard her when she leaned over and told Pastor Franklin that ain't nothing 'pared to losing no child, but this one here done suffered long enough. She better with the Lawd.

Our Daddy, he still living, but barely. Naw, that ain't right for me to say, 'cause he seem to be fairly good, except for that li'l limp he walk with. He had polio as a boy and it twisted his right leg some. But he fine now. So I guess I'll go on and take what I said back. I only said he barely living, 'cause of his new wife. She the one who put a dampen on his living and everybody else's round here.

That woman stood in line with the rest of the widows and unmarred ladies in our town, all hoping to court Daddy now that Momma was gone. I thought it was a shame how they carried on over him with they smiling and giggles. We couldn't even get Momma in the ground good before they all started showing up, one after the other. They knocked on our front door so much the hinges got loose.

We found that out the evening skinny Miss Ophelia came by with some hot soup. That woman barely weigh ninety pounds, but when she knocked on the door to come in, it fell right out the frame into the sitting room. That was a lucky day for ol' big behind Miss Pansy. See, right after Miss Pansy, who was also visiting that day, stepped away from that same door to hug Daddy and offer her condolences, for the fourth time, the door came crashing down. Dust flew everywhere and that loud bang scared her something awful. She nearly fell running cross the room. I do believe she wet herself.

The crash and commotion didn't scare Granny Rose none at all. Just caused her to fold her arms real tight and narrow her eyes in the direction of Miss Pansy. She finally leaned over to her best friend, Miss Maggie, and said, "That doe shoulda fell on her. Pansy need to go and sit her big behind self-down somewhere. Need to put on a girdle, if you ask me, with all that butt rolling going on."

"A man can't help but to look at it. Good Lawd, her behind say how-do for she do," Miss Maggie added with a nod.

Now, why Miss Pansy's behind riled up Granny Rose and Miss Maggie so much, I don't know. But me and the others in earshot got a good snicker out of the whole fuss.

The constant door knocking following Momma's burial day was irritating; however, it did guarantee one thing, food and plenty of it. We ate real good. Them women brought mo food than the entire Colored Army could eat. Sweet potato pies, rhubarb pies, blackberry dumplings, lemon cookies, and chocolate cakes was spread all over the kitchen. Boiled and barbequed pig feet, ham with cola poured on it, baked and fried chicken, polk salad, collard greens, turnip roots, yeast rolls, corn and crackling bread kept us full as hogs.

It musta been 'bout three weeks later when the knocking finally slowed down. The ladies stopped coming so much like they first did. Well, all except for one.

Granny Rose said, "That one there done put her hooks in him. She like a mangy dog with a bone."

Granny was right. Wasn't long before Daddy made his decision. One we all thought coulda been a better one. He soon introduced us to his new wife and our new step momma, Miss Jean.

Just plain old mean is how I would describe that woman; I might even add evil too. She was a big woman with funny-looking big hands and feet to match. And she stood well over

Daddy at least three feet. Fussing and complaining or finding fault with us was routine for Miss Jean. She was just happy being unhappy. She had no children of her own, no friends, not even the dog liked her. The main targets of disgust were usually me and my sistah. Although her unruly tirades on occasion could be quite random. *"Them chillun eat too much. Ate up every bit of that stew I made last night. They always into something. That postman, know he always late. Ain't he suppose to be here earlier in the day? Come sometimes at ten in the morning, then other times late as three in the evening. Probably somewhere slippin in some of that devil water. I should tell his bossman on him. Next time I go to town, I just might do that.*

Daddy was a mild but proud man, not like his *lovely* wife. She had a big mouth and was bossy. "Wallace!" she'd yell out to him, always in an irksome tone of voice. It wasn't a yell or scream, just odd and bothersome. She'd rattle him and anyone else nearby. Her behavior, along with the house, land, and money her father left her in his will, allowed her to control him. We all knew who was in charge.

Over the next few years, Miss Jean went from secretly disliking me and Honey to making it no secret at all. She made it real clear that if she had her way, me and my sistah would be out of her hair. We was nothing but a pain to her and she shared this with anybody that would listen. I once heard her tell a lady from the church, *Ifin I had chilluns of my own, I woulda did a much better job of raising them than Wallace and that dead wife of his. Seem to me that them two ain't do nothing but feed them; no raising at all.*

My little sistah was no taller than a stalk of collards when I took over. Right before Momma passed on, she made sho to tell me, look out for everybody real good. I do believe she would be proud. I wash, comb, grease, and plait Honey's hair. Though at times, it gets hard on me and her 'cause she real tender-headed and always be snatching away. I make certain she wash herself, eat right, brush her teeth, and don't wear no dirty clothes. That's one thing I remember 'bout my Momma. Even when she was sick, she hated to see folks walking round with dirty clothes on. She used to say, *You may be po, but ain't got to look like it.*

So, that's what I do. I take care of everybody. Though, since Daddy got his new wife, he don't need much tending to. I still make certain he eat his oatmeal. It seem to keep him regula. He get mighty fussy when he ain't regula. Now, Honey on the other hand, she need plenty tending to. She always into something, getting a whooping for this or a pinch for that. Before Momma died, she would send Honey out to gather three switches 'bout every other day. And they'd be all for Honey. When she come in with two, she got turned right round to go make three.

"Something ain't right 'bout having to get yo own whipping switch. And can you believe that woman make me braid them too? Just ain't right," Honey would say with a bit of confusion on every trip to the hedge bush.

Things round here have changed since Momma been gone. Even the sun don't seem to shine as bright. All of us miss her something bad. Daddy try and hide it, but I know he do. Sometimes, I catch him staring out the window. When I ask him what he's looking at, he just mumble *nothing* and walk away. One thang that ain't changed, though, is that Honey.

That sistah of mine done had a thing for boys ever since she was a teeny thing. Seem like she always had a fella here, a fella there. They was always somewhere "sniffing around," as Momma would say. I believe Momma first took notice of Honey's peculiar likings in church.

"Turn yo hine-tail round, little girl. And what you smiling and waving at with yo fast self? Lawd, ain't nothing back there but some bad-tail boys. Stop all that right now before I's get my switch in this here church."

Honey would always wiggle herself around on the pew and end up looking to the rear of the church where the boys sat. She did this when the singing got loud and Momma got to shouting. All the noise and praising in church kept Momma busy and preoccupied. This way Honey could get out all the flirting she desired.

"I ain't neva seen nothing like it before, Momma. Gone have to watch this chile of mine," Momma told Granny Rose, who very much agreed.

I'm sho Momma had no notion of just how much watching Honey would need. I sure didn't.

"No need for you to get upset with me, now. I'm just calling it like I see it. And would you stop all that crying?" I said.

"Well, you act like it's my fault."

"Well, ain't it? Alls um saying is looks like every boy that comes yo way seem to end up like this." After noticing a large splatter of blood on the chifferobe, I pointed it out to Honey to clean up. "Look ova there. You missed a spot. And put some more soap in that bucket and pass it to me."

"That ain't exactly so, Louise," Honey said 'tween sniffles. "Ain't happen to Norris, Hudson, Clement or Ulysses. Bo, well, he just the third one. And it was an accident anyway.

Didn't mean to do it, just scare him is all. Didn't know it could go off like that."

"Honey, that's what guns 'pose to do. Go off. Goodness," I said, wound up.

"I done told him a million times bout sneaking up on me like that. Scaring me. Jumping out like a rabbit at folks. Wasn't funny to nobody but him."

"Well, you ain't got to worry 'bout him doing that no mo, now do you? Or much else, for that matter," I whispered under my breath.

Me and Honey worked real hard in the sitting room scrubbing the walls, baseboards, and floors. Our mix of bleach, soap, and a drop of turpentine was sho to clear up the splatter that Honey had created, and hopefully the smell too. The entire mess was making me a little dizzy and sick on my stomach, but I knew I had to keep it together.

"See, my plan was to do the scaring this time," Honey shared while wringing out the soiled rag she had just removed from the bucket. "Last night, I grabbed Daddy's baby out of the cabinet and set it on my lap. I must have dozed off 'cause when he come round the corner and jumped out at me, I-I hopped up and dropped it. Heck, I didn't know the thing was loaded. Neva saw Daddy put one bullet in it. Just didn't happen like I planned, is all."

"Clearly. And what 'scuse you got bout Joe and Ned?"

"Ain't no 'scuse and ain't right for you to bring that up now, Louise, but since you did. Well, how was I 'pose to know Joe 'lergic to turnip roots? What Colored boy you know can't eat turnip roots? He was sitting there stuffing that fat face of his, just eating away, running his mouth as usual, and then all of a sudden his face started turning blue, then red, all kinds of colors, I tell you. His eyes got real big and scary, and the next thang you know—his face plopped right down in that plate. Scared the life out of me."

"Yeah, and him too," I said.

"Hush yo mouth, smarty pants. And I ain't gone talk "bout no Ned, so don't you ask. You thank this gone leave a stain right here?"

"A stain?" I asked in disbelief. She was worried 'bout a stain and a dead young man lay less than two feet away from us? Shaking my head, I told her, "Never mind. Just keep scrubbing."

We both worked real hard to remove any evidence. The room had to reflect the same order it had before the return of Daddy and Miss Jean. The pair had driven up to Lumpkin for a tent revival and would return sometime later.

Once our task was complete, we burned the rags that we cleaned with and scattered the ashes out back behind the shed. It was the perfect place since Daddy didn't go back there much and Miss Jean never did. We made sho to wash out the buckets that were tarnished with his blood and placed them exactly back on the iron hooks attached to the shed just as we had found them.

"Everythang put away? Did you scatter those ashes like I told you to?" I asked Honey.

"Yes."

"Okay, good. Now we got to get him on out of here with his big ol' self."

We both grabbed a leg apiece and began to drag Bo out of the back door. It was a good thing he was dead. His poor head bobbled along the floor like a bouncing ball and even got hung up on one of the nails that popped from the floorboard.

"Be careful, Honey."

"Gurl, he don't feel nothing anyway. Good grief. Man, he heavy."

"Pull and stop complaining. Shoot, Daddy be back sooner than later. Last thang he needs to see is me and you dragging Bo back here."

"Um pulling."

We finally got Bo's body out of the house and in the backyard. We sat him upright and leaned him against the old oak tree. Just in case an unexpected guest showed up, he'd look like he was out there sleeping. Honey walked around to the back of the shed and found that old wheelbarrow we used to haul any and everything in, including bodies. Finally, after several failed attempts, we hoisted him into the barrow, nearly breaking both our backs. We rolled him over to Miss Jean's car trunk and, with all our might, we flipped him in. Honey quickly tucked a quilt over him, saying he might get cold back there. I just looked at her.

"You remember how to get there?" she asked me.

"I remember. You just keep quiet and pray we get back before Daddy and Miss Jean."

We climbed in the front of the car and faced the same problems we did every time we'd snuck that old Chevy. Neither one of us was quite tall enough or permitted to drive yet. However, those things never stopped us before and tonight would certainly be no different. Since I couldn't see over the steering wheel, I piled two of Miss Jean's Sears and Roebuck catalogues for me to sit on. Now, they made me taller, but that also presented a predicament for my feet. I'd sit up so high, my feet would dangle away from the pedals. So, to remedy that, Honey would scoot down on the floorboard and press both the gas and brakes as directed. Fortunately, we never got caught. Although one time Old Man Purtis, who lived up the way, told Daddy he could have sworn he seen us girls out driving one night. Daddy paid him no mind since Mr. Purtis is blind in one eye and can't see real good out the other.

After driving an hour from the house, we reached the old Coleman cotton plantation. Way back when, Daddy said this field was prosperous, that all you saw for miles and miles was bright white cotton. He also said that the prosperity started and stopped with Rhett and Savannah Coleman and they rotten chilluns. The Coloreds that worked the fields made next to nothing, barely enough to feed themselves, much less they family. Most of the workers were sharecroppers that lived on his land and worked off they debt on that back-breaking red dirt. Once old man Coleman passed, his wife and chillun foolishly stop paying they taxes on the land and lost everything to the government. All that was left was an old withered field that no longer found a reason to bloom.

Driving through that dark and high weeded field unnerved both of us.

"Louise, I hate this place. It's spooky out here."

"Nevermind that. What's in the trunk of this car is a lot mo spooky."

After arriving at the location we had used twice before, we stopped the car.

"Is this the spot, Honey?"

"Looks like it. Last time we was here, I stuck a tall iron rod in the ground. Just in case we came out here again, I'd know where we was the last time. Can you see it?"

"Yeah, there it is over there."

We both nervously got out of the car and opened the trunk.

"Yep, he's still back here," Honey said.

"Was you 'specting him to have other plans? Good grief, Honey. Grab one of those shovels and get to digging. Rememba now, we gotta make sho this hole is as deeper than it is wide. Just like before. Got it?"

"Okay."

We began digging and slinging away the dirt from where it rested. We dug and dug until I gave the nod that the hole was plenty.

"Come help me pull him out of this trunk," I said to Honey as she stood there completely exhausted and scared.

"I'm tired and I want to go home."

"We both do. It's almost over," I said to her, both irritated and protective.

We finally hauled him out of the trunk, which was no easy task. It was more challenging getting him out than was putting him in. It almost felt like he was pulling away from us. Though I know that wasn't the case. Once his body hit the ground we rolled him to the hole. I bet we were a sight to see, two girls rolling a dead man to his grave in an old cotton field.

"Push, c'mon and push, Honey. He's almost in."

"Okay," she said, grunting with her final push as he landed in the hole. "Now what?" she asked as though this was all new to her. I shot her a quick look with the belief she read every word I was thinking.

We packed the dirt real tight on top of the ground. Next we kicked some loose dirt on top of that, to disguise any hint of disturbance. Then we recited a quick prayer of "God bless the dead and us too." It was the same prayer we'd prayed the last two times we were out here.

"Okay, Honey, this is it. I can't do this no mo. You understand. Not one mo time."

"Okay, but you know they was all an accident."

"I don't care what they was. This the last time, you hear? And we will never, ever talk about this again. Ever. Now give me your finger."

Grabbing each other's pinkie and spitting two times on each side of us was a ritual we created long ago. It was our way of sealing a promise. We were fortunate and we both knew it. Bo, Joe nor Ned would be missed and if so, very little.

I worried over that while I was driving home. Bo often left Preston for long periods of time, looking for work in different counties. However, when he was around, he was always drinking, carousing, and fighting, creating a ruckus wherever he went. Those behaviors made his absences hoped-for and pleasing, for anyone unlucky enough to have been in his presence.

As for Joe, he was a hobo that lived more on trains than not. Honey met him one day while she was out picking blackberries. After noticing he did more eating than picking, she felt sorry him and decided she'd invite him over one night for supper. She chose a night that would line up with Daddy and Miss Jean's church outings. It turned out to be a dreadful meal. For supper that night, she served strickalean, butter beans, and Miss Jean's favorite, turnip roots.

As for Ned, to this day I'm not sho what happened. All Honey told me was that she was out picking dandelions and he joined her to pick them also. He was a little sweet on her, so he followed her around like a li'l puppy dog. They walked up to Pleasant Grove and had picked about six of them when a bee started buzzing around. That bee was getting on her nerves so much that when it landed on Ned's arm, she swatted and killed it. Po Ned, he musta been 'lergic too. She said he dropped like a rock. A man did come round looking for him, but he didn't look long.

We finally got back to the house and not a moment too soon. Good thing for us Daddy kept Miss Jean's car in the back of the house. Otherwise, he would have surely smelled its fumes and noticed that it had been moved.

"Time for church, get to getting up," Daddy yelled from the hallway early the next morning after our latest adventure. "My, it smells awfully fresh round here. You girls been cleaning?"

Both of us lay in our beds just as awake as we were when we laid down the night before. Hearing his voice was a reminder that last night was not a dream.

"Louise?"

"Yes, Honey."

"You all right?"

"Yes, Honey, I'm fine. We fine."

"You think we ought to tell Daddy?"

"Tell Daddy what?"

"You know."

In an almost whisper I began to scold my sistah. "No, I don't and you don't neither. Now look-a-here, what you thank happened last night didn't happen, and you better get that in yo big head and right now. We already done planted two men 'cause a you, now it's three. You understand. You done forgot our promise already?"

"Naw, but—"

"No buts, lessen of course you want to go and wear one of them fancy uniforms and break up some rocks with Uncle Vern."

"No, I don't. Sides, ain't no girls on the chain gang anyway. Miss Know-It-All."

"It ain't? Oh yes there is. Where you thank Uncle Vern's wife Glory been all this time, on some fancy ship sipping tea with the Queen of England? I'll tell you where she is, right there in Milledgeville at the prison camp for Colored women."

"For real? Daddy said she just moved up north."

"Uh-huh. She moved north, all right, from the bottom bunk bed north to the top one. Now, any minute Daddy gone knock on that door. You better get yo self together now and wipe away them tears. Hear me?"

"Yeah, I hear you."

"Good. It's time for church anyway. Whatcha wearing?"

"I don't know, don't really care."

"Hope it ain't that yellow, orange, and brown dress Miss Jean made you last Easter. That dress got to many toos."

"Huh? Too many toos?"

"It's too big and too ugly. The zipper won't zip, and the sleeves and hem is uneven. She always pinning something up on somebody. Got us walking round looking like two Colored pok-e-pines with all them pins and needles."

"Yeah, and it hurt something awful when they pop loose," Honey said, rubbing her side remembering the last pinch.

"Who told her one-eye self she could sew anyway? Always telling me, *thread this, thread that*. I can't see them li'l holes in her needles no better than she can. Boy, she get on my nerves."

Giggling, Honey made sure not to wear that outfit.

We continued to dress as a second knock came from the door.

"Hush up all that playing and get ready for church. Ya'll know I don't believe in being late."

"Yes suh," we both said.

❧

"What ya'll girls been into?" Mr. Percy said when me and Honey bumped into him in the feed store after church.

"Suh?" I said surprised to see him standing there.

"Hump. You two into something. I know that for sho." He said.

Last we seen Mr. Percy was when we drove by him on our way to bury Bo. He noticed us when we walked in the store. Daddy sent us there to buy flour for Miss Jean to burn some chicken for supper that evening.

"Ya'll still staying in trouble?" he asked, looking at us with his good eye.

"Naw suh. Ain't been in no trouble at all," I said, as Honey snickered and walked away.

"Uh-huh. I know what I seen that night," he mumbled to me. "Ain't fooling nobody."

"Have a good day suh," I said and pulled Honey out the store with me.

"Ain't funny, Honey."

"Oh, yes it is."

2

We were not going to stay home for long. Not with Miss Jean climbing up our backs all the time. Honey was the first to jump. She's been gone a while now. Since she left, my life of church and cleaning has changed to a life of church, cleaning, and raising chilluns. Honey never was happy sticking around after those boys we put in the ground. As time passed, the young men's absence did not prove to be a concern for anybody in our town. This was a sad truth for the men, but a fortunate one for me and Honey.

Still, that did not change her nature. Sides falling in love every time she turned around, Honey was feisty and sassy. Her tongue was swift, matching her temper. She was quick to fight anyone, man, woman, or child that she felt teetered on any line she drew, literally. During a confrontation, she was known to take a stick and draw a line in the dirt. *No need in crossing it*, she'd say, *I'll just step right over and save you the trouble.*

Me, on the other hand, had no desire to end a fight, much less start one. As her big sistah, I was thoughtful and protective of her. I had to be. Whenever she needed me, which was mo times than not, I'd always be somewhere near. Always just in time to save someone from Honey or simply save Honey. Maybe she was experiencing some divine intervention by way of me, or maybe the devil was just having fun at my expense. Either way, it got on my nerves.

"Yo temper is awful bad, Honey. I'm tired of breaking up yo dumb fights. You always somewhere into something. Getting too old for this."

"It's called defending myself, Louise. I don't start nothing, I's just finish it. "

"You don't finish nothing. I do. Seem like I have to stand in the corner at the schoolhouse more times than you do."

"Well, Granny Rose said standing good for yo back anyway. Oughta be thanking me. Did you a favor."

"Humph, naw you didn't. Some favor. Almost got hit in my eye the last time breaking up your foolishness. Don't take much to get you riled up at all. Just looking at you seem to stir you wrong."

"Depend on who doing the looking," Honey said right before she sprung a surprise on me. "Guess what?"

"What?"

"I been thinking 'bout moving from here."

"Moving? Where? You know Daddy ain't gonna let you go nowhere."

"What you talking 'bout, ain't gone let me? We out of school and um almost grown."

"Yeah, and that almost the only part he looking at."

"Well, I'm leaving anyway. Too many bad memories here. Just time to go is all. Been thinking on Columbus or maybe LaGrange. Been to both a few times with Granny Rose."

"For what?"

"To help with them babies. Sides, they betta than this place, anythang is. I figure I'll get me a job cleaning, since that's all I do round here anyway. Why not get paid for it?"

"Cleaning what?"

"Folks' houses, stores, I don't know. I can do some washing too."

"And where you plan on staying? You don't even know nobody in Columbus or LaGrange."

"Don't need to know nobody. I'll find somewhere even if it's at the Salvation Army for a little while. I hear they gives you a hot meal and a cot to sleep on too. Even heard the white folks nice to you there. Mr. Earl told me that they has to be 'cause they's preachers for everybody, not just the white folks.

"Un know 'bout that, Honey. Don't sound right," I said, at the same time thinking I was no more ready for her to leave than I was watching summer turn to fall. She needed me and by the way I was feeling, I needed her too.

"Well, um going, Louise, I got to. Sometimes I feel like I can't breathe round here. Ain't nothing to do here but pick cotton and I ain't neva eva going to a cotton field again."

"Salvation Army huh?"

"Not sho yet, but I'll find somewhere to stay. But you can't say nothing to Daddy."

I hadn't even considered that side of it, lying to Daddy. "How am I not gone tell him?"

"Easy. Just keep yo mouth shut. Won't take me long to find a place and some work. Something different be good for me. Not sho when, but I'm leaving soon. Just know, the day you wake up and I ain't here, I'm gone be in Columbus or LaGrange."

We continued to walk down the dusty road, some in conversation, but mostly deep in thought. Us two were thick as thieves and this was anything but a good idea to me. Not to mention, Miss Jean would turn her attention from me and Honey to just me. This was one time that being the center of attention was something I did not look forward to.

In less than a month, that day finally came. I woke up to a note folded on my pillow.

Louise, stop starring at this letter and give it to Daddy. Thank you kindly.

> *Dear Daddy,*
> *I know you gone disagree with this and call me contrary, and a few other thangs not so Christian like, but I'm 17 now and can make my own decisions. I moved to Columbus. It's only a few miles up the road. Thought it be best that I get out on my own and make it. I'm fine and not scared one bit. Just time is all. No need in you driving up to Columbus and branging me back, 'cause I'll just leave again. Just causing you mo headache and mo worry.*
> *When I get good and settled, I'll write you again.*
> *Love always,*
> *Honey*

After Daddy and Miss Jean finished yelling and threatening to whoop me for not telling him of Honey's plans, he finally calmed down. Those several minutes of him chasing me around the house tired him out. I swore up and down—with my fingers crossed, of course, because I was sho lying—that I was just as surprised as he was and that this was purely an act of hers alone. Clearly, saddened by her departure and concerned as well, Daddy decided against his better judgment to let her go. Columbus was only an hour or so up the road and if need be, he could always bring her back home.

"That gal always been headstrong and contrary, Mr. Wallace," Miss Jean said. "Ifin I was you, I'd go up there and tan that hide of hers. Who she thank she is, just no respect what-so-eva." Like usual, Mr. Wallace, also known as Daddy, just ignored her.

I followed him out to the porch as he walked out with his head down and hand shoved in his pockets. I could sense the hurt in him. He wore it like a suit jacket.

"Got room for one more, Daddy?" I asked as I sat down next to him on the porch swing.

"Uh-huh."

"She be all right, Daddy. You know Honey can take good care of herself," I said that with as much confidence as I could muster. Not that I totally believed that myself. Shoot, Honey had a temper and somehow, someway trouble always found her. "She'll be fine."

"Guessing you plan on leaving me too?" he asked, looking away from me.

"Me?"

"Naw, that hound dog running cross the yard. Yeah, you, gurl. Who else would I be talking 'bout?"

"Naw, suh. I ain't going nowhere," I said, secretly wishing I had half the courage of my crazy sistah. Ifin I did, I'd be right with her.

"You sho?"

"Course um sho. Sides, who would take care of you?" Whispering, I added, "Not 'tending to be disrespectful,

Daddy, but somebody got to feed you. Miss Jean cook bout good as she sew."

Looking at each other, we laughed. It was a decent attempt to shield the sorrow of my sistah's departure. It worked, but only for a while. I cried myself to sleep that night. I believe Daddy quietly did the same.

A lot has happened in these years. It's been a doozy for this here family. Well, mostly me.

I'm a momma now with two babies, a girl and a boy, to be exact. They names is Pearline and Felton. They daddy is a fellow I care not to remember, much less mention, so I won't. I would call him a mistake, 'cept I got my chilluns and ain't nothing a mistake about them. My girl Pearline is smart, I tell you. She started walking and talking before most babies gets to crawling. I do believe she gone read soon. She always pointing at something or the other for you to say.

"Momma, that?" she says as she points at her new discovery.

"It's a pan, Pearline."

"Pan, Momma," she'll repeat and quickly look for some sort of praise.

"Good gurl. Just so smart," I'll say.

I do get tickled every time she learn something new. Makes me feel good. My Felton, he still a li'l thang. I think he gone be short. Hopefully, not as short as his Granddaddy, though. He a good boy too, but I tell you, seem like he stay sick. This past winter he had a cold and a bad cough for what seemed like months. Way too long for my nerves. It was a good thang Granny Rose know babies 'cause I thought I was gone lose my mind with all his crying and hacking. After making a salve of tallow and turpentine to loosen up the cold stuck in his chest, he finally settled down. I'd just scoop out a small gob of the oily gunk and then rub it on his chest, his back, and belly, even his legs. Granny Rose told me I was overdoing it, but I was determined to get rid of that awful cough. The salve finally slowed the rattle in his chest down and he was able to breathe much better. Plus, I was able to finally get some sleep. That is, until the rain came.

Been a bit worried 'bout the rain coming through Preston like it has lately. The constant pouring is causing problems for everybody. The ground done got real wet and soggy. Make me feel like I'm gone sink all the way to China when I walk out there. Mud, dirt, leaves and mosquitoes is everywhere, and starting to make theys way in this house. With all of us having to go in and out the house every day our floors stay dirty. No matter how many times I scrub, wipe, and mop, seem like I'm scrubbing, wiping, and mopping again.

This is the first year since Honey been gone that it rain like this. Just the sound of it coming down tends to make me uncomfortable. Thumping, like somebody knocking hard on the rooftop. I don't like it one bit. Last night, I counted eight days since it started and had not stopped. I sho hope the good Lawd ain't planning on thirty-two mo. But just in case he decides to, I need to get with Honey as soon as possible. With a lot of rain comes floods, and with floods things start to rise and float. My only choice is to write her, since I can't drive to her in this terrible weather. Lawd, I hope the postman come on time today, he been late this entire week.

Dear Honey,

I hope this letter fines you well. Me and the chilluns is fine and so is Daddy. I know us four is 'bout all you care to know, so I'll stop there.

I been a li'l worried 'bout all this rain coming. Not sho if it's raining hard in Columbus, but from the looks down here, Noah could show up any day now. Been thanking a lot 'bout Colemans. Not sho what it is likely to wash up. I'm sho thangs the same, but I need you to come on down, just so we make sho.

I love you.

Louise

The next week didn't pass for Honey showed up at Daddy's. Smiling and singing with a gleefulness that was unsettling. That gurl strolled in here with her usual carefree attitude. 'Cept, this time it bothered me. I made a quick decision not to pay her no mind. I had other things to worry about.

"Where them babies at?" Honey asked me as I opened the door.

"They in there with Daddy. And how do to you too. Yo rude behind. Come in here not speaking," I said.

"Didn't I speak when I said, where them babies at. That's speaking, Louise. Is the old hag home?"

"Honey, I still live here," I quickly said to stop her. "Watch yo mouth. And no, she done gone to the church."

"For somebody that seem to keep devil in them all the time, she always in church, rocking and fanning." She walked to the parlor to find Daddy and the chilluns.

"Hey, Daddy," she said with a gleefulness that always made Daddy smile.

"Well, hey there, gurl. Louise didn't tell me you was coming." It was obvious he was happy to see her, but curious at the same time. "What done brought you down here in all this rain?"

"Can't a gurl come home to see her people?

"Sho you can. I'm always glad to see my chilluns. Just a li'l surprise you come down here in this weather is all."

"I miss ya'll, Daddy. Well, most of ya'll," she mumbled under her breath as Daddy stood to hug her.

As I leaned on the frame of the door, I watched her float through the room without a care in the world. My little sistah still wasn't connecting the dots. We had a potential problem on our hands, and from the looks of her you'd never know.

"Come here, boy. Give Auntie a kiss," Honey said right before she planted her wet lips against Felton's cheeks.

"And you bet not wipe it off," she said to him, since he had the tendency to do just that. "Pearline, Auntie brought you something."

"What is it?" she asked.

"Here yo go, baby."

"Oh my, a picture book. Thank you," she said in response to her gift.

"You welcome, sweetie. Lawd, that child talk like she grown already. Is she three or thirty?" she asked with a laugh.

"I'm three, Auntie. I'm just smart," Pearline said.

"And humble too," I added, embarrassed. I was the one who told her that all the time.

"Anythang in the kitchen to eat that Miss Jean didn't cook nor burn up, Daddy?" Honey asked.

He shook his head at her crack. "Louise cooked tonight. Gone in there and get you something to eat. Got plenty in there for you."

As she and I walked into the kitchen, she bumped me with her shoulder in a playful manner like when we was chilluns. Usually, I'd bump her back. Tonight I didn't and she noticed it.

"Look at all this mud. Look like you need some help cleaning round here," Honey said.

"What I need is for you to straighten up and stop playing. You hear me?" I whispered.

Honey didn't take kindly to my scold and that was very clear. Her lips got tight, shoulders high, and she gave me that look. It was the same face I always got when I had to straighten her up. And as usual, I couldn't have cared less.

She went over to the basin and washed her hands and dried them on the rag. After taking a plate down from the rack and searching for a fork, she began loading her plate with food. "Now, what's this note of yours bout this rain? A good rain ain't neva hurt nobody."

"Really?" I said. "And keep yo voice down. You know how nosy Daddy is. And there's two people this rain can hurt, namely me and you."

"Louise, you worry too much. We planted them real good. It would take more than this li'l rain to wash them up."

"Well, just to be sho, we going out there. And would you please stop saying we planted them? Like they some cabbages or something. Lawd."

"When?"

"When what?"

"When we going out there?"

"Tonight."

"Tonight? We can't see in the dark."

"We gone use Daddy's kerosene lantern. Sides, we don't have a choice. What if day breaks and they is out floating somewhere? I'm not quite sho how you can sit there and eat like you is, but hurry up. As soon as I gets these chilluns down and Daddy and Miss Jean get in the bed, we heading out there."

"Fine," she said, dismissing the subject. "Where the pepper sauce? How Miss Mabel been? I hear she got bursitis and the sugar."

I was finally able to get the chilluns settled. Daddy fell asleep in his chair and Miss Jean was upstairs snoring very loud as usual. Me and Honey tucked our beds to give the appearance we were still in them just in case Daddy got up and peeped in. He had a habit of walking round the house late at night after everyone was sleep, checking on thangs. We got in the jalopy and I quietly backed it out of the yard. We looked at each other and couldn't help but giggle a li'l bit. Thankfully, the rain had slowed to a drizzle and we could see ahead.

"You worried 'bout nothing. Everythang is just fine. Gurl, did I tell you about Hattie?" Honey said to me as we drove down the dark road.

"No."

"Well—"

"I don't care 'bout no Hattie, Honey."

"Lawd, I don't know how that man stay with that big-foot woman. She can't cook nothing, she mean, and she snore like a bear."

"Honey," I said, interrupting her. "I don't care 'bout no Hattie nor that crazy Miss Jean. Alls I care 'bout is them three bodies not floating when we get to the field."

"Well, let's pray 'bout it."

"Gurl ... How we gone go to the Lawd wit dis. *Dear Lawd, me and my sistah buried three mens on this plantation that she kilt by-the-way. Can you please make sho they ain't floating with all this rain you blessing us with? Thank you and Amen.*"

She looked over and laughed. Then I joined her. It was hard not to. There was something about Honey, even in dark times that could make you do things you hoped no one was watching you do.

As we drove along the rugged path, the sound of the gravel beneath our wheels played an eerie tune. The darkness of the night and slushing of the pools of rain didn't make it no mo' pleasant. We finally made our way to the same cotton field we promised never to speak of again. When we got out of the car, I stood there for longer than I was aware of.

"Gurl, come on. We ain't got all night. What you standing there for?" Honey said to me.

"I-I know. Give me a minute. I can't seem to get my legs to move."

"Well, something better get to moving. Ouch," Honey said without notice.

"What you ouching for?"

"Something just bit me."

"Hold this while I get the matches."

"Okay."

Honey stood there holding both lanterns while I tried to light them. My hands were shaking so hard, I couldn't.

"Give me the matches, Louise, for you burn yo-self."

Once the lanterns were lit, the dreaded field seemed to light up, as if to say welcome back. The old shed was still standing, the red paint that once covered it was now a faded rusty brown and peeling. The Big House far in the distance had lost its glory. It looked so fragile, like an old man bent over with a cane. One strong wind could probably knock it over. Down the way, I could also see the iron rod that served as our marker. Though now leaning and slightly covered by brush, it was still serving its purpose.

"Ain't that it?" Honey asked as she pointed in that direction.

We tipped over to that rod as if it was likely to turn and see us coming.

"See, I told you. Ain't nothing changed."

"Thank goodness. It looks like it," I said with relief as we walked toward the burial ground.

"Lawd, I hope I ain't stepping on Bo's head out here."

Did I just hear her correctly? This sistah of mine done really lost it. She bout to make me add her to this here graveyard. Goodness.

"Are you serious? Jesus, Honey. Stepping on his head? I can't believe you just said that. You best hope he ain't sitting up waiting on us."

Fortunately for us, neither, Bo, Ned, or Joe had risen with the rain. Their burial sites were wet, intact, and undisturbed.

"You satisfied now?" She asked me as we sloshed through the high weeds.

"Gurl, I ain't gone neva find no satisfaction from this."

"Where ya'll two been in this here weather?" Miss Jean asked as we entered the kitchen through the back door, returning from the field.

"Whew, you scared me," I said, surprised that she was up and creeping around so late.

"Me too," Honey said.

"Uh-huh. Seem to me you two should be in this here house with it being so late and all. Yo daddy thought ya'll was sleep. Least, that's what he said to me."

"What you doing up so late, Miss Jean, you all right?" I asked, hoping to get her mind off me and Honey.

"Not that it is any of yo business what I'm doing up in my own house, in my kitchen, but I got gas something terrible. It woke me up and yo daddy. Lawd hab mercy my stomach is aching. Not sho what I ate, but it sholl is disagreeing with me. Can't seem to put my hands on that cider vinegar and cream of tartar. A spoonful of each tends to gives me some relief when I gets to feeling like this."

"Oh, I know where they is," I said as I fumbled through the cabinets.

"Miss Jean, have you ever tried a little rubbing alcohol with a pinch of turpentine?" Honey asked.

"Naw, I ain't heard of that remedy before. Sound mo like poison if you ask me."

"Do you real good. Loosen you up right quick," Honey added.

"Here you go. Miss Jean," I said, cutting my eyes at Honey while also handing over the spice and vinegar.

"Good night, Miss Jean," Honey said.

"Uh-huh," she mumbled back as she walked from the kitchen.

"Turpentine and rubbing alcohol, Honey?"

She just looked at me, smiled and headed to bed. Too tired to fuss with Honey, I followed her. We were both finally done.

"Can't you stay a li'l longer than just ova night?" Daddy asked Honey at daybreak. "You leaving mighty early. Don't believe the rooster done crowed yet."

"He has, Daddy. He done wiped his eyes, even had a cup of coffee. Sides, I'm catching a ride with Ernie back up to Columbus. He got some deliveries to make and told me he had room."

"Yeah, she best be leaving, this house full enough." Miss Jean piped up.

"Jean," Daddy said bothered. This was one of the rare times she was able to rouse him enough to respond to her rudeness.

The chill of the morning had us all hugging ourselves as we stood outside on the porch with Honey waiting on Ernie to pull up. Although the weather was damp and cold, I found some comfort in knowing that the adventure me and Honey went on last night was over. I could rest in peace.

3

I t was Watch Night 1945 when my momma first met Mr. Edgar. Edgar Theocious Abraham Lincoln Scott, to be exact. I remember that night so clearly. It was a month or so after my seventh birthday, Aunt Honey was visiting, and it was New Year's Eve. Momma had been nervously bustling around earlier in the day, trading jokes and insults with Aunt Honey, and trying to decide if she'd go on to church or stay at home like she really wanted to. We both encouraged her to go, it was time. Aunt Honey, as usual, had a comment or two for the occasion. The one that lingered with me was when she told Momma that staying in this house won't change nothing but one day to the next. It was time she got her ass out them doors. Those were her words, not mine, although I firmly agreed.

I suggested to them that Momma wear that pretty new blue dress which hung in the rear of her closet for a special occasion. I considered this occasion quite special. Aunt Honey wanted her to wear a red lace one that she brought with her all the way from a fancy boutique in Columbus.

"I'm going to church, not a juke joint, Honey," Momma firmly responded.

She selected the blue dress. It was the one she'd purchased from Jeb's Five and Dime. It was a great find, hidden behind the odds and ends section in the back of the store. The dress took well over eight Fridays of putting away money to buy it. A nickel here, a dime there, finally covered the entire two dollars. It had big gold buttons in the front and white lace on the sleeves. And it caught her in her waist, giving the impression she had bigger hips than the good Lord had blessed her with. With her narrow frame and little legs Momma always had the desire for a *little extra,* as she'd say. Occasionally she'd joke that the women around Preston had more than their fair share of hips, butt, and breast, and in her opinion, some to spare.

The decision to go to church was made after she contemplated for more than two hours that day. Aunt Honey said this hiding in the house was getting plumb foolish and wasn't nothing else to talk about. She was going to church tonight. Momma finally relented. To my surprise, and I think hers too, she pulled out that shiny pink pearl necklace to wear along with her new dress. Truthfully, it wasn't all that shiny anymore. The thick dust on it had dulled its sparkle; nevertheless, she resolved to wear it anyway. She'd asked me to catch it around her neck, since the broken clamp made it hard to fasten. I did, but I was a little uncomfortable. That old necklace had a lot of sentiment and sadness strung through it. It was the necklace her dead beau, Raymond Crump, had given her.

After gathering her Bible, handkerchief, and purse prior to heading out to church, she all of a sudden returned to the long mirror in the hallway. She gazed at her reflection almost as if she recognized an old friend. I knew why Momma lingered and I knew I had to do or say something; otherwise, she just might not make it out of the house.

"Momma, go," I said as I flopped on her bed, exerting kindness, but with a hint of authority.

"You sho, Pearline?"

"Yeah, she sho, Louise, goodness," Aunt Honey interjected. "All this twisting, stopping, and turning bout to wreck my nerves."

"Yes, ma'am, I'm positive. You've been in this house long enough. You're liable to disappear in the walls if you don't. I promise it'll be fine. Besides, Aunt Honey is with you and look how pretty you are. Bet you'll both be eye candy for somebody's son tonight."

That must have been the right thing to say, because she smiled and nodded to herself in the mirror.

I pulled out her heavy winter coat, the one with the shedding fox collar, from the hall closet. That coat was never a favorite of mine, but for Momma it represented a bit of glamour. She likened it to the coats the Hollywood stars like Lena Horne and Dorothy Dandridge wore in the fancy magazines. Except, hers was almost a real fur coat, but not quite. All I saw was an old coat with a spooky dead animal hanging around her neck. I always felt like that that dead fox took a peep when no one was looking.

To make sure that she would leave, I opened the coat and held it for her to put on. She took a deep breath and slowly slid her arms in, one at a time, delaying her exit just a little longer.

"You know, you better hurry, Momma," I said, noticing her intentional delay. "Granddaddy is probably already over at the church, and I'm sho he's sitting there watching that door like Jesus's second coming about to happen, waiting on you two. Can't you just see him there, fidgeting with his old Timex pocket watch? Open, close, open, close. Not even giving poor time a chance to change, looking at it every second or two. Plus, you know how he gets really perturbed when you walk in church after devotion. That's not to mention that the ushers won't let you all in once the deacons' start, especially if Sistah Lucille is in charge tonight."

"She still over the usher board? Thought they would have retired her by now," Aunt Honey said.

"Naw, retire her from ushering? Have a better chance of snow in July than taking that job from that one," Momma replied.

"That woman has the strength of ten men and two bulls when she grips those door handles. You'll be stuck outside in the cold until devotion is finished, which by the way, could be forever if your cousin Joe is leading prayer tonight," I added.

Glaring at me with a curious look, she tilted her head and said, "Honey, yo niece doing a whole lot of talking tonight. You thank she been sneaking Daddy's Sanka again?"

"No, ma'am, of course not," I said, hoping to put on a believable look of shock that she'd even ask me such a question, especially since that's exactly what I'd been doing. My discovery of coffee and its perks had occurred at a very early age. Aunt Honey knew I was fibbing—because she slipped me the coffee.

"Uh-huh," Momma said with a look a disbelief as she glanced at me and Aunt Honey. Knowing the truth wasn't in either of us.

"And them big words of yours. I have no notion what pert-er means, Pearline."

"Momma, it's per-turb-ed," I said, but when she gave me a look indicating that my tone was teetering on disrespect, I quickly adjusted. "What I mean is, he's going to be upset with you if you enter church after devotion. You've known him longer than I have. Hopefully, luck is on your side tonight and your cousin isn't leading devotion. I swear, it seems like he forgets there's more to church than just his praying. And that hymn he loves to sing, 'Hey Charles,' could run ya'll least another hour or two. Goodness. He's so longwinded with all his sanging and praying. Good Lord, Momma, I do believe Jesus himself nods off for a nap when that man is praying."

"Okay, Pearline. Gurl, you so silly," she said with a slight chuckle. "Look, we leaving now, but don't let midnight catch you nor yo brotha and ya'll not in bed, you hear me?"

"Yes, ma'am," I said, with no intention to do that at all. Me, asleep before 12:01 a.m., January 1st? Who does that on New Year's Eve anyway? My cup of coffee, although cold now, was nicely tucked under my bed along with my oh-so-delicious book just waiting on me.

Right before they walked out the front door, they both turned to me with a look of confusion. Aunt Honey said, "Wait a minute, one more thang. What, pray tell, hymn is 'Hey Charles'? I don't believe I eva heard that one before."

Annoyed, I said, "Huh? Of course you have. My goodness, he sings it *every* Sunday." I began to sing, "Hey, Charles—"

She quickly interrupted me with a hearty laugh, shaking her head in disbelief. "Lawd Jes-us. What he saying is *A charge* child, *A charge.* It's the hymn 'A Charge to Keep I Have.' He ain't saying no hey Charles."

"Oh! Well, that's what it sounds like to me and every other child in church."

"You mean to tell me all this here time, you been thinking that man been calling on somebody by the name of Charles?" Momma asked, amused as well.

"Yes, ma'am. I sure did," I said, responding boldly, as if she was the nutcase who'd just mistaken a classic hymn with a greeting and a person's name.

"Ooo, Louise, that chile of yours is blessed with plenty of book sense, plenty, but the rest of her brain. I just, I do declare, I don't know sometimes about her." Aunt Honey was tickled by this notion about an old hymn. Then she sobered up, remembering her night's mission. "Well, okay, you right, we better get on outta here. Daddy liable to tap a hole in the church floor if we take too much longer. We off now. See you in a li'l while."

As they left, I grabbed Momma's hand to offer one more bit of reassurance. I just felt like she needed it. "It'll be fine, I promise."

She winked at me and headed out.

"Bye, baby. I'll take care of her," Aunt Honey said as they walked down the steps.

"And who gone take care of you?" Momma asked as they playfully bumped into each other.

Ever since Raymond died, we felt Momma had given up on pretty much everything, including ever meeting, much less loving, another man. I remembered Mr. Raymond well. He was quite a nice fellow with a pleasant demeanor. Physically, he was tall, with a wide smile and strong shoulders. There was never a time he didn't ask what I was reading, and he seemed to take a real interest in my *schooling*, as he called it. I believed he loved Momma and I knew she loved him.

Unfortunately, death visited him earlier than anyone would have ever hoped for. One day while walking home from fishing, a large branch snapped loose from an old oak tree and hit him square in the head. It was almost an entire day before someone found him lying half dead near the Kinchafoonee Creek Bridge. Funny how a simple walk home can change everything. The men who stumbled upon him carried him down to Dr. Mitchell's. He never awakened from the injuries. Sadly, he passed a few days later.

Dr. Mitchell told Momma death was the best thing for Raymond with that kind of injury. He said it would have been a cruel thang for him to keep living. When he finally crossed over, Momma was with him. She'd been curled up right next to him the entire time he laid unconscious in his death bed. After his passing, she stayed cooped up in her own bed for over a month—that is, until Aunt Honey came back. After pulling Momma from her bed and dragging her to the tub, I heard her tell Momma one morning, that was enough.

"You getting out this here bed. Gone brush your teeth, comb yo hair and wash yo face, Louise. Goodness. You done mourned Raymond long enough. The good Lord know better than you do where he belongs. And if he saw fit to take him, then that's that."

Yes, Momma's venture out of the house was a welcomed one, even if it was just two streets over to the New Missionary Baptist church.

It was well after two in the morning when they finally came home. I was still up reading the last chapter of *Uncle*

Tom's Cabin when I heard them. They walked to my room as quietly as they could, but the old wooden floor's crackling revealed their presence, as it always did. With the floor's timely notice, I quickly blew out the candle and fanned the smoke before Momma could open my door. Turning over on my side and snoring just a little, I hoped to give the impression that I was lost in sleep.

I heard Aunt Honey say she was tuckered out and going to bed, but Momma had other plans. She entered my room. Once in, she gently scooted onto my bed and shook my shoulder. With a slight whisper she asked, "Pearline, you sleep?'

"Huh?"

"You sleep?"

"Yes."

"No, you ain't, Miss Smarty. I saw that candle burning through the crack in the door and I smell it too. You probably in here reading again. You know, your granddaddy done told you 'bout doing that so late. You aiming to burn this house down."

"What candle? I-I don't—"

"Stop that lying for I gets my switch!"

Once I realized that my deception was revealed, I said, "But, Momma, you wouldn't believe some of those characters in this book. I couldn't stop reading. Unbelievable!"

"You gone be unbelievable and with a sore behind ifin your granddaddy catches you with this candle burning late like this again. What if you fell off to sleep and burned this whole house down with you and Felton in it? I oughta make you go get the switch myself."

She continued to fuss about that candle so much that she'd forgotten why she came in my room in the first place.

"Momma?" I said, attempting to interrupt her tirade.

"What?"

"You were saying?"

"I was saying, no more candles. You hear me?"

"Yes, ma'am."

"All right, then," she said as her tone softened. "Chile, you done got me all off track with you and them candles. Well," she added after taking a quick breath and clearing her throat, "I was saying, I met somebody at the church tonight."

"You did? Somebody like who?"

"Hold on, I'm fixing to tell you. His name is Edgar Scott. Edgar, something with a president's name, Scott. He told me his whole name, but it was way too much to remember." She tried to remember for another moment, then continued. "Well, he kinda tall, got good strong shoulders and smiles a lot."

I quickly interrupted her, "Ooo, Momma, he sounds a lot like—"

"Be quiet. Sometimes you too grown for your britches. You just like yo auntie, goodness. She said the 'xact same thang. He ain't no Raymond. I's clear on that. I do believe we buried him two months ago. Now, can I finish telling you about my night please?

"Yes, ma'am"

"Thank you," she said sternly. "Well, right off I noticed that he can sang. Sho can. He must be a praying man too. Looked like he knew all them scriptures Pastor was reading. I saw that for myself, 'cause I kinda kept watching him."

"Kinda, huh? Momma, can't this wait till morning? I'm sleepy."

"Naw, it sho can't. Now listen."

She nudged in next to me, a little closer, shoulder to shoulder. Then she started sharing with me how she and Aunt Honey arrived at church a bit late and had to wait outside for the ushers to open the doors. Three of their lady friends, Miss Lutrell, Miss Bessie, and Miss Emma Lou were also waiting outside. When they noticed them, they rushed over to embrace both Momma and Aunt Honey. Once the hugs and kisses concluded, the gossip began. It was their duty to catch her up on everything she'd missed during her absence. Miss Lutrell was happy to launch the session.

"Louise, ump, ump," she said as she stood there with her arms folded. "You know that Maybell, the youngest daughter of Moochie and Odessa, is pregnant."

"Do tell," Momma said.

"Yep and guess who the daddy is? "

"Who?" Aunt Honey asked

"That dim-witted Waylin."

"Waylin?" Momma said, unsure of who this person was.

"Rochell and Mackey's oldest boy."

"Don't believe I know him," Aunt Honey said.

Yes, you do. He the one always walking round here putting rocks in his pockets," Miss Emma Lou said.

"Naw, not him?" Aunt Honey said, shaking her head.

"Yeah, him. Shame, ain't it," Miss Lutrell said with her arms tightly folded. "That boy gone actually be somebody's daddy. Lawd have mercy."

"Now, that Odessa been lying all summer," Miss Bess said.

"Is you surprised? You know lying run in they family like cross tires down a track," Aunt Honey said, laughing.

"Bless her heart, talking 'bout Maybell done gained a lot of weight. Humph. As many chillun been born round here, you'd thank she know we know a pregnant chile when we see one," Miss Lutrell said.

"Uhmmm-ump," Miss Emma Lou said in agreement while nodding her head.

"Yeah, you'd thank," Miss Bessie said. "Whenever I see her down at Jeb's, she tell me that same old fairy tale time after time. Say stuff like *That girl of mine sho nuff eats too much. I keep telling her she needs to push back from the table.* Humph, that table ain't the only thang she needs to push back from. And from what I know, collard greens and hog-mog known to give you gas, but I ain't neva heards they gives you a baby."

"And did you hear about Deacon Earl?" Miss Lutrell asked.

"Can't say I did," Momma said.

"Uh-huh. Deacon Earl and Shuga."

"Talking about his crazy goat Shuga?" Aunt Honey asked.

"Yep. Well, sometime last month Shuga got loose and tore up Clyde's yard. And you know how Clyde is bout that piece of dirt of his," Miss Lutrell said.

"Yeah, he funny bout that yard," Momma said.

"Well, they say it was like that goat was possessed by the devil hisself. He started digging holes, chasing folks, knocking over garbage cans, and ripping clothes down off the line," Miss Bessie said.

"He did all of that?" Momma asked.

"Sho did and the next thang you know, Clyde got so mad, he done ran in his house and grabbed that ol' pellet gun of his. That fool came outside and yelled, 'Drop the shirt, Shuga like he talking to a person. Next thang you know, he shot Shuga," Miss Bessie said.

"Aw hell, he shot Shuga?" Aunt Honey said.

Nodding her head, Miss Lutrell chimed in and said, "Yep, shot Shuga. And you know that Earl just bout went crazy. He got to running round, crying and screaming that Clyde done kilt his Shuga."

"Lawd have mercy," Momma said.

"And gurl, that ain't all. Next come the fighting 'tween Earl, Clyde, and Earl's wife Ubeena. She come branging her ol' fat self on out there just making thangs worst, screaming for Clyde to get off of her Earl. All of them out there cuttin the fool in the front yard for everybody to see over that old goat," Miss Bessie said.

"What?" Momma said, laughing and confused right along with Aunt Honey.

"Then all of a sudden, a miracle happened. Folks say Shuga sprung up like a jack rabbit and ran right back to Earl's yard. Heard he wasn't limping or nothing. Said the goat sat there shaking his head too, like he was embarrassed them fools was acting like that. Girl, they said Ubeena looked over at Earl and said, *Oh, you done forgot you learned Shuga how to play dead, baby.* "Humph," Miss Emma Lou said, "I tell you, Louise, it's a was good thang that damn goat lived, 'cause they probably woulda had to dig two holes, one for that goat and one for Earl."

"Naw, one hole woulda been just fine, 'cause he woulda climbed his crazy behind right on in next to his Shuga," Aunt Honey said, laughing.

Listening to all that foolishness gave both of them a good laugh, Momma said. She said she actually forgot just how cold it was outside while she and Aunt Honey waited to enter the church. Finally, to everyone's delight and relief, the church doors began to slowly open. Sistah Lucille had let her grip go and released the knobs of the door. As ritual called for, she raised her white gloved hands and motioned for everyone to begin entering the church.

All worshippers were expected to behave appropriately when crossing the threshold. The look alone on Sistah Lucilles' face gave that command without her saying a single word. She was about reverence, silence, and decorum and all in that order. No fast walking or running, no chewing gum, and certainly no loud talking or laughing upon entering the Lord's house.

Unfortunately, neither silence nor decorum was to show up that night. It was just too many people. Watch Night, Christmas, and Easter would always draw large crowds and tonight was no exception. Everyone hurriedly entered in hopes of grabbing one of the last remaining chairs, being that all the pews were full. With all the people shoving and pushing behind her, Momma stumbled but was caught by a nice gentleman grabbing her arm.

"Scuse me, ma'am. You okay? Guess folks done forgot we in church."

"Why I-I guess so. I'm fine. Thank you, suh, for asking."

That easy exchange between the two sealed the deal. Neither one of them could keep their eyes off of the other one for the rest of the night. Their gazing must have been obvious to others, including Granddaddy. She said right after the benevolent offering and right before altar call, Aunt Honey pinched her to warn of Granddaddy's gaze.

It was too late. Granddaddy began coughing really hard and clearing his throat in an attempt to gain her attention. He did this more than a couple of times and the last time he coughed so hard he nearly choked himself. Momma said, the next thing you know, Miss Jean, like a fool, rushes over to Granddaddy, pushing grown men and "chilluns" out of her way. She starts punching the po' man in his back real hard like, "thanking he really choking." Being the big woman she is, she almost sent him flying over the pew. Laughing, she said all that nonsense, along with everybody else's snickering, broke the eyeballing between her and Mr. Edga, at least temporarily.

She swears to this here day, she couldn't tell you if you paid her real cash money what the Preacher talked about that night. All she could remember was bumping into her future.

"And guess what else, Pearline?" she asked with the excitement of a school girl. "He even waited for me after church. Sho did. Once he saw me and yo auntie, him and his friend walked right over to us and introduced they selfs like gentleman. Said he'd like to see me again if he could. Yo crazy aunt made it clear to his friend an introduction wasn't necessary on his part. She just stood there stone-faced with her arms wrapped tight. Just rude she is. Then of course, here comes yo Granddaddy walking up and pulling us away before I even could answer the man. But I turned around and nodded yes for I got too far from him."

Giggling and smiling in between sentences, she continued to share how she felt it had to be a good sign being that they met each other at church and on Watch Night at that. I hadn't seen Momma smile like this in a while. Well, not since Aunt Honey's last visit. We all perked up when she was around. It was nice to see happiness visit Momma again.

"Got's to be the start of something new for us. I can feels it!" she said.

Those were the last words I remember hearing right before I dozed off to sleep. After that night, we began to see a transformation in Momma. She was becoming her old self again. She smiled and certainly laughed more. To my delight, I would often catch her humming while working, like she used too. She stayed lost in her own thoughts, daydreaming. I once heard her tell Granddaddy that she couldn't tell where meeting Edga (as she called him) would go; she just hoped it would take her and her chillun to something better, and maybe out of Preston, Georgia.

"Goodness. I think I done burned these here collards too. Lawd, my nerves bad."

"Smells like it," I said as I stood in the doorway watching Momma. She was surely having a hard time preparing this meal. Milk was spilling, clouds of flour was everywhere and nearly everything she cooked, she was burning. Why she was so nervous that Mr. Edga was coming over was beyond me.

"Stop that laughing, put that book down and come look. What you think? Can we still eat these?" she asked while tipping the smoking pot so I could look in.

"We?"

"Yes, little girl, we."

"Well, Momma. Truth be told, those greens are only suitable for one person in this house."

"My, it smells good in here," Miss Jean said as she walked in the kitchen interrupting me.

"And here she is," I said with a snicker.

"Hush yo mouth, gurl," Momma whispered, hoping Miss Jean didn't hear the onset of our conversation.

Momma didn't know much about this new fellow other than his people were deceased. She said he mentioned a brother, but he was dead also. Mr. Edga was a dapper fellow who was keenly aware of his looks and somewhat charming, at least that's what he and Momma thought. Me, I wasn't too impressed and neither was Granddaddy. Now, Granddaddy's wife, Miss Jean, liked anything that represented a route for us to leave "hu house," as she loved to put it. We had been living with them my entire life, and she was clearly ready for us all to make a collective exit. More than occasionally, she'd ask Momma as only she could, in her annoying voice *"You thanks that Edga boy coming by today? I sho hope he do. He seems like a right fine young man, fine young man. Yes suh, indeed."* I do believe she had more anticipation for his courting than Momma did.

You'd always catch Mr. Edgar dressed to the nines and with a wide grin. He loved the finest of whatever twenty-five dollars a week could afford him. Normally, that would include a brand-new–looking used suit and tie from the Goodwill over in Lumpkin, a brim, and some *not so pleasantly smelling* smell-good. His eau de toilette, which is French for cheap perfume, kinda reminded me of sweat meets pork ribs. In my opinion, it was too strong and musky. I always knew he was either coming or going, whether I saw him or not. He was also especially partial to those funny-looking two-toned black and white brogues. Those shoes looked uncomfortable and a tad bit girlie to me and apparently to Granddaddy also. I once overheard him jokingly say to Miss Jean, all that Edga boy was missing with those shoes on was a dress and a dandelion glued to his head.

Mr. Edgar would gladly walk and sometimes hobble all the way to Lumpkin to update his attire as long as Mr. MacAfee paid him on time and what he was really owed. South Georgia roads were layered with hard red dirt, rocks, and pebbles, all wrecking havoc on the bodies of its frequently walking guest. He seemed oblivious to the discomfort of those long walks, or at least he pretended to be. His vanity prevailed over achy feet and legs any day. Granddaddy would just shake his head and mumble when Mr. Edgar would limp up to the front door all dressed up. "Look at him, ol' damn fool. No, he can't ford all that mess. Gone need a cane afta a while hobbling like that." Momma, on the other hand, was so smitten with him, anything he did met with her approval.

Miss Jean was especially excited that Mr. Edgar was a working man with employment over at MacAfee's Slaughter House, more commonly known as the "House." He began work there when he was a boy as an apprentice with his daddy and granddaddy. He was the third generation of butchers, and he loved to brag about it.

"My daddy did it, his daddy did it and now I's doing it." We all heard that quote recited on more than a few occasions. He said that his granddaddy took him aside and "learned him everythang he knew on butchering." So, by now he was quite capable and skilled at his craft. As a boy, he started out hosing down the floors, cutting tables, hangers, and knives. He said whenever he got a chance, he'd sit and study as much as he could on how those men would slice those pigs up with care and lightning speed. It didn't take too long before he was butchering the pigs as well as becoming quite proficient at it. His expertise earned him a reputation and a nickname.

"Quicks is what they call me," he loved to say. "Ain't nobody able to cut them pigs quicka than me."

At the House they killed everything killable. The unsuspecting victims pretty much included pigs, hogs, cows, and chickens. But if you looked hard enough, you might run across a deer, goat, raccoon, or even possum occasionally. Old Man MacAfee, while chewing on a brick of tobacco and spitting in between, would happily share with anyone in earshot, his annoying motto: "We don't scriminate here. If you can eat it, we here at this here famous MacAfee's can kill it, clean it and, if you got enough money, cook it too!" Sarcastically, I thought, "How appetizing."

Old Man MacAfee and his two sons Elroy and Beau ran the place, but there was only one "Bossman" over at the House, and that was the old man. I would always cringe when I heard Mr. Edgar refer to Mr. MacAfee as his Bossman. What kind of word is that? I thought. It's just too feeble-sounding and it reminds me of some of the subservient, head-scratching, shuffling characters from a few of my books. "Yes suh boss, no suh boss, I got this here boss." That one word nearly drove me crazy.

One day it occurred to me that I could remedy my annoyance and educate Mr. Edgar at the same time by assisting him with his not so apparent need. I'd help him replace the word Bossman. I decided I'd explore word selections more fitting and suitable than that particular title. Hoping to locate something synonymous with *bossman*, I pulled out my reliable Webster's Dictionary, the hardback edition I'd gotten for my birthday a couple of years ago. After thumbing through it, I finally located exactly what I was looking for, a more noble replacement for that horrid word "Bossman." Magically, the words *supervisor* and *manager* appeared. "Perfect," I thought, either word would be sufficient. The day finally presented itself where I could share my results with Mr. Edgar: a Sunday afternoon, right after dinner. We were all sitting on the porch when Momma went inside the house to grab her shawl for their evening walk. Her timing could not have been more perfect; I was left alone with him. I thought, what better opportunity than now to enlighten him?

"Mr. Edgar, got a minute?"

"Yep, what's going on?"

"Well, I noticed you refer to Mr. MacAfee as your 'Bossman'?"

"I do."

"I thought I might have a solution for you?"

Looking at me perplexed, he said, "A solution? What I need a solution for?"

"A solution is a—"

"I didn't ask you what a solution was, I asked you what I need one for?"

"Hmmm, you're right; substitution is probably a better description. I was thinking of a substitution for that word Bossman. You may not know this, but Bossman is not really a word. I looked and looked. It's not even in my Webster's Dictionary and every word is in there."

"It ain't, you say. Uh-huh, and what might you suggest?" he asked, while simultaneously lighting a pipe.

"So glad you asked."

I politely recommended my selections of manager and/or supervisor, and shared that either would be adequate. I even took the time to point them out to him in my dictionary. After he stared at me and then laughed for at least a few minutes, quite enthusiastically I might add, I realized my efforts were in vain, essentially a waste of time. I grabbed my books, gave him a look of irritation and kindly departed his presence. Momma walked out of the house right as I pulled the screen door open to walk back in. I heard her ask him what was so funny. I know he told her, because she began to laugh too. She didn't laugh long, though. When she came in later from their walk, without a word, she popped me on my behind. I didn't have to ask, I knew why. Correcting grown folks ran a close second to cussing.

Before Granddaddy finally gave his blessings for Momma and Mr. Edgar to marry, Mr. Edgar hung around our house all the time. It seemed like he was forever somewhere near or trying to be near Momma. To better charm her on his visits, he never came courting empty-handed. Instead of bringing flowers, chocolates or other romantic gifts, like other suitors, Momma got swine. That's right; he'd never fail to show up without some pig with him when he came a courting.

"Here he comes again," I'd say to myself, as I'd watch him from the window, still grinning, while walking up to the porch with a bundle of something in his hands and wearing those squeaky, ugly shoes he loved so much. "Bet he got some swine with him again."

It was either the pig's feet, ears, tails, tongue, or even its guts or chitlins, as they're called around here. To my disappointment it was always the scrap.

"Don't they have some bacon or ham over there?" I'd mumble with irritation.

One time he showed up at the house with the pig's whole head. It was for Momma to make some hog head cheese. A culinary delicacy I chose not to indulge in. Because our icebox wasn't big enough to store the head temporarily, she placed the head in the sink on a large pile of ice. It would have been nice if she had warned me that a pig's head would be smiling from the sink when I strolled in the kitchen for a glass of milk. There is nothing like walking in the kitchen to be greeted by a big old pig's head, eyeballs, teeth and all, looking straight at you with a wide smile.

Who knew I could run that fast or scream that loud heading out of that kitchen? I broke two vases, a chair and nearly my neck getting out of there. Everyone got a good laugh at my expense that day. I, on the other hand, found absolutely nothing joyous about that encounter at all. Even today I still get a little queasy when I pass the local Piggly Wiggly. They have that awful smiling pig's head on their building as their mascot. I swear the eyes on that pig follow me and wink when I pass by.

4

The leaves had begun to shed from the trees and gather in piles throughout the town. Some of them were a golden orange, a few freckled with yellow; others were tinged with red with a brownish hue. The potpourri of colors was indeed beautiful, especially as they fanned through the air after being kicked by playing children. Along with the beauty that showered the landscape, the shedding of leaves also showed that the summer heat would finally take a break, that the season of fall would soon come, and Momma and Mr. Edgar would marry.

There would be no jumping of any broom or throwing of any matrimonial rice for their ceremony. Momma had my other brother in the oven, so time was of essence. Our pastor married them quietly one night over at the church. Granddaddy, Miss Jean and my Aunt Honey stood with them. Aunt Honey surprised Momma and caught the bus all the way from Columbus to stand with her.

Since Momma was clearly with child, the pastor chose his back office instead of the church's sanctuary to marry them. He made everyone squeeze in that tiny space of his. Rationalizing that it just wasn't proper or dignified to marry them in his church with her like that, unmarried and pregnant that is. I know the whole backroom thing hurt Momma's feelings. This wasn't her idea of the church wedding she'd dreamed of. Not to mention, Aunt Honey was not happy with his decision and was quite verbal with her irritation. More than once, she called the pastor a plain old lying hypocrite amongst other things.

She expressed when she initially learned of the nuptial's relocation, "Louise, I can't tell you the number of times I done seen yo pastor—that's right, the W. H. Low hisself—leaving Wilhelmina's house."

"His name is Bow, Honey. Pastor Bow."

"Well, it should be Low, Low-Down, if you ask me. More times than I can count, for sho he done bumped into me drunk, fixing his clothes, leaving that Wilhelmina's. The nerve of him to even thank bout judging somebody. Humph."

"It's all right, Honey. Just let it go," Momma said. "If he ain't nothing but a wife-cheating, dranking hypocrite, then so be it. 'Tween him and the Lawd."

"Him and the Lawd? Gurl, please? From what I know, the Lawd said, keep him out of it."

Early the next morning after their marriage, I was awakened by the floor again. Momma was on her way to my room to greet me with her news. Excitedly she said, "Pearline, Pearline, you up? Wake up, sweetie. I got something good to tell you! Wake up!"

"Huh, I mean, ma'am?"

"I just got married. Me and Mr. Edga is now husband and wife. Folks gone call me Mrs. Scott now. Can you believe it?

Holding her ring hand out in front of me, she said cheerfully, "He even done got me this here ring. Look, it even got a few diamonds in it. And guess what else?

"What, Momma?"

"He said you and your brotha can call him Daddy now."

Annoyed and a bit confused from being roused out of my sleep, I reached over to locate my reading glasses, which I kept on my nightstand. I always felt like my hearing improved with my ability to see. Once I clumsily put them on, I asked, "Momma, what time is it? And what did you just say? Ya'll did what?"

Speaking to me in a tone that indicated I'd better wake up and listen, she said, "I said we just got married."

"Oh, okay," I replied somewhat still asleep and irritated with all the commotion.

"Just okay, Pearline?" I noticed the tone of her voice changed. Apparently, she was anticipating more excitement from me than I was able to muster, especially so early in the morning. "Look like somebody round here be happy for me. Daddy nor yo Aunt Honey doing too much celebrating. Well, he a good man and I love him."

Honestly, I wasn't overly thrilled with Mr. Edgar. I found him to be quite exasperating at times, especially his jokes, but he'd do. I did want Momma to be happy and she seemed happy with him. So, I guess I'd live with it.

"Momma" I said, making sure to look her straight in the eye, while grabbing one of her hands, a ritual we created long ago. "I'm happy for you. Congratulations."

Relief cloaked her like a warm blanket on a cold night when I said that. I could see the disappointment of my initial reaction melt from her face. Praise and approval from me was always important to her. We were so close in age. Sometimes she felt more like my sister than my Momma.

She had given birth to me when she was barely out of her teens. From the little I have acquired and I do mean little, my birthplace was right here in Preston, on the old Coleman plantation. I do know that my Granny Rose delivered me right in her kitchen. She was my great-grandmother on my momma's side. Momma said before she could make it to the bedroom and lay down like normal pregnant women do, I was already here. There I was pushing my way through so fast that she had no choice but to have me right smack on that cold kitchen floor. Every now and then she reminds me of my entry into the world. It normally occurs whenever I'm rushing her or ready to move a bit quicker than she approves of. I might hear, "Gurl, you showed up in the world with no patience. Everythang, I means everythang, is always in a hurry with you. Slow yo behind down, chile!"

My Granny Rose, who I have limited memories of, was the midwife for all the Colored babies and the white ones also. And because she had, as the old folks put it, "special hands," people from counties all over would come for her help. She was mostly known for delivering babies that tried to come out crooked, feet first, or with no intention of coming out at all. Blessed with the ability to turn babies while they were still in the momma's stomach without killing the momma or the baby, she was in high demand. It wasn't unusual for her to stay away from home overnight and sometimes for days.

One of her favorite stories passed down was her trip to Lexington, Kentucky. Proudly, she shared how the people of this very sick pregnant woman drove all the way down from Kentucky in need of her help. They were some white folks, but she didn't hold that against them. She felt babies were just that, babies____"wasn't they fault who the good Lawd signs them to," she was known to say. Although she was reluctant to go to Kentucky, especially with white folks, the desperation in the eyes of the family, especially the father, made the decision easier. So she went. Unbeknownst to her, she had to go up and down an Appalachian mountain to get there. Going up a hill was one thing, but a mountain was another. Since she had never been a fan of anything too high off the "solid ground," as she'd say, that mountain soon became "that damn mountain." She said that drive felt like she was riding on up to glory, a journey she thought would be much more pleasurable. Fortunately for that lucky woman, Granny Rose thought herself to be a good Christian woman. Otherwise, she said she would have "turnt her ass right round" to get off that mountain.

My great grandma, her special hands, the plantation, and my birth date pretty much sum up all that I know about my beginnings. My grandma had already died when I was born, so I never got the chance to meet her. Although I always heard growing up that I was just like her, a description I accepted as a compliment. Momma never spoke of my real daddy and strangely enough, no one else would either, not even a whisper. Whenever I'd bring it up, I'd usually get a pop on the behind or a "Didn't I tell you not to ask about that again" look. I finally gave up on that pursuit, although I knew I didn't get here like Jesus did.

Shortly after the nuptials, my parents decided that we as a family would head north. Leaving Preston was first and foremost on both their minds. I knew Momma wanted a fresh start. Not too many days passed where she didn't remind us of that, especially when it rained for some odd reason. Plus, she hated Miss Jean. Her only hesitation lay in leaving my granddaddy. He was getting old and she worried about him, like she did everything else. Daddy was ready to go also. Other than his job and a cousin here and there, there was nothing to keep him in Preston either. We never saw much of his family anyway.

The last time I saw one of his family members was at the county fair, which is really popular around here. Folks travel from nearby towns to watch the circus troupe, eat the greasy food, and enjoy the games and music. I especially loved it. The oddity of all the people was like a picture show for me, but in real life. Last year I saw an elephant, a man that could swallow a sword, a bearded lady, and I also met Mr. Elroy, Daddy's cousin. I remember strolling along with my family distracted by everything we saw and heard when we bumped into this couple. Neither Momma nor I had ever seen them but Daddy clearly recognized at least one of them. I thought he was gone trip over his own two feet as they approached us. After failing to maneuver us in a different direction away from them, the gentleman yelled our way.

"Edga? Boy is that you?" He said leaning in to get a closer look. "Hot damn, I knowed that was you, boy. Come here. Been a long time."

Daddy just stood there almost like he was embarrassed, and for the first time probably in his life, unable to speak.

"How do, ma'am. Look like the cat done got Edga tongue," this stranger said as he tipped his hat to Momma.

"Well, hello," Momma responded with as we all stood in awkward silence.

It was obvious even to me that this man and the woman he walked with had been drinking and too much at that.

"Hey, Elroy." Daddy mumbled.

"Is this yo pretty wife and chilluns?"

"Yep."

"Yeah, I heard you got married a while back. Nice to meet you, ma'am. How thangs been going?"

Before Daddy could answer him, he said, "Oh, pardon me for being rude. This here is Lanette. My woman friend. Say hey to these good folks, Lanette."

"Hey ya'll," she said with an unnecessary wave of her hand.

"Would you like a sip?" Elroy said as he snatched the bottle away from Lanette's lips, causing a little of the brown liquor to slush around and splash onto her face. Unfazed, she wiped away the dripping liquid with the back of her hand and kept smiling.

"Naw, no thank you," Daddy said with clear irritation.

"Humph. Don't drank no mo? Okay, then. How has it been going? Heard you over at the MacAfee's cutting. They still calling you Quicks? Don't know if you know this, ma'am, but yo husband sho can cut up some hog. That's how he got's the name Quicks."

"Yes, he's pretty good with that knife." Momma said.

"Speaking of knives, you heard from yo brother?"

That question immediately caused Daddy to gather all of us and motion for us to walk away before he could barely complete the question.

"Good seeing you, Elroy. Take care."

"Now, Edga, you ain't got to rush off like that."

"Yeah, Elroy, I do. Nice meeting you, Lanette."

"Edga!" Momma said. "That's a shame you acting like that. And did he say brother?"

"Don't know what that fool said. Drunk as he is, hard to tell. I ain't seent him in a month of Sundays. Sides, look at him and that woman he with. Both of them drunker than Cooter Brown on Election Day. I don't think he even know what he talking about."

"Who's Cooter?" Momma asked, confused.

"It's a saying, Louise. What folks say when somebody real drunk like Elroy is. Got to get you out mo often."

"Humph, I gets out just fine," Momma said right before Mr. Elroy yelled, "Ya'll take care, Edga and family" as we walked hurriedly away.

I was more curious now than ever. I noticed that Mr. Elroy and Lanette remained in the same spot, just watching us. He wobbled a little, but Lanette made sure he didn't fall. He had a pinched look on his face as he twirled that toothpick in his mouth. Once Daddy noticed my distraction, he nudged me to look ahead.

"Edga, you ought to be ashamed of yo-self acting like that. Thems yo people."

"Uh-huh, yeah, they my people alright. Best we keep moving."

After that exchange at the fairground our departure time seemed to move up. Momma had her eyes on Columbus, and Daddy agreed. Both felt that city was north enough for us. Aunt Honey lived there already, so Momma said it just felt right to go there.

Our exodus to Columbus covered a whopping sixty miles, hit or miss a mile or two. Regardless of the distance, we were finally getting out of Preston, Georgia. Our departure also meant we were getting away from Granddaddy and Miss Jean. Now, I loved my Granddaddy, but my feelings toward that Miss Jean could not ever be twisted, molded or shaped into love. Terms more like disdain, contempt, and ill will quickly came to mind, though there were others. I was just too young and too scared to repeat them.

To my surprise and disappointment, my brother Felton and I had to stay a little longer alone with Granddaddy and Miss Jean. The initial trip to Columbus would be without us two. In exchange for me not having a hissy fit, I made Momma promise that she would be gone no more than a day or two. Leaving us with Miss Jean without her was likening to pulling wisdom teeth without lidocaine, being kicked in the shin by a mule or worst having to eat Miss Jean's rhubarb pie. I'd never experienced the first two personally, but from what I heard, both were awfully painful. The latter I knew for certain was downright torture. Simply put, the stay would be one of torment. So, before she and Daddy left, I made her swear on two Bibles, a three-leaf clover, and a picture of white Jesus that I'd shaded in black that she would return to Preston as soon as humanly possible.

After securing the promise of her timely return, out of curiosity, I asked if she'd ever considered New York as an option for our next move. After reading about spectacular New York City and how it was home to some of my literary heroes, like Langston Hughes and James Baldwin, I thought I'd ask. It couldn't hurt. She just rolled her eyes and attempted to shoo me out of the kitchen.

"Wait, Momma, I been thinking. I just finished a really good novel, rather a fantastic novel, about a family moving from one settlement to another. It got me to wondering what our expedition north might be like."

"Expedition?" Momma asked as she pinched biscuits for dinner.

"Yes, our trip."

"Really?" Momma said.

"Yep." I ventured back to one of my classic readings. "Might it be a dark, dusty, and dangerous journey with little food to eat or water to drink? Maybe we'll bump into armed men on the highway that'll keep us from moving to our new settlement. We might even have to smuggle a convict in the back of the wagon under some hay for added protection. You and Daddy can ride in the front of the wagon, while me and Felton cram in the back as we bump along the unchartered and the unknown."

She looked at me like she always did, shook her head and said, "Chile, please. I know you my chile 'cause I had you. But sometimes I do wonder... what is you talking about, armed men and wagons? I sho hope we won't be on no dang gone wagon. They got's cars now and we do plans on driving one. We just going up the road some. Lawd, you and yo magination. Look now, been decided we gone live with your Aunt Honey for a spell, then get our own place. She tells me Columbus is a good place. Say me and Edga can get a job real easy there. Told me white folks hiring maids and yardsmen all the time. Even said it's a slaughterhouse there for Daddy maybe. Be a good place, real good place for us. You know it ain't as country and backwoods as this here Preston. Everybody ain't got to go and pick cotton like they do down here or work at the mill. She even says they got a Colored hospital."

Momma was especially excited about that hospital. Ever since Raymond passed, she'd gotten a little paranoid about any of us getting sick or hurt. A cough, sneeze, scratch, or God forbid a fever was definitely a guarantee to visit Dr. Mitchell's office. And I'd do almost anything to camouflage any of my aches or pains. I'd put a piece of ice on a bruise, a cold cloth on my feverish head, and once I even drank some of that horrid stuff, Black Draught all on my own. What was I thinking? I clearly didn't know it was a ghastly tasting laxative. I might as well have opened a can of motor oil and just drank that. I stayed on the toilet cramping for three days and two nights.

Dr. Mitchell's office was always crammed with plenty of people hacking, sniffing or something. Right before leaving, Momma got in her head that I needed to go to the doctor. *Just to be sho,"* as she said. I fought against going, but like always, I lost.

"But, Momma, I'm fine. It's only a sneeze."

"Girl, you feel hot. Can't take no chances. Folks dropping round here like flies."

Sarcastically, I said, "Take Miss Jean instead. She's closer to dead than I am."

"Hush up that mouth and let's go. Grab yo brother's hand. Ought to be grateful we can walk to Dr. Mitchell. Some folks can't even do that."

"Yes, ma'am."

Dr. Mitchell was the only Colored doctor around for miles. I liked him and found him to be quite intellectual and interesting. He came to Preston as a young man and decided to stay. Occasionally, Dr. Kraftin, the first Jewish person I'd ever met, would come down from Columbus and lend a hand with his practice. His visits mostly occurred during flu season when the waiting room would burst at the seams. Those two met each other at a medical conference in Atlanta many years ago and a lifelong friendship began.

I found Dr. Mitchell's desire to settle in Preston somewhat curious, I must say, especially since he was originally from California. I was so curious about this, on my last visit I decided to ask him about his choice of residence.

"Dr. Mitchell, why on earth did you decide to practice in Preston, of all places? I bet you could live anywhere."

"I could, but I like this place. It's a quiet and slow and I like the people here. Besides, my internship was assigned here and I just never left."

"What's an internship?"

"It's a duration of time when physicians, or rather residents, like I was at the time, are sent to live and work with patients for the most part free of charge. We treat patients and gain knowledge all at the same time. It's a great learning experience."

Looking at him intently, I said, "Soooo, basically, you residents" —I formed quotations with my two fingers—"get to practice on poor Colored people like us huh without actually being bona fide doctors. Is that legal? It doesn't sound like it. I better go and look that up."

Pulling his glasses down from his nose, he said, "Well, hold on there now, child. I tell you, Pearline, of course it's legal. All physicians, regardless of specialty, have to do an internship." He peered down at me intently. "I have to wonder sometimes if you really are a child or an old woman disguised as one. And that's a rhetorical question, young lady."

"A what? Rhetorical?" I asked.

"Never mind, and be still," he said while taking my pulse.

🌀

Momma and Daddy were away a couple of days before they came back to pick up me and Felton. Our stay without Momma felt more like of an eternity than less than seventy-two hours.

Ecstatic is the word which totally summed up my feelings the day of our departure. Finally, no more Granddaddy, and "thank you God" no more Miss Jean. I do believe the feeling was mutual, at least from Miss Jean. She'd made it quite apparent that our time with her was no more enjoyable for her than it was for us. *Now, when you say they momma coming back to get them? Don't make no sense she leaving them here like this. I tell you in my day, folks didn't do these kinda things.*

"Shut up," I'd scream in my head. "Momma's coming back not a minute to soon, old hag." Occasionally, she'd catch me eyeballing her. And of course I'd catch it, but the punishment was well worth it.

I remember the day so clearly when Momma and Daddy returned to Preston to pick us up. Felton and I stood on the front porch fully packed and ready to go. We were both a sight to see, standing on that porch. The night before, I packed both our bags and stacked them right beside the front door. I even slept in my clothes and made Felton do the same so we would wake up ready.

Right after daybreak, I grabbed a biscuit and sat out on the porch to keep a watchful eye for their arrival. It looked like every car that approached our house might be Daddy's. They were all the same color, big and loud like his. I'd perk up, and then deflate as the car would pass right on by.

"Still not them," I mumbled with disappointment.

The crunching sound of the tires rolling on the pebbles and dirt along with the dust flying finally signified that Daddy was driving up. When I turned around to the sound, excitement overcame me.

"Here comes Momma," I said, almost singing. "Felton, they're here."

"Hey, Momma!" I said as I ran toward Daddy's shiny black Buick.

Getting out of the car for Momma was with a little difficulty. Her pregnancy had created quite a large stomach.

Granddaddy and Miss Jean heard the commotion and walked out to the porch. Once Momma saw them, she walked up and hugged him and greeted Miss Jean.

"Ya'll ready, I see," Momma said.

"Them chillun been ready since last night. I do believe they slept in they clothes," Granddaddy said.

"Take this, Daddy. It's the least me and Edga can do to thank ya'll for allowing the chilluns to stay while we was gone." Momma attempted to put some money in his hand while he shook his head no.

"Why, thanks ya." Miss Jean said as she snatched the money from Momma's hand and counted it. "We was 'specting a li'l bit mo, but I guess this a do." She stuffed the folded money in her brassiere.

"Yes, I guess it'll have to," Momma said to Miss Jean. Then mockingly added, "I sho hope it don't get lost down there," referring to Miss Jean's enormous bosoms.

"Pearline and Felton say your goodbyes and thank Daddy and Miss Jean for 'lowing ya'll to stay. We got to get on up the road now."

"Yes, ma'am," we said in unison prior to hugging Granddaddy and mumbling thanks to Miss Jean.

Right before we made our final exit, Miss Jean took the time to happily share every infraction she could remember or make up about my brother and me.

"I thank it's only fitting that I tell you before you leave a few thangs bout yo chilluns."

"Jean, leave them chillun lone. Goodness," Granddaddy said.

"Naw now. She needs to know how she ain't raising them right proper. Somebody need to learn them 'bout cleaning up behind theyselves. Had to stand over them to make sho the dishes was washed. And that Pearline, she sho got a fresh mouth. And all that Felton want to do is play with his trucks. I tell you, in my day . . ." Miss Jean rattled off to Momma.

"She can remember that far back, Momma?" I said under my breath.

"What she say?" Miss Jean asked, not clear of what she'd just heard.

"Oh, nothing." Momma said quickly, while slightly pinching my arm.

I knew Granddaddy didn't necessarily agree with her comments, but he just looked on. She continued to complain about everything from us eating too much, us not cleaning up behind ourselves, to us just breathing more air than we needed. In her opinion, surely we could have breathed a little less. After all, what would be left for the birds and bees to inhale?

Since Daddy didn't like Miss Jean either, he stayed near his car waiting rather impatiently to head back to Columbus. While I was leaning against the porch column, waiting for the conclusion of this tirade, I couldn't resist the temptation rattling in my brain. So I didn't. I crossed my eyes and licked my tongue out at Miss Jean, thinking no one was looking. To my dismay, Miss Jean was looking straight at me.

Next thing you know, she screeches, "I see you, gal, come here!"

"See what?" Momma nervously asked.

"What you talking 'bout, Jean?" Granddaddy asked.

"That ungrateful gal just... come here!" Miss Jean said.

She tried to chase me down the steps, hoping to catch me for one final whooping. Unfortunately for her, I was too fast. I was down those stairs and behind the car next to Daddy before she could take two steps. Fortunately for me, Miss Jean's feet moved faster than her big body was able to keep up with. The conflict in motion caused her to slip and fall right on top of Granddaddy.

"Bam" was the loud thumping sound of their collision. He moaned, "Oh Lawd, Jean, get off me. You gone kill me. I can hardly breathe."

That was the loudest I'd ever heard Granddaddy speak. I guess being crushed will do that.

The sight of it all rattled Momma so much, she shooed Felton along, rushed down to the car, and told Daddy to drive. He pulled off so quickly, the car's tires spit gravel.

As we drove away, Momma said, "Humph, that woman ain't had chicken naw chilluns. Always talking 'bout how to raise somebody else's, the nerve of her. Wish Daddy never married that old hag."

I scrunched my face and licked my tongue out at Miss Jean one more time and doing so felt great. She saw me and tried to get up but couldn't. She and Granddaddy were too tangled up.

As I turned back around, giggling to myself from my last display of disrespect and personal glory, I found Momma looking directly at me. My eyes widened, but before fear could set in, she winked and smiled at me. She clearly hated Miss Jean too.

"Momma?"

"Yes, Pearline."

"I've been concerned that I may not make any friends in Columbus."

"Why? You don't have none now," Felton said with genuine curiosity.

I greeted his comment with a sharp twist to his arm.

"Ouch. Why you do that? She pinched me, Momma."

"Yeah, you lucky that's all you got. Knucklehead," I said.

After a hearty laugh, Daddy said. "That's enough, ya'll."

Momma laughed also and then offered me a bit of reassurance. "You will baby, you will."

5

Simee

"Is ya'll watching?" I said to the crowd standing around my table. "You got's to look real good now. Don't wanna miss nothing." Humph, I done got real good at this here card trick con. This old Mexican down in Jackson learned me how to do it. Said it was best to reel them in first by letting them win a couple of times. Said I had to act real surprise like and mad that they keep winning. Once I let them win a few times, then let the losing begin. The longer the stay, the mo they lose and the mo I make.

"Pick a card, any card. After you lay yo dollar down, that is," I said as folks stood and watched. Finally, two chumps put they money on the table.

"Ready?"

"Yeah, we ready," one said.

I began snapping the cards and shuffling them so fast, I almost got confused. Then I kissed the deck and said pick yo card.

"Uh, I'm gone get this one."

"Looks like you pick the wrong one. Next."

"This one," the other sucker said.

"You lose too. Next."

Before I could convince another sucker to play, I noticed a white man staring at me. He finally walked over and spoke.

"Don't I know you, boy? You look like somebody I know."

"Naw, suh, don't believe you do."

"Humph. I believe I do."

"Naw, suh," I said again, hoping he'd go away.

"Yes, hell I do. You that Nigger from down in Jackson. Ain't you?"

"Naw, suh. That ain't me."

He walked closer to the table, then said "Let me see them cards."

"I can't do that. These here is special cards. Not anybody can touch them."

"Boy, give me them damn cards."

"You know what? I'm done. See ya'll good people another time."

I started packing up my things to walk away. In my hurry to leave, I left my deck of cards. It didn't take long for one of men to thumb through them and realize what I had done. Next thing you know, I was standing before the county judge. I had been arrested and sent to the county jail.

"How long you say you in here for?" my cell mate, Lester Green, asked me again. Before I could twist my mouth to answer him one mo time, he kept talking like he never asked me a question.

"Me? Got bout another thirty years, I reckon. Shit, after nineteen I stopped counting. Hey, guard!" he started to yell. "Can't a man get some water up in here? And brang a clean cup this time. I's prefer not to share my water with the vermin round here ya'll call pets. Damn, it's hot in here. Humph. You marred? I am. You know, my wife and my woman done stopped coming to see me. Now, how is that possible? Gertrude, she my wife. She a fat, mean, yella thang. Told me when I met her, she be part Injun. Humph. I say mo like part barracuda. Gerty, that's what I calls her, is bout yeh high and yeh wide," Lester said as he brought one hand up near his chest and then opened his arms wide in front of him.

"Really?"

"Uh-huh, and can you believe she done marred again?"

"How's that? Thought you said ya'll was still marred."

"I did. She say we divorced. I didn't. Come telling me she needs a man round to help feeds our chilluns. I told her if she ain't eat so much, be more food left for the chilluns. I don't know much, but I do know one ham should accommodate more than one woman. We ain't divorce. I know 'cause I ain't never signed nothing and I never will. Damn straight. Now, Maggie May, she my woman. She fat too but she ain't yella, mo like dark molasses. One yella woman is enough for me. You know yella womens sleep with they fist balled up."

"Naw, didn't know that."

"Yeah they do. Now, 'cause Maggie May so big, it take a minute or two to get her moving, but when I do, Lawd hab mercy. She got the biggest legs and thighs one man can handle. Which by the way, she most certainly needs. Her legs is what the fancy folks calls a necessity."

"A necessity?" I asked.

"Yeah, she needs them."

"Why?"

"Something got to hold hu big ass up."

"Lester?"

"Yeah man?"

"Do you ever shut up? Damn, you 'bout to make my ears bleed."

"Just making a li'l small talk is all."

"Small? That's what you call running yo mouth like that. Damn. Look Nigger, you ain't shut up since they moved me in here with you which, by the way, is some bullshit," I yelled through the bars.

"No need for all that, man. Trying to be friendly is all."

"Well, friendly yo ass on way from me and shut the hell up."

After shutting him up, I sat down on my bunk to think a minute. June 5th is finally here. Today is my last day here at the Mississippi State Penitentiary. A place inmates call Hell's second home. Man, I can't get out of here fast enough. Specially, since they put me in here with Lester. He talk mo than any woman I know. Yap, yap, yap, all he do. For my entire sentence, I was in stockade number four, then was moved to number five with his ass. Hell, ifin I knowed I'd have to listen to this here fool every day, I would have begged to stay in number four with the sisses. Most time, this stockade is where they put you when you bout to be freed. Though I don't think Lester going nowhere. Looking at him, you would never suspect this to be true, but he in here for killing two men. I know it was hard for me to believe.

This ain't no easy place to be, but being locked up ain't nothing new for me. Humph, the law started locking me up when I was a boy. I did li'l thangs like stealing. You know, a pie here, a wagon there. I even killed a couple of cats. They deserved it. Seem to me like they always walking round like they owned the place. And I didn't like the way they looked at me, all uppity like.

From thieving and killing cats, I moved on to conning. That profession offered mo money. Over time, it became quite easy for me. All I had to do was talk, smile, and look these womens and girls straight in the eye. I got so good, one time I had a gal and her momma giving me money and other thangs. The preacher got wind of it and told my momma something was wrong with me. He said that I was messing with some real fire, sleeping with a momma and her child. He even told her that something bad was gone happen if I kept going the way I was. My momma didn't pay him no mind. She shooed him away like a gnat buzzing about her head. I was just fine in her mind. The only thing that woman ever cared about was my daddy. Not me, not her people, just my daddy.

It was clear Daddy didn't care much about me either. Although he did love my brother Edga. "The good one" is what he called him. Truth be told, he is much different from me. Mostly 'cause he stay out of trouble, while I on the other hand, stays in it. I haven't seen my dear brother in a long time. Probably for the best, since he don't care for me much after what happened. None of that was my fault. He can thank our low-down Daddy for that.

"Simee Scott?"

"Yeah, boss."

"You ready, got yo bags?

"Yeah, boss."

"Follow me," the fat suma-bitch guard said as he unlocked my cell.

"Good knowing you, Simee. You take care. Don't forget where you came from, now. Make it a lot easy to find on your way back," Lester said laughing as I walked out of the cell, then yelled: "Would somebody bring me some damn water."

Walking away, knowing that I was not walking to another cell, made my knees shake a little. My mind knew I was leaving, but a fear came over me like none before. I was afraid the guards was gone change their minds and say I ain't going nowhere. I knew that could happen, I'd seen it many times before.

Finally, after what seemed to be the longest walk ever, we arrived to a back office in the prison. This part of the building was clean, lights were bright, and it smelled fresh like Pine-Sol. I walked through like I was walking on glass floors. Made sure not to walk too hard. Felt like if I did, I might break something and be right back in stockade number four.

"You can stop right here," the guard said to me.

"Yeah, boss."

"Unlock his shackles," a voice from behind us yelled out.

Even with that command to the guard, I stood frozen. As the chains fell from my wrist and my ankles, I watched them bounce on the floor, but I dared not to smile.

"On behalf of the great state of Mississippi and the Mississippi State Penitentiary you free to go. Don't make yo way back round, Nigger. Next time we gone bury you here," the fat-bellied warden said as he pulled the keys from his belt to unlock the iron door that separated me from my freedom.

"Yeah, boss."

6

Louise

I still was feeling poorly the day after we arrived in Columbus. All the excitement from our departure had taken a toll on me. Even in Edga's prized Buick, the drive to Columbus was hot, bumpy and uncomfortable. I complained, yes complained the entire way. Prior to arriving, I told Edga I was gone throw up if he didn't get me out of that car and right quick like. This was my seventh month of carrying and it was surely hard on me. Edga noticed a Phillips 66 filling station for gas on Macon Road and stopped not a minute too soon. I hopped out of that car so quick I stumbled and almost fell. The next thing you know, I'm throwing up right on the side of the car. Edga, being Edga, foolishly asked that I watch my aim. His comment was met with some rare cussing from me.

"Edga, you go straight to hell and you can take this here car which-cha."

He just ticked me off more by laughing. Like to see him carry all this extra round, specially in this here heat.

"You all right, ma'am?" this friendly voice coming from a friendly face asked me as he walked up to the car, wiping his oil-stained hands with a dirty cloth.

"Yes suh, I'll be fine in just one min—" I said right before I gagged and threw up again.

"My, my. I got's some saltine crackers and ginger ale in the station, if that'll help some. They seem to help my wife."

The thought of food, even saltines, just made me throw up even harder. I waved my hand to motion him away and shook my head.

"Well, all right then. Hey, how ya'll doing?"

"We fine," Edga said as he exited the car.

"Now let me guess, I betcha ya'll them new folks from down in Preston, ain't cha!"

Edga looked surprised and answered, "Why yes, suh, and you is?"

"My name is Robert, but folks call me Rev. Evans. Rev is short for Reverend. I pastor the church here named Mount Pleasant Baptist Church and run this here filling station too. Me and a fellow named RaShay, but he ain't here right now."

"Well, it's a pleasure meeting you. This is my wife Louise and as you can see, she 'specting too. Them is my other chilluns in the back seat. Ya'll say hello."

As those two chatted with each other, I continued to unsuccessfully battle my morning, noon, and night sickness. Leaning against the car, I noticed both Edga and the Rev quickly look at each other and grin quietly at me. I saw nothing funny 'bout this at all.

"Just curious, Rev. Evans. You did say Rev?

"I did."

"How'd you know we were from Preston? We just pulled in here," Pearline unexpectedly asked.

"And yo name is, young lady?" he asked. Looking at her a bit bothered, probably thanking surely this here chile ain't interrupting us grown folks.

"My name is Pearline, suh. I'm the oldest."

"Pearline," I called out. "What I done told you? Stay outta grown folks' business. You hear me. Igno her, suh. She know better."

"That's all right, that's al-right. Children much more curious these day than in ours. Well, if you must know, young lady, this here is a very small place. Ain't many secrets round here. Sides, Honey described ya'll to a tee and she told me ya'll would be pulling in sometimes today. Most likely before sundown so, it wasn't hard to figure out. Now Miss Pearline, do you mind if I ask your daddy a question?"

"Of course not, sir." She looked like she knew he really wasn't asking for her permission but that he found her entertaining.

"Is ya'll church-going folks?" Rev. Evans asked.

"Why yes, suh, we sho is," Edga said.

"I figured as much, being Honey people and all. I'd love to see you and yo family come to church first chance ya'll get."

"No trouble at all. Of course we be there. We 'preciate you asking."

"Ok, now, anything you need I'm just a stone's throw away. I live in The Quarters too. Four houses down from Honey. Me, my wife Mary, and my seven chilluns would love to have ya'll over when you get settled in. Ain't bragging or nothing, but nobody fry chicken and make buttermilk cornbread round here like my Mary. Just let me know."

"Gone do that, Rev, and thank ya," Edga said.

"See ya'll soon." He waved to us as we pulled away from the filling station.

We finally arrived at the main entrance to The Quarters. As we turned onto Shepherd Drive, I told Edga, "My, it's beautiful. Look like they keep it up real good in here. My eyes can't seem to catch it all."

Pearline thought it was beautiful too. The wide smile on her face gave that away. As we drove in, she rolled her back window all the way down and rested her head on the car door to get the best view. Though the community seemed a bit small or rather "quaint," as my chile would say, we were all still excited about this move. Couldn't help but notice the streets were nicely paved and cleaned. They was narrow but wide enough for two cars to pass by each other. Edga even said he liked how all the houses neatly lined both sides of the road. He said they set by each other like a row of dominos. Families could even park they cars, if they had one, in a shared driveway 'tween each house. To our surprise and delight, most of the houses was brick, with only a few wooden ones scattered about. But all of them had front porches with rocking chairs and plants hanging from the porch. Lawd, we even saw flower beds and vegetable gardens one after the other in every yard we passed. Even the playing chilluns was a pleasure to see. Made me feel good to know my chillun would have others to play with.

As we drove through, people turned their attention to us newcomers. Most seemed friendly enough with the waving of hands. 'Cept, a few did look over they glasses with folded arms, being what I considered to be a little uppity. I reminded Edga and Pearline that every community has a "Miss Jean" or two and The Quarters ain't gone be no different.

After finally making it to my sistah's home me, Edga, and Pearline stretched outside the car. Our legs and feet demanded some relief following that long ride. Since Honey wasn't home yet, Edga and Pearline had the pleasure of unloading the car. Our stuff was everywhere, suitcases, boxes and of course Pearline's books. Edga fussed each time he moved a box telling me and the chilluns, *Ain't this much reading good for nobody, I tell you.*

"How ya'll doing?" a stranger who appeared out nowhere asked. Every last one of us jumped when she spoke, even my little Felton. Not one of us saw her coming or crossing the street.

"So how ya'll doing?" she repeated, irritated we'd missed her first greeting.

"We fine, ma'am. I'm Louise, this is my husband Edga and chilluns, Pearline and Felton."

"Uh-huh, I'm Addie, Addie Mae Harris. I live rights cross the street from here. Looks like ya'll got a load here. Needs any help 'cause I'll make them boys cross the way come and help."

"No ma'am. But we thank you anyway."

"Guess you Honey sistah?"

"Why yes, ma'am, I sho am. We just come up from Preston."

"I figured ya'll them. Yeah, I heard ya'll was coming. Well, welcome."

"Good to meet you too. We just pulled in," I said.

"Like I said, I lives right cross that street. I keep a good eye on everythangs round here. Everythang. Not much get pass me, specially these here chilluns," she stated, gazing at both Pearline and Felton, while at the same time pointing to some children playing next door. I could see that Pearline knew at that very moment she met Miss Addie "that she was that neighbor." The nosy, busybody, child-watching, I'm gone tell your momma neighbor.

"Yes ma'am. Me and Edga sho 'preciates that. Ain't nothing like having nosy—I mean, nice neighbors," I said.

"You welcome."

"Uh, 'scuse me, Miss Addie, me and my husband is both looking for work right now. If you know of anything we sho be thankful for your help. We came up here before looking and didn't have no luck finding nothing. "

"Luck ain't what you need. Don't know why that Honey didn't just ask me from the start. Well, I just might know of something. I hear you a butcher, Edga."

"Yes ma'am, I am," he said proudly.

Distracted by the playing children, she interrupted him. "Scuse me a minute, Edga, these here chilluns gone run me ragged. Boy, stop that running, you hear me? Slow yo-self down. Just wait to yo Momma get home." Turning back toward Edga, she says, "Now you was saying."

Disturbed by her rudeness, Edga continued, "I was saying, I'm real good at it. They calls me 'Quicks' down in Preston."

Not too impressed, she twisted her lips and said, "Uh-huh. Well, gone down to Southern Mill, on Third Street tomorrow morning first thang. My brother Booker run a shift over there. He can probably get you on. I'll tell him you coming tomorrow."

"Yes, ma'am. Why, why, thank you. Me and my wife 'preciates that."

"Yeah, you welcome. Remember now, I keep a good eye on these here chilluns. All of them, old and new."

We all let out a sigh of relief when she walked away, Pearline especially. After that session with her she knew Miss Addie would be the one to watch, because she'd sholl be somewhere watching her.

No one realized just how much stuff was jam-packed in and on that car of Edga's. Taking them boxes down seemed never ending for them. Pearline complained that it felt like the bags and boxes were sprouting from the car. Every time they got one down, another one popped up. We were all pretty worn out, especially me. For a while I felt like this here move and carrying this baby was gone be the life of me. After they pulled the last bag down from the car, we could finally head on in the house. I opened the front door and everyone trailed in behind me. Once in, we just stood there, at least for a minute or so staring.

"Boy, look at this place, Momma. I've never seen a cleaner house in all my life, except yours, of course," Pearline said mindful not to show no favor with her aunt's housekeeping over mine. I did agree with her, just kept it to myself though.

"You sho she living here? Don't look like nobody live in this place. Look like what they call a mu-zium," Edga said.

"Edga, what you know 'bout a museum?" I asked him.

"I know this place look like one."

All the beds was tightly made, the sink was free of dishes, not a dust ball in sight. That Honey always took great pride in keeping a clean house. And she made no exception this day. As we all continued to wander through the house, admiring everythang, Edga tripped and fell but caught hisself against the door frame.

"You all right, Daddy?" Pearline asked

Gathering himself, he said, "Now, why in the world would she put this dang on thang right here? Somebody likely to kill theyselves falling over it."

Honey had placed a potted plant in the most unusual place. Right in the walkway of the door entering her room.

"Never mind why. You just watch where you walking is all. Gone and walk round it next time. Her house, her plant," I said to him.

I walked to Honey's room and noticed three men's jackets hanging on her door. "Lawd, this girl can't be without one," I said, forgetting my chilluns was in earshot.

"Without what?" Pearline asked.

"Neva you mind."

"Whose jackets are these, Momma? I thought Aunt Honey lived alone."

"Depend on what time of day it is," Edga joked.

"Shut up, Edga," I said.

"It looks like one of those fancy hotels I've read about, huh, Momma? Pearline chimed in. "She has roses on the coffee table and the kitchen table. It even smells good in here. Look, even the windows and countertops have a sparkle to them."

Honey tended to keep each item in her house in its rightful place, even the canned goods. She was all about order. I guess order helped to keep her mind clear. She would always say, "*Everythang had its place.*" That girl even had a thing for turning the can food labels to the front and stacking them by what they was, vegetables or fruit.

All of a sudden, the back screen door screeched open and snapped close. Honey had just walked in.

Laughing and yelling as she strolled to the front, she said, "Edga, is that you I smell? You and that damn cologne. Whew-we." She entered the front room holding her nose and fanning her hand in front of her face.

"Go to hell, Honey!" he shot back.

"Edga, watch yo mouth!" I said, quickly interceding.

"I thought so! I tell you, Edga, I smell you for I see you every time." Clearly, she enjoyed picking on my husband.

Honey walked right past him, smiling from ear to ear. With her arms extended, she headed to Pearline, me and Felton. Looked like she was just as happy to see us as we were to see her, 'cept for Edga. It was hard to measure much with those two. They had what I called an interesting relationship. At any rate, both my chilluns and me pretty much raced each other to her arms.

"Aunt Honey!" Pearline yelled.

"Hey, Unt Hunee," Felton said.

"Hey girl!" I said.

"Hey there babies." She said. "Glad to see ya'll done made it here good. My, my, my. Come here, let me look at ya'll chilluns. Pearline, you done got so big and pretty and Felton, you just as handsome. Just look-at-cha. How was that ride up the road?"

"Other than the heat, the flies, and your sista thowing up at every turn, I guess I'd say it was delightful," Daddy piped up.

"Oh, shut up, Edga! It was fine, Honey," I said.

Looking at Pearline and winking at the same time, she said, "I guess they honeymoon is over huh?"

"We just glad to be here and thankful we can stay with you for a spell. Shouldn't take us that long to get settled." I wobbled over to the couch, holding my stomach to sit down. "Oh, by the way, your neighbor Miss Addie cross the street, walked over and introduced herself. I asked her if she knew about any work. Hope that was okay?"

"Uh-huh," she said.

"She told Edga to go down to the slaughterhouse tomorrow, said her brother could help him get a job."

"She did, huh? Yeah, well, gone down there. Booker can probably get him on since he been down there fo-ever, with his lazy behind. Funny, he known to find you work but seem contrary to doing any himself. Always sitting and pointing. Do this, move that. And Addie, I tell you, that's one nosy woman, her and them sistahs up the way, MinLee and Carrie. They keep up with everythang in The Quarters. You bound to meet them two and the rest of them."

"The rest of them?" I asked.

"Yep, the rest of them. They gone make sho of that. Watch them now: if they don't know your business, they sho to make some up. I bet Addie popped up like a ghost. Didn't she? Seems like you never see that woman coming and most times don't see her going. The chillun call her Caspar, 'cept they say she ain't so friendly. Just plain spooky sometimes. Well, kick your shoes off and rest some. I got everythang ready for ya'll. Louise, you and Edga take my bedroom, and Pearline and Felton can share the spare room. It's more than enough space."

"Where you gone sleep, Honey? We can't take both your beds. Them chilluns can make a pallet on the floor. "

"Naw, they can't. And yes, ya'll can. I'm fine, I'll sleep right here on this couch. Sleep here most nights anyway. Just glad ya'll here. Gone and wash up and sit a while. I'll get supper on. I got it all planned out. Fried chicken, collards, crackling bread, okra, candied yams, and sweet tea, make me hungry just saying it. And for my favorite niece, I made a chocolate cake with pecans on top and all through it. Just like you like it."

It was routine for Honey to call Pearline her favorite niece. A title she accepted proudly. Although she was without any competition, since she was her only niece. As far back as I can remember, Honey was always her favorite too. Honey was a beautiful, spirited woman, forever somewhere laughing and awfully quick-witted. Charm and charisma seemed to seep through her. Someone was always saying, *That girl sho is some-em, she just a mess,* and they were right. She could make you laugh or at least pull a smile from you, just by a look. Something funny was sho to show up in her presence.

"Aunt Honey, I just love your home. It's beautiful. I'm not surprised, though. You've always reflected a sense of style, class, and sophistication."

"Why, thank you, baby. I try."

"Yeah, you try, all right," Edga said. "Look like you'd try and move that killa plant out of the doorway for somebody kills they self. I nearly bout fell over it."

"Done told you to walk round it, Edga. Her house, her plant," I said again.

"It's all right. I'll move Shakespeare. Would sho hate to have to drag Edga outta her. Ain't that right, Louise?"

"Shakespeare? Lawd, this crazy woman done named her plant Shakespeare," Edga said.

As Edga and Honey went back and forth with silliness, I was stuck on that last comment from Honey. My eyes got bigger than saucers and I could hardly believe what she'd just

said. For a minute, it was like I was frozen. Ain't heard her
mention nothing like that since we was chilluns. Specially
since the last time we drugged anythang together it was a
dead body. Now to add to my worry, what is she doing with
them jackets in her closet? I tell you one thing, them mens
better still be round to wear them.

"Why on earth would she make a joke like that?" I thought.
"Lawd Jesus, what's going on with her now? Never in a hundred years did I thank she'd say something like that. I sho
hope this girl ain't got caught up in no mess. I done got too
old for her foolishness."

"Momma, Momma, Momma," Pearline said as she shook
my shoulder to gain my attention.

"Huh?" I said, turning toward her voice and noticing all
three of them staring at me.

"You OK?"

"Yeah, baby, I'm fine."

"No, you're not. You look like you've seen a ghost or
something."

"Naw, baby, ain't seen no ghost,"

I step outside of the house, pretending to admire Honey's
tomato plants out back, then I called her. "Honey, come here
for a minute."

"Yes, Momma, I mean Louise."

"Who them coat jackets belong to?"

"What coat jackets?"

"Girl, don't play with me."

"Them is from friends of mine. Herbert Lee, James Alan,
and LeRoy. Why?"

"So you was seeing all three at the same time?"

"Louise, why is any of this yo business?"

"You know why I'm asking."

"Goodness, it was a while back. They was just some company to pass the time with. Sides, I ain't seeing them no mo."

"You ain't seeing them no mo? Where is they now, Honey?"

Laughing, she said, "Don't worry, they ain't gone wash up nowhere."

"That's not funny."

"But the look on yo face is."

7

Honey

On Sunday of their second week in The Quarters, when it was time to go to church, my brother-in-law decided to do some shopping. He had promised Rev. Evans of his family's attendance, but he felt it only fair to mull over all of their options for worship. That old fool could mull all he wanted to, there wouldn't be any change for me. Mount Pleasant was my church home. However, nearby The Quarters were three other choices for service, the Sanctified & Holy Church of God and Christ, Kingdom Hall, a Jehovah Witness church, and the 4th Street AME church. After much careful consideration, he felt his selection was a pretty easy and clear pick for his family.

As we all sat having supper one night, Edga decided to share his rationale in selecting a place of proper worship.

"Them Jehovah Witness bothers people way too much. They always show up at folks' houses uninvited. Folks get tired of hiding in they own house. And them Holy Ghost people do too much dancing, running, and screaming. It's a wonder they don't hurt they selves running round like that. But I tell you, they co-or-dination is awfully suspicious if you ask me. Look like somebody be hurt by now. Just too much for me, get on my nerves bad. Oh, and them ol'Episcaling Coloreds."

"Episcopal, Daddy." Pearline corrected as me and Louise both shook our heads.

"Epissing, Egyptions, Episcaling, humph, whatever they call they selves! They just too damn uppity. Always trying to sang like they know that opry or something—who wanna listen to that all day? Plus, they boring, bore-rang, with a capital B and a capital R. Always sitting upright, back straight as a board. Do they even say Amen over there? Put me plumb to sleep. Mount Pleasant Baptist Church will do us just fine."

"Hurry on up! We gone be late. Felton, fix you collar and Edga, take off that hat. You know you ain't sitting in church with no hat on," Louise said as we were walking up the steps to enter the church.

"Woman, I'm gone take my hat off," he grumbled. "My goodness, I been going to church thirty some years. Don't need you to tell me to take my hat off. "

"I'm just like my daddy, don't like walking in nobody church late. Folks turn round looking at you funny. Make me uncomfortable," Louise said.

"From my recollection, the good Lawd said come as you is and if late is as you is, I reckon he'd still like to see ya." Edga grabbed Felton's hand, telling him, "Come on, boy, for I hurt yo momma."

As we all walked in the church, the heat greeted us first. It was awfully hot this Sunday and sadly, them slow spinning fans they'd propped up in the windows didn't offer any relief. Looked to me like the fans was sweating too. To fight the heat, to they best abilities, everyone was fanning away. As we continued walking down the aisle, most of those present took a moment to share a nod and smile. They of course recognized me, but my kin caused some speculation. I could see the eyes squinching for some and widening for others. There goes that Robert Lee and Homer. I wish they would stop smiling at me. It ain't gone neva happen. I don't like neither one of them. One too fat and the other too country. Sides, they terrible in bed.

Once we got to our row, we were noticed by Reverend Evans. His demeanor changed and he seemed to light up as we all sat down. He even nodded at us as he stood behind the podium. I noticed that Pearline was taking in the scenery. That chile, she always thanking, thanking on something. I saw Louise looking around herself. Our church was nice with more fancy stuff than the one they left in Preston with that old fool Bow, Low or whatever they call him. We was good at keeping the wooden pews polished, not one sight of chipping paint from the ceiling or walls. The gold-plated collection plates were neatly stacked on the front table, right next to the communion glasses, and praying chairs, and the brightly lit cross on the pulpit was always a sight to see.

"And now for the announcements, gone head Sistah Smith," Rev. Evans said. This was his cue to the church secretary to begin with this week's past, current, and future events.

"Good morning, saints!" Sistah Smith began with as she walked in front of the congregation.

"Good morning" bounced back from the congregation, with a shameful dull response.

Annoyed, she repeated herself. This time she was a bit louder and stern in her delivery. "I said, Good morning, saints!'

We all replied with much more enthusiasm the second time around: "Good morning!"

"That's better," she said, peering over her glasses. "Here are the announcements. Brother Hezekiah and Sistah Ernestine is still on the sick and shut-in list. Ya'll need to make sure to stop by and take them a plate, some hot coffee, or dessert. Ain't nothing worse than being sick and nobody stop to check on you." Amens began to ripple through the sanctuary. "Now, Mr. Job's home-going service is this Saturday at eleven. It's gone be crowded, so get here on time. And as I always say, early is on time and on time is just about late, and late is, *well, just keep yo behind at home*"—the crowd said in unison with her. "Now, if anybody in here got's some extra chairs they can loan us, please see Deacon Buster. With all them people here next week, we don't want to run out of seats. As you know, we is still collecting for the building fund. Rev is de-termined to build us a new church up the road on the land Mr. Job left us. So give what you can, every bit counts. On your way out, Sistah Hall gone have a basket for you to place your contribution in. Now last Sunday, we didn't do so good, but I know this Sunday gone be better, amen?"

"Amen," flowed from the congregation.

"Last, but certainly not least, the missionary society is having a bake sale for pastor's anniversary right after church, so make sho to buy some of them cake slices. I believe Sistah Dean made one of them lemon pound cakes, and we all know, can't nobody make them lemon pound cakes like Hester. Oh, for I forget, make sho you knock hard when you stop and visit Brother Hezekiah. I thank sometime he don't hear so good and he's been missing some of his visitors."

"Oh, 'scuse me, one mo thang I forgot to mention. I'm sho by now ya'll done noticed the new fans from Heavenly Rest Funeral Home," Sistah Smith said. "Ya'll can thanks Rufus and Bernice for them."

Amen's, thank you's, clapping, and head nodding flooded the church almost in unisons.

"Now will all the visitors please rise?" Sistah Smith continued.

As we looked around, it appeared my family was the only visitors or at least the only ones to stand. Once they rose from they seats, they was greeted with more hand clapping and "welcomes."

"Would you please tell us your name, your church affiliation and any other thangs you'd like to share?"

Edga uncomfortably looked at Louise and she returned the same look. Finally, he cleared his throat and said, "We the Scotts. This here my wife, Louise, and chilluns, Pearline and Felton. We come up here from Preston. My wife's sistah is Honey. Thank ya!"

"And your church affiliation?" she asked with an air of judgment.

"Uh, Pastor Low, uh, I mean, Pastor Bow from New Harvest."

Almost before he could finish, Reverend Evans popped up from his chair and happily chimed in. "I'd like for everybody to welcome the Scotts and make them feel at home. Like he said, they just moved here up from Preston and they's Honey people. I met them first time over at the filling station. Now, he a man of his word, I tell you. He said he and his family would be in church and here they is. Praise Gawd and Hallelujah!"

Amens, sho nuffs, and other praises flowed through the church like an orchestrated symphony. Louise and Edga looked around nodding and smiling, Felton was preoccupied with the little toy truck he snuck in, and I'm sho Pearline was wondering how much longer we would be in this heat box. Worshipping was fine, but it was just difficult to pay attention. It was just too hot. All the singing, praying and preaching in the world couldn't lessen the discomfort of the heat. Every last one of us was more than ready to go when the congregation was finally dismissed.

Right after the benediction, we stood patiently and waited for the crowd to disperse so that we could follow. Once we finally entered the center aisle to leave, we were quickly surrounded. As I expected, fellow church members anxiously waited to introduce themselves. One after the other, they extended handshakes, *how ya'lls* and other pleasantries our way. I noticed one man in particular nearly bout break his neck to get to me. I was not happy with his pursuit. I nearly knocked Pearline over to get away from him.

To add a touch of oddness, a lady dressed in all black, including a black veil, asked in this eerie voice. "Is ya'll related to Vondell Scott down in Preston?"

"Yes, ma'am, that's my third cousin on my Daddy's side. Sad to say, we buried him last month," Edga said.

Cheerfully she snapped her finger. "That's where I know ya'll from. I was there for his home going. I sat right on the second row, on the left-hand side, right behind his wife." Then with a hint of bother she added, "Woulda sat on the front row, but the ushers said the front row was for family only. Humph. Oh, I'm Prudence, Prudence May Jenkins, by the way."

Louise noticed as she spoke that I, as well as a few others standing near, slightly shook their heads and rolled their eyes

"How do, ma'am?" Edga said.

"And I'm Wilhelmina, the Sunday school superintendent; I'm in charge of the Sunday school," said a woman who stepped in front of Prudence, looking directly at Edga. "Anythang to do with Sunday School come through me first. And if you need anything, I means anything, don't hesitate to ask."

"Well, okay. We's make sho to remember that," Louise said as she stepped in front of her husband and reached to shake her hand in place of Edga's. I think Louise was rattled at the tone of this Wilhelmina. Not to mention annoyed that she seemed to be flirting with her husband right inside the church.

We continued to stand, hoping this greeting would soon come to a close. Without fail, another oddity occurred. A white hand made its way through the crowd toward Louise. Of course I knew who it was, but with all the other foolishness I just stood there.

"Hello, I'm Agatha, Agathe Deneuve," she said. "I live *deux*, which is two, doors down from here."

"Deux?" Edga said as both Louise and I rolled our eyes at him.

Since Agatha was from France, her way of talking was much different than ours. It was thick and foreign. The sound reminded me of one of them actors, sorta like the ones on the radio. Pearline nervously looked at me, but I just ignored her. I didn't rightly know what else to do.

"How do you, ma'am?" Louise finally said.

"Very well, thank you. And young lady," she said to Pearline, "I teach French. If you'd like some free lessons, you are welcome to come by my home on Saturday's between noon and three. *Entendu?*"

"Yes ma'am." Pearline said. Without a clue to what *entendu* meant.

"That means, do you understand? Don't worry, I'll teach you."

"Agatha, ain't nobody interested in no French. Do we look like we anywhere close to France? Poly vu frenchie yo-self on outta here. How ya'll doing?" this very short man said, as he interrupted Miss Agatha. "They call me Turnerd. Turnerd with a T."

"We good. Good to meet you too," Edga replied.

"See ya'll made it," Miss Addie said, while glancing over at Pearline and Felton.

"Yes ma'am, good to see you again."

"Now, I'm Gloell Randle, and this my here my son Spudnick."

This last introduction caused all four of them to stop and stare. Even Felton was distracted momentarily from his truck. They looked a bit longer than they should have, but I couldn't blame them.

"Ah, she means, her daughter," Spudnick said as he extended his/her hand in a very dainty fashion toward Edga. "I'm Spudnick."

They were all taken aback. It was obvious that Spudnick was a man, but he was completely dressed as a woman. He always wore a dress, a flower in his hair, and the highest heels you could find on those big feet of his. Not to mention he also painted his lips and fingernails a bright red. This sight was clearly one neither of them had seen before. Finally, after time seemed to shake loose from standing still, I elbowed Louise, she pinched Edga and he nudged Pearline. Each move was in step to disrupt they gawking. Following a couple of ouches and shoves, it worked. Lawd Jesus, they finally stopped. I heard Mr. Buster whisper to Edga, "I'll explain later."

"And Edga, we Beatrice and Rufus Jones," Rufus said, pointing to his wife as he handed him a business card with one hand and rapidly shook his hand with the other.

"Nice to meet you," he said, almost exhausted, clearly hoping this final introduction would allow us out.

After all the introductions concluded, we hurriedly returned to our car to head home. Before the first car door closed completely, Edga started:

"Them some crazy ass folks, I tell you, Louise. Crazy."

"Edga, watch yo mouth . We ain't even left the church grounds yet."

"Naw, woman. In all my days, I ain't neva seen so many clowns in one place, 'cept when the circus came to town last summer. Look like all of them bout nuts. And Honey, I remember that woman in all that black—you should too, Louise. She was the one that bout turned over Vondell's casket at his funeral. Hollered 'Lazarus, rise, rise' the whole damn time. Couldn't even hear the preacher man finish po Vondell's eulogy. And you know she ain't even our kin. Nobody even knew who she was. Just showed up. Folks still talking 'bout that to this here day."

"Edga. That's enough."

"Naw, it ain't, woman! You done brung me and my chillun to this here crazyville. Funny-talking white woman, man shorter than even yo daddy, another one dressed up like a woman, Lawd. I believe I done seent it all." As he drove, he nervously attempted to light the cigarette dangling from his lips.

Time would shorly tell and show that he was wrong on that assumption. Unbeknownst to them all, the adventures in Columbus, Georgia, had just begun.

It didn't take them long to get settled in The Quarters. Thankfully, everything started to fall right in line. They got they own place only a road over from me. Louise and specially that niece of mine was thrilled that they were so close. That Edga, on the other hand, preferred at least another mile or two. He did get that job down at the slaughterhouse, and Louise started working as a maid for the young white couple by the name of McLands. They lived in the white part of town, right cross the railroad tracks.

She stepped right into her new job. Since she was always good at cleaning, washing, ironing, and folding, she was ready. Don't know to this here day how she got them pleats just right and starched them shirts like they'd crack, but she did. Louise and Edga both stayed busy working and running that house of theirs and now managing three chilluns. Sometimes they both be so dogged tired, looked like they'd fall asleep standing up. They kept Pearline pretty busy as well, though she wasn't too happy about it.

"Pearline, gone in the room and brang yo brother to me, time for his feeding. Then I wants you to walk over to the McLands and pick up them clothes. When you drop them clothes off, come back by here and get a plate to take on over to Sistah Ernestine. And when you finish all of that, and I do mean all of it, you can go over to Miss Agatha and then to the library before it gets dark."

"Uh, would you like for me to build a bridge while rescuing some sheep and walk the dog we don't have too? Geesh!" she mumbled.

"What you say?" Louise yelled from the front of the house.

"That gurl, she ain't said nothing. Yo hearing getting as bad as yo cooking," I said, trying to keep my niece from a pop on the butt.

"Nothing, Momma. I swear, sometimes I believe that woman has antennas on her ears."

"Uh-huh, that's what I thought, missy," Louise yelled back.

"Watch yo mouth. You want us both in trouble?" I asked Pearline.

"No, ma'am."

"All right, gone and do what yo momma said."

Pearline left the house in a hurry. She always did come Saturday mornings. She knew once she finished all her chores and her momma's extras, both Miss Agatha and that library would be waiting to greet her. I always felt like that chile's love of books outweighed pretty much everythang else. Never was a time you didn't see her opening a book or finishing up one. Though sometimes she'd get too lost in reading, so to speak, she made all us proud.

I walked up to the kitchen once Pearline was clear of the house. I wanted to make sure she was gone before I shared with Louise what was troubling me.

"Louise, I been thinking."

"Bout?"

"I think I'm sick."

"What, why?"

"Been to 'fraid to tell you, but I can't sleep at night. Seem like I sweat up every nightgown I put on, and I'm tired all the time. My mood seem to be always changing. Good one minute, pissed the next. Even get these headaches that won't go away."

Louise began to smile. Her smile moved to a giggle and her giggle turned into a laugh that proceeded to fold her over laughing more with tears.

"You ain't sick, fool. You just mean as hell and it sound like you going through the change."

"What change?"

"The Change."

"Ain't I too young for that? I thought that only happened when you're old like you or something."

"Ha. Ha. For some folks it happens sooner than later. Once I heard Granny Rose say some womens start early, specially if they ain't had no chilluns. If you ask me, you need some...."

"Some what?"

"You know."

"No, I don't."

"S-e-x." She spelled in a whispering tone.

"Sex?" I replied loudly.

"Girl, watch yo mouth. Got chilluns round here."

"You're the one who said it. And that's the last thing on my mind. What that got to do with me not sweating at night?"

"I figure you can get some loving, have a little fun, and make me a niece or a nephew all at the same time."

"Humph."

"Well, who's the prude now? A little loving ain't never hurt nobody."

8

Pearline

I've been told time and time again that I'm special. Depending on who says it constitutes how I receive it. Coming from Momma and Aunt Honey, it's always flattering, but there are others around here who say it and I know it's not a compliment.

"That gurl sho is special" followed by a slow shaking of the head with twisted lips immediately identifies the true meaning. I can't help that I'm bright and intelligent. It's a gift from God. At least that's what Momma has always told me. She laughs when she shares that as a baby I would look at words like I actually knew what she was reading. Yes, I love to read. Novels, magazines, the newspaper, anything I can get my hands on, it really doesn't matter. Words, their sound, their meaning, and how they can be twisted and manipulated to construe any thought or idea has always been fascinating to me. And I love using what Momma call "them big words," although I am respectful and conscious of my surroundings.

I'd never say or do anything like "talking down," as Momma would say, to embarrass anyone, especially her.

I started reading really soon, maybe by three but certainly by four. Miss Ginny Mae taught me. She was this really old woman who kept me when Momma went in the field. She was the child of an actual slave and she had been taught to read by their owner. Her book of choice was the Bible. She'd read it so much, the pages seem to turn themselves. I'd just sit and listen, and then one day I started repeating what she'd say. Next thing you know, she'd point her finger to a word, and I'd sound it out and read it to her. Stories of Adam and Eve, Cain and Abel, Jonah and the Whale, the Great Flood, were a collection of the best mysteries, short stories, drama and comedy all wrapped up in one place.

I still think about Miss Ginny Mae. My thoughts of her mostly occur when I'm outside, like today, for instance. The memories aren't full, just bits and pieces, but memories just the same. Whenever, she pops in my head, I try to remember as much as possible. I'll always feel like I owe her something. After all, she introduced me to my first love, a good book.

Walking in the heat was always quite annoying. The sun, as usual, was ridiculously hot again today. I felt like there was a target on my back and the sun's beam was hitting it. Nevertheless, I needed to complete my chores or else, no library and no Miss Agatha.

As I walked on down the road, making my way out of The Quarters, I saw quite an unfamiliar and interesting-looking man. He had long braids, a funny-looking beard, and he wore a green, red, and yellow beret. I knew it was impolite, but I had to look twice. He was totally out of the ordinary for these parts. After he observed my double-take, he struck up a conversation.

"What's going on der, gurl?" he asked, while loading up some crates of fruit on his truck.

"Not much," I said, noticing that he spoke really funny.

"You one of them new people, huh? One of Honey folk, right?"

"Why, yes suh, I am."

"My name is RaShay, RaShay Francis, to be exact. I'm Gloell's brother-in-law. You might call her Miss Randle."

"Oh, yes, Miss Randle. I met her and her son—er, daughter—Spudnick in church." I was a little embarrassed—well, more like a little unsure of how to refer to Spudnick.

"That's them, all right," he replied. "And what be your name?"

"Oh, I'm sorry, sir, I'm Pearline. I don't mean to be rude, sir, but you speak uh kinda funny."

Laughing, he responded, "I actually think you speak kinda funny. Just kidding, I'm Jamaican. That's what you hear, a Jamaican accent."

"A real-life Jamaican, huh?" I said, fascinated with him immediately. I could now attach the sound with the accent. "Wow, so this is how they sound," I thought

"What are you doing here in Columbus, all the way from Jamaica?"

"Oh, Gloell was married to my brother Roscoe. When he died, I came here to help her."

"That was nice of you. Are you married?"

"No."

"What do you do for a living? My daddy's a butcher."

"I'm a salesman of sorts, and I work down at the filling station with the Reverend."

"Oh, okay. You're *that* RaShay. You have any children?"

"No, and you ask a lot of questions for a little one, my dear. 'Remember this,' Hog say, 'de first dutty water mi ketch, mi wash.'"

"Okay," I said, completely clueless as to the meaning of his last comment.

As I stood there wondering what the heck he meant, he motioned for me to walk over. I obeyed, but with caution. Friendly or not, he was still a stranger. As I approached, I noticed he was smoking something that looked like a cigarette but it was much fatter, not slim like the cigarettes Daddy smoked. It also smelled much different than the ones I was accustomed to. I guess it was from Jamaica too.

"Here, take this home and ask ya momma to slice it and fry it. Be real good. They called plantains. Look like bananas, but taste better."

"Plantains huh? Well, thank you, suh."

"Got good manners. They take you a long way, gurl." He handed me this bag of really large banana like things. They were green, a little hard, and quite different. But of course, I graciously accepted it.

Mr. RaShay would eventually become my friend. I'd always pass him in my comings and goings. When he did see me, there was never a time that he didn't strike up a chat or hand me a treat. Although I rarely understood anything he said, I did enjoy listening to his rhythmic language, and those plantains weren't too bad either. He would always wear that same beret and smoke what Momma called those "funny cigarettes."

As I strolled down the street, daydreaming about some ice-cold lemonade, I saw the sisters, Miss MinLee and Miss Carrie, or as Aunt Honey called them, Nosey and Just as Nosey sitting on their porch rocking away.

"Hey there," Miss Carrie yelled from her porch. "How you doing, Pearline?"

"Fine, ma'am."

"All right then, how's yo momma and daddy?"

"Both are well, thank you for asking."

"I tell you, you sho talk good, Pearline. Don't know no other chilluns round here talk like you do. Sounds like you been to one of those fancy private schools, like them real smart white chilluns, though I knows you's ain't." Miss MinLee was clearly taking delight in the fact that I was not white, or in private school.

"No, ma'am, I haven't attended private school. But thank you," I said, and then mumbled beneath my breath, "I think." I wasn't quite sure if that was a compliment or not.

After finally arriving at the McLands', I walked around to the rear of the house and knocked on the door. This was a routine I found quite annoying especially since I had to pass two doors that were nearer, the front and the side doors, to enter the home.

"Yeess," Mrs. McLand responded in her uppity voice, like she had her pinkie elevated in the air while fanning and sipping sweet tea.

"It's Pearline, Mrs. McLand. Momma said I needed to pick up your laundry."

"Why, come on in, Pearly."

Pearly, who the heck is Pearly? Didn't she hear me say Pearline? I thought, rolling my eyes. "I probably should be happy she didn't call me gal. That was her other name for me."

The McLands were considered good white folks, well, at least one of them was. And I'd have to say that honor went to Mr. McLand. His other half was lumped right there with Miss Jean. She was unpredictable, unattractive, and unbelievable, literally. She lied a lot.

When I entered the house, I found Mrs. McLand, as usual, in the dining room. Today she was circling the table intently, studying an array of fabric swatches she'd selected for her new draperies. I took a quick count of ten. It was quite apparent that color coordination was not her strong suit. She had proven that by the décor that illuminated the living room: a pink couch, burgundy wing-back chairs, bright red lamp shades, and a dark purple throw rug she'd purchased from Montgomery Wards. It looked like a sick rainbow had thrown up in there.

Lost in her activity, she pointed in the direction of the clothes for me to gather. "They're in there. His shirts, dress pants and socks are all on the kitchen counter."

"Yes, ma'am."

"Now, when you see Louise, tell her and Honey that the next time I'd like those whites to be as brilliant as possible."

"Brilliant?" I repeated.

"Yes, brilliant. You would not know this, of course, but that is the new way to say real white. I read it myself in my latest issue of the *Ladies' Home Journal*. That's a real popular and fancy magazine for white housewives like me."

"For real—I mean, yes ma'am," I said, catching myself before I revealed my surprise that she read or that she desired to extend her vocabulary. Come to think of it, I'd seen a couple of those gossipy *Confidential* magazines laying around her home, although I wouldn't call those periodicals real reading.

As I gathered the clothes to leave, Mrs. McLand noticed my book bag and asked. "So, what you got there?"

"Oh, this. It's my book bag."

"Book bag?"

"Yes, ma'am. I carry all my books in it."

"Excuse me, but I do believe I know what a book bag is, gal. Just surprised you read is all."

"Oh, yes, ma'am. I love to read. When I finish all my chores, Momma said I can go to the library and to Miss Agatha's."

"Agatha, huh? That woman, French or not, shouldn't be colluding with you Coloreds. It's a major topic of concern with the ladies auxiliary. Agatha and her Colored associates comes up on the agenda every Saturday, every Saturday."

"Colluding?" I said, questioning that description. "She's teaching me French."

"Well, whatever. She's still white and a woman at that. It's just not proper. Not proper at all."

After pausing to catch a glimpse of her face in one of the many mirrors she hung in the house, she said, "Anyway, what might you be reading?"

"Actually, I'm reading several books, but the one I just finished is the *Grapes of Wrath*. It's a novel by John Steinbeck."

"Oh, really?"

"Yes, ma'am."

"I see. You're reading about grapes, huh?"

"Grapes?" I asked, not quite sure what she meant. "No, ma'am, it's about—"

She interrupted me, "Well, my favorites grapes are the green ones, although the red are quite tasty too. Did you know they come in purple too? I hear they are just as wonderful, though I've never tried them. Well, good for you. You'll do real good on one of those grape-picking farms. I guess that's better than picking cotton huh? You keep that up, now."

My mouth gaped open slightly, causing her to ask if I was okay and if I needed some water.

Stuttering a bit, I responded, "No, ma'am, I-I'm fine."

Momma always said Mrs. McLand had rocks for brains. After that exchange, I thoroughly disagreed. It was more like sand.

"Oh, one more thing, Pearly." There she goes again in that annoying syrupy voice as I turned to leave. "Don't forget, brilliant, brilliant, brilliant."

Nodding my head, I said. "Yes, ma'am, I won't forget – brilliant, brilliant, brilliant."

"Where you off to, Pearline? Mr. McLand asked as he entered the room, right as I turned to leave.

"Oh, hi, Mr. McLand." I said, happy with his timely intervention. "I have to take your laundry to Momma's and Auntie's."

"Okay. Well, good seeing you. I heard you mention to Harriet that you love to read. If you'd like to ever borrow a few of my books, just ask. Your aunt loves to share how well you're doing in school and what a big reader you are. I've got some really good novels in my library you might enjoy. Just let me know."

"Yes, sir," I said, really surprised that he offered me access to his books, in his own library. "I appreciate that."

As I turned to leave he said, "Oh, wait a minute, I'll just give you one. Hold on a second."

Mr. McLand was a well-read man. Often when I would stop in, he'd be somewhere nearby reading a thick book with his pipe. For some reason, he'd always be suited up with a crisp white shirt, dress slacks, and a tie. I enjoyed my encounters with him, they were always pleasant. Now that he'd opened his library to me, I was ecstatic.

"Here you go," he said as he handed this heavy book to me.

"*Moby Dick*, by Herman Melville. Wow, thanks. I haven't read this one before," I said, curious and anxious all at once.

"Well, good. I'd like a report on it soon, young lady. Melville is one of my favorites."

Excitedly, I responded, "Yes, sir. I'd love to. Thank you."

As he and I stood chatting away, I could feel Mrs. McLand growing irritated and he could too. She was displeased because my interaction with him "wasn't proper" as she was known to say. After all, I was just a "Colored."

"Okay now, Pearly. You best hurry along. Your momma will be waiting," she said.

"Yes, ma'am. And thanks again, Mr. McLand."

He opened the door for me and smiled at me as I left their home.

"No hurry, now. I'm on my way out of town for a couple of weeks. I'm in, then gone again. This is travel season for me. Enjoy, young lady."

"Yes sir, and thank you again," I said, aching to pop open this new adventure.

I had just turned the corner of the house when I heard her distinctive voice. "I simply don't understand why you're always chatting up a storm with them Colored's like you do. It's not right and frankly quite embarrassing, Bill." I stopped, wanting to hear what these white folks said when they thought I wasn't listening. "And I would like you to know, it's been brought to my attention on more than one occasion. It just doesn't look right for you to be shaking their hands, standing round with them and treating them like you do."

"Like um what, Harriet? People?"

"You know what I mean."

"Don't start, Harriet. You know *exactly* why I'm always chatting up a storm with *them*. And why I treat *them* like I do. Or has your memory failed you once again? And for the last time, don't use that word."

"What word?" she asked, although it sounded to me like she knew full well what he was referring to.

"Harriet. I'm not in the mood."

"From the looks of it, you haven't been in the mood in a while now."

"Oh, my goodness. What was that about?" I thought. "Hmm, I wonder."

9

Simee

Lucinda Crowell, more commonly known as Tight Lucy, was a reputed loan shark. Reputed is probably an unfair designation, given that her criminal activities were well known and documented. On more than one occasion, she considered retirement from her life of crime, but as it turned out, it was only a consideration. This graceful, diminutive and soft-spoken Creole woman truly enjoyed her banking enterprise especially with the twenty-five percent interest she tagged onto her loans. Panic, coupled with regret and doom, were the typical immediate emotions of those who failed to meet their financial obligation to her. Their delinquency was sho to guarantee a fitting introduction to the barrel of her shiny gold-plated .45 caliber pistol. In addition, she would happily extend to those unlucky fellows a pleasantry, a smile and without fail, would always offer a portion of whatever she was eating or drinking at the time. *Kinda like they last supper,* she was known to say. Her kind and unexpected gestures would 'cause many to think that maybe, just maybe, grace and mercy had miraculously showed up and granted them a second chance. Unfortunately for them, neither grace nor mercy had any intention on ever being in the same room with her.

I met Tight Lucy at Rudines Tavern late one Friday night. I wandered into this smoky, crowded haven to delight in the flowing bourbon and partake in a game of poker. Tight Lucy, a card shark herself, was a frequent guest of Rudines. She made sho to make herself available for the next fool who'd need her services. It was inevitable that someone would require a desperate loan to stay in the game, get out of the game, or for that matter, live through the game.

After wandering through the tavern and tossing back some Wild Turkey, I scanned the room for an empty seat. *Shouldn't be too hard to make a dollar on these busters in here,* I thought.

Eyeing the room, I noticed several tables. One in particular caught my attention. It was short one man and those that sat there appeared easily conquered.

"This seat empty?" I asked a rather rough-looking man sitting at the table.

"From what I see it is," the ruffian said without looking up at me.

"Mind if I sit in?"

"Don't mind at all, long as you got yo money, pretty boy."

I smirked, pulled my chair out and took his seat. I joined a crew of four, becoming number five. As the night progressed, we played passionately for a couple of hours before, one by one, each began to fold.

"Damn, I'm out," said one player as he placed his cards down and pushed away from the table.

"Me too," came from the second player shortly thereafter.

"What you got?" I asked one of the two remaining gentleman seated at the round table.

"Me?" one said.

"Yeah, fool, you. What you got?" I asked.

Sweating and stuttering, he wiped his brow and said, "A straight."

"Like I thought, not a damn thang. Next", I said with as much cockiness as I could muster, then looked over to the last remaining competitor.

"What yo ass got?" I brazenly asked the clearly calm foe who sat directly across from him.

"What I got is three thousand dollars on this table." He looked around and spoke more to the audience that had collected than to me. "And what I see you need is more money than it seems that you got."

"Look, chump."

"Chump? This fool crazy. Coming in here calling me a chump," the stranger said, insulted.

"Call it like I see it. My money is the least of yo worries. I'm good," I said confidently as I continued to glance at the straight flush nestled in my hands. I was almost salivating over it. "I'm gone ask you one mo time, what you got?"

I watched with disgust as my adversary slowly laid down a royal flush.

"Damn. What the hell?" I mumbled as I eyed the room for the closest exit.

"Who the chump now?" asked my winning opponent.

"Pay up, asshole," roared from the voice across from him.

"Uh, uh, you gotta give me some time. Just need a day or so to get the balance."

"Is you crazy? Talking all that shit and your ass don't have my money."

Before I could get up from the table, I was quickly grabbed from behind, punched and knocked to the floor. I bellowed out in pain as I watched my hat fly from my head. To no avail, the punches and swings kept coming. I finally staggered to stand up, putting my hands over my face.

"Look at him, covering up that girly face of his," someone yelled from the crowd.

"Kick his ass. Can't stand no pretty boy anyhow," another unknown patron yelled.

Before another punch could be landed, this woman sitting at the bar raised her hand and motioned for the chaos to stop. "Sons, that's enough for now." Her interaction quickly caused the crowd to disperse.

"What's your name, handsome?"

"Simee, Simee Scott." I nervously straightened my tie and picked up my hat. Once composed, I found a seat at the bar.

While motioning for the barkeep to pour a shot for two, she asked, "How much you need?"

"How much I need? What are you talking about?" I said, confused and a bit dazed.

"I said, how much money you need?"

"Lady, who are you and what business is it of yours what I need? Hell, you plan on giving it to me?"

"Give isn't exactly what I was thinking of, more like loan."

"You must be hard of hearing or a little touched up there. I said, who are you?"

"Naw, I hear quite fine, thank you. And believe me, slow is good sometimes. My name is Lucinda, but they call me Tight Lucy."

"Tight Lucy? What kind of name is that, Tight Lucy?" I asked, shaking my head, still thanking on my escape.

"It's a name that belong to a woman that can save your ass and possibly your life. You know what? Never mind, take care of this shit yourself. Smart ass. You starting to get on my nerves anyway." She turned away to leave her seat.

"Now, wait a minute. Calm down. I'm just saying. Not often a man meet a woman named Tight Lucy. Just caught me off guard is all. You say you can get me that money. From who?"

"From me."

"You?" I asked, perplexed.

"What, you thank a woman can't have money like that?"

"Didn't say that."

"Naw, but your eyes did. Anyway, you want my help or not?"

"I do."

"For somebody in a world of trouble, seem like you would talk less and listen more. I charge twenty-five percent interest."

"Twenty-five percent? Damn. I might as well just gone and get my ass kicked, Tight Lucy. Tight is right."

"Huh-uh, I wouldn't recommend that route. They likely to do more than a little ass whipping. I promise you that. Look, I don't live far from here."

"And?"

"And, I was thinking, why don't you walk me on home and we discuss this a bit further? We just might be able to work something out."

"Sounds good, but I don't think they gone let me through them doors. Look at them eyeballing me."

"They will. You with me. Dust yourself off, grab your hat, and let's go."

I slung back one more shot of bourbon and pushed back from the bar. I found it odd that the remaining patrons shook their heads and snickered as they watched us leave through a bright red door in the rear of the building. A few folks even held their glass out as if to offer a toast. I later learned that door, which provided the exit, was a very special door. One either walked through it with Tight Lucy or was carried through it by some not so kind thugs. Given the choice, walking was preferable.

I was surprised I wasn't stopped or followed as we headed out to leave. I was so surprised that I had a hard time walking through the door without glancing back, even stumbling a time or two.

The walk to her house was no more than half a block away from the tavern. Her home was very large, with stained-glass windows in the front.

"So this where you live. Nice place. It kinda reminds me of a church, though."

"Thank you and it should. Used to be one. The city was selling it and I bought it. Liked it so much I just moved on in, after I had it gutted, of course. Can't rightly sleep on no pews."

"Yeah, that would be a little strange," I said sarcastically.

"Best thing about this place is, I don't have to worry about going to church, since I wake up in one every day."

"OOOOOkk," I said. Finding the used-to-be church, now my home a bit strange, but hey, she said she could help with my debt, so I'll just go with it.

"No chilluns?"

"No time for that," She said as we entered her home. Once in, she removed her coat and gestured for me to hand her mine.

As we walked into her parlor, I couldn't help but notice the elaborate décor. The space was dominated with dazzlingly colored walls, fancy curtains, beads strung from the ceiling to the floor, and a funny-looking mask hung from the wall.

"Have a seat."

"Thank you," I said as I fanned the strung beads away.

"What's all this?"

"What's all what? She walked over to her record player and placed a vinyl disc on it. When she lifted and carefully placed the nickel-weighted needle down, Duke Ellington's "Black, Brown and Beige" smoothly flowed through the room.

"Oooo, I love this song. Come dance with me. You ever been to New Orleans during Mardi Gras?" she asked as she swayed to the music.

"Yeah, I been to New Orleans and been to a few Mar-dee Gras," I said as I continued to sit and take in everything.

"Well, all this, you see, reminds me of home. I miss that place, the gumbo, the beignets, the men, Bourbon Street, ooh mercy, every thang. Come on now and move with me some."

I stood up and grabbed her waist, then her hands, then her waist again. I was uncertain as to how to proceed. When she motioned for me to move in one direction, I clumsily moved opposite to her directions. This un-orchestrated dance caused her to stumble. She couldn't decide if I was leading, leaning, or leaving.

"Humph, I see God passed right over you with rhythm. What is you doing? Laughing, she said, "Never mind, you have a seat. Won't be no dancing tonight, at least with you. You pretty, but them two left feet of yours bout to break mine.

"Would you like a shot?" she asked as she took a break from her swaying. "Got some Jack here."

"Wouldn't mind if I do. Me and Jack been good friends for a long time."

She pulled a bottle of Jack Daniel's from the same table she kept her Bible on. Uncomfortable with the placement of the good book so close to the sin-in-a-bottle, I said, "Girl, you keep your Bible by all this liquor and booze?"

"Sho do. They drank in the Bible. I do believe Jesus hisself took a sip or two. Didn't you read the part where he turned water to wine? It didn't say nothing 'bout turning water to no milk. "

"You crazy."

"Straight or with ice?"

"Woman, everythang bout me straight."

"So, Mr. Simee Scott," she said, tilting her head to the side as she walked around me slowly, touching my shoulder as I sat at her table. "It's very clear yo ass is broke. Now, if looks was money, you'd be a wealthy man, but since it ain't, you ain't. You broke and from what I can see, very broke. I saw that when you walked in all high and mighty. I said to myself, *Look at his ass, I bet he broke.* I can spot ya'll kind of Niggers from a mile away."

"Wait, wait, wait a minute now. I ain't exactly broke. I'm just momentarily monetarily deficient in my funds is all," I responded with a slight laugh.

"Where you read that at? Can't even say it yourself without laughing. Momentarily monetarily ..... Hell, I can't even say that mess myself. "

"Let me help you, then."

"Ummm-humph," she said, as though she knew exactly what I could do. "There's some good news for you."

"And that would be?"

"I can help you, but you will need to comply with a few things."

"Comply?"

"That's what I said. I don't make no deals without having an agreement first. A signed agreement. Strictly business. You still interested?"

"For sho"

"Humm-uh. Well, first, you'll make love to me tonight."

"I thought you said this was strictly business."

"I did."

"Sound like more than business to me."

"Don't care what it sound like. Is you in or is you ain't?"

"Hell, that ain't no problem. When you want to start, right now, let's go." I quickly removed my jacket and shoes, then socks.

"Hold your horses, big fellow. Sign this."

I took her black fountain pin and that agreement as she called it and signed on the dotted line. No need to read it. My intentions was clear. I'd sleep with her, take her money, then adios.

"Here you go. What else you got?"

"Well, you gotta do something a little different for me."

"No problem with that. How you like it, on top, the bottom, from the back. I'm here to please," I proudly said.

"First, what size shoe you wear?

"A fourteen, why?"

Tight Lucy opened her closet door and began rummaging through a large pile of shoes. She dug in the stack for well over three minutes, heightening my curiosity.

"What you doing, woman?" I asked, finally revealing my annoyance with her hunt.

"Here we go, a thirteen and a half . Guess it's gone have to do. Might be a li'l tight. " She handed me a pair of ladies high heels.

Before I could ask the obvious question, she walked over to a large dresser and from the top drawer, pulled out the largest lace nightgown I'd ever seen.

"And put this on with it. It's a twenty-two. Should work."

"What? Put what on? What the hell you thank I'm gone do with all this?"

"Wear it. I told you I needed something different."

"Yeah, different, this what you talking 'bout? I rarely call on you, but Lawd have mercy, this crazy as hell." I immediately stood up, looking around for my own clothing.

She calmly lit another cigarette, tilted her head and asked, "You want that money or not?"

"Wait a minute, now. You expect me to wear them shoes and this here lady's nightgown?"

"The French say lingerie."

"I don't give a damn what they say."

"Okay, have it your way," she said causally as if she knew I would eventually comply.

I reached to put my own shoes on and stopped. The memory of the last butt whooping I'd received less than an hour ago held. My jaw was still hurting and the black eye I caught was more purple and blue now. "Shit," I said after taking one more look at the shoes and the "lingerie," as she called it, and took a deep breath.

"You finish thanking bout it? Good. I'll loan you your balance, which I believe is fifteen hundred dollars. Based on your abilities, I may consider lowering your interest from twenty-five percent to ten percent. Keep in mind; this is all based on how good you is. Now, from my calculations, this will bring your balance to me to sixteen fifty, but only if I like you. And if you real good, that might drop a little further. I've had a few to surprise the heck out of me. That boy from over in Newnan bout killed me, but in a good way. He walked with a dragging leg, but that was the only thing that dragged on him. And from the looks of you, you might have a couple of surprises up your sleeve too. If thangs don't turn out the way I'm 'specting they will, I want the whole eighteen seventy five by Friday of this week. Don't care how you get it, but I want my money. Got it?"

"Yeah, I got it," I reluctantly said as I thought back to the way the men at Rudines laughed as I left with her. I agreed to the terms.

After she disrobed, she sat and watched me do the same. While I painfully stuffed my foot in that shoe, I could only shake my head. I fared no better when I could barely slip the gown on, thinking, *this some crazy shit.* She lit another cigarette, poured me another shot of bourbon and handed it to me as she crawled in her uncommonly large bed, and invited me in. The sex began and to my surprise and delight, I enjoyed every bit of it, even with her bizarre request. And based on the unnatural wails that flung from her throat, so did she.

After my final release, I concluded that I had never slept in a bed this big, or in a vagina this small. "So that's why they call you tight, huh, Lucy?"

"That's what I hear."

"Can I take these damn shoes off now? Please."

"Why, sho you can." She began stroking me for another round. "Oh, and don't forget about Friday."

I hi-tailed it out of Atlanta that very same night I bedded Tight Lucy. While she nestled quite satisfied in a deep sleep from that never to speak of again romp we had, I quietly dressed. I put my shirt on and as I reached over to grab my pants, I noticed a tall stack of dollar bills sitting on top of this big piece of furniture in the corner of her bedroom. *What we got here?* I asked myself. I took them down and began to fan through them. Then I got to thanking, *Hmmm, be awfully wrong of me to leave Ulysses, Andrew and ol' Ben here with her crazy ass. Best I take you boys with me. Ya'll can thank me over a glass a gin.*

So, I grabbed them, as well as a couple pieces of jewelry, and slipped away into the early morning. As silently as possible, I navigated through those dangling beads in her home. Each time I moved one, it moved another. My navigation required a little savvy, but I managed. I discreetly managed to make my way to a highway heading south. As I stood there contemplating my next move, a truck driver pulled over and asked if I needed a ride.

"Where you headed?" he asked, more cheerful than anyone should be so early in the morning.

"Where-eva you going," I said.

"Hop on in. I'm headed back home to Columbus. My name is Buford by the way," he said as he extended his hand.

"And you is?"

"I'm Simee, Simee Scott."

"Well, nice to meet you, Mr. Simee Scott. Boy, what you out here so early for? Dangerous, being on this dark road like this."

"Safer than where I came from," I muttered.

"Yeah, don't mean no harm, but you looking pretty beat up. Thanks you gone be okay?"

"Um, I'm fine. Thank you."

"Hmmm. Scott, you say? Got's some Scotts down in Columbus too."

"They's Scotts all over, I reckon," I said with a hint of annoyance, not really in the mood to talk. After all, it was around three am in the morning.

"Let's see Edga and Louise. Yeah, that's them," Buford said.

That name was like a lightning bolt in the sky. "Edga, you say?"

"Yeah, he and his wife Louise, them and they family moved up from Preston a while back. Good, hardworking, church-going people." Buford shifted his gears in the truck. "Well, sit back and enjoy the ride. Won't take us long to get there at all. Don't have much to offer you, but I do have some moon pies left over. Would you like one?"

As I took the moon pie from Buford and unwrapped it to eat, I thought, *My luck just can't get no better. Humph. Edga, my long-lost brother, is down in Columbus, Georgia, of all places.* "Damn this is good. What kind of pie is this again?

"They call them moon pies. Guess 'cause they shaped like the moon."

"Got it. Moon pie. It sho is good."

10

Pearline

Old Glory has finally called Mr. Job on home. Daddy told Mr. Buster that Old Glory should have been ashamed of himself letting Mr. Job live so long. He said it just wasn't right for any man to outlive Methuselah.

Crundale Bishop Lewis, better known as Mr. Job, was the oldest man most people had ever known. When he finally died at age one hundred and ten, the Guinness Book of World Records recorded him as the oldest living man, Colored or other. The nickname Job, which he reveled in, was derived after he turned ninety. He once said that since Job was so close to the Lawd, that extra name of his was a good thang. It was what the edu-ma-cated folks call a *compliment*.

I had the good fortune of attending Mr. Job's funeral. Yes, one doesn't normally attach "good fortune" and "funerals" together, unless it's someone you felt death was way past due on, or, it's the reading of the will and you happened to be an expected or, even better, unexpected beneficiary.

However, on this particular occasion, I was lucky to be there and I could thank Deputy Beauregard and Miss Prudence Jenkins for that.

Upon Mr. Job's passing, everyone in the community, and some outside of it, made sure to pay their respects. This was not only a big deal for The Quarters, but for the city as well, due to Mr. Job's celebrity. Both the white and Colored newspapers would be in attendance at his funeral to take pictures and interview his family and others who knew him well. This would be one of the rare times a Colored was in the white paper, outside of being arrested, of course. The mayor even took the liberty and assigned Deputy Beauregard to help control and manage the expected large crowd. We all knew that this particular deputy controlling, much less managing, anything was more of a hope than a reality.

Cletus Beauregard the II was unfortunately the deputy assigned to patrol The Quarters. He was not too pleased to be "stuck" with the "Niggers," as he so ignorantly referred to us, so his visits were far and few in between. With Cletus having little to no sense, common or otherwise, a strong disregard for Coloreds, and pretty much reigning as a bumbling idiot, folks in The Quarters were extremely happy to see him infrequently as well. However, because he was the grandson of Robert Shaw, a very influential and powerful city leader, he was given his job and allowed to keep it in spite of his consistent buffoonery.

Poor Cletus had demonstrated his ineptitude early in his career. No one knows exactly what happened that 4th of July weekend, but rumor has it that after an evening of heavy drinking, Cletus and his two friends Bubba and Elmore all staggered back to the city jail. Cletus, anxious to show off his new high-powered Dupont Remington .22 hunting rifle, insisted they leave the festivities. This was a definite no-no since the last time he held a rifle unaccompanied resulted in disaster. It's said that in his drunken haze, he pulled out the "loaded" rifle, pointed it and foolishly fired it. The bullet ricocheted. The outcome of that misfire resulted in Cletus losing his entire right arm, crippling Elmore, and nearly collapsing the jail ceiling. Following that fiasco, he was put on desk duty. After months of Cletus begging and pleading to be on active duty again, his grandfather eventually gave him The Quarters as his sole responsibility. How anyone expected him to serve as law enforcement in any capacity was anybody's guess.

"Tweeeeeeeeee!" erupted from Cletus' ever present whistle as he poorly directed the crowd during the funeral.

"If he blow that damn whistle one more time. Ooo whew, I wish he'd swallow it," Miss MinLee said.

"Why in the world they sent that Cletus over here is a mystery to me, I tell you. That boy can't direct his willie over the toilet, much less some traffic. And how you suppose to direct traffic with one arm anyway? Look at him. Look like he waving at folks," Aunt Honey said, laughing.

"Girl, I couldn't tell you. I'm hoping he don't cause another accident—bout near caused Lillie and Ma Sally to drive right smack into one another. I'm sho he can't wait to get from down here either. Po thang," Momma said as we all stood and watched deputy Cletus create more chaos than calm in his attempt to direct traffic.

"Wait a minute. Is Cletus waving at you, Honey?" Miss MinLee asked

"Look like he is to me," Miss Carrie said laughing. "Ya'll make a cute couple, Honey."

"Uh-huh, anyway. I likes men for sho, but that Cletus ain't exactly my type. Is ya'll finish?"

Incredibly, Mr. Job's death was of great annoyance to at least one other person. That one person was Miss Jenkins or, as she's more commonly known behind her back, The Funeral Lady. To her great inconvenience and irritation, two people had the nerve to die in the same week, Mr. Job and Miss Katherine. Their mutual untimely deaths created a dilemma for her. She finally concluded the only way to decide fairly which funeral she'd attend was to do a toss-up. It was heads for Mr. Job and tails Miss Katherine. To her disappointment, Miss Katherine won. So, she concluded that immediately following Miss Katherine's burial and before Mr. Job's repast, she would hurry on over to Mr. Job's burial site at the Blessed Angels cemetery. And to everyone's disappointment, that's exactly what she did.

Me, Momma and Aunt Honey stood together, dapping tears and exchanging pleasantries with the rest of the mourners, following Mr. Job's service. Miss Jenkins gleefully rushed toward us and squeezed herself in our little huddle.

"Evening," Miss Jenkins said once she was comfortably wedged in.

"Evening," Momma replied. Aunt Honey just looked away.

"So just how was it?" she asked.

"How was what?" Aunt Honey dryly responded, while ignoring Momma's *be nice* look.

"Job's home going, silly. Why, the funeral, of course. Did they make him up nicely? I sho hope so. He was always a good-looking man even in his elderly years. Shame on them if they didn't. You know, a little rouge and powder can do wonders. I called Bernice, and she promised her and Rufus would make sho he looked no mo than eighty. Lawd, I hate I missed him. You may not have known this, but Job was sweet on me."

"Naw. We missed that bulletin," Aunt Honey said.

"Can you believe they closed the casket for I could get to his viewing last night? Hump! So how was it?"

Aunt Honey let out a heavy sigh and said, "We thought it was just lovely, Prudence, especially when he sat up and thanked us all for coming."

The look on Miss Jenkins' face said it all. She narrowed her eyes, clutched her purse and walked—rather, stormed off—quite hastily. The entire group of women who stood together laughed so hard, each had to lean on the other to keep their balance.

Aunt Honey kept a straight face and proceeded to yell toward Miss Jenkins as only she could, "Hey, Prudence, one mo thang. Job asked about you too, said he sho hope to see you soon."

"Tweeeeeeeee!" from Cletus's whistle as he attempted to stop Miss Jenkins from walking into traffic.

"There he go again," Miss MinLee said, shaking her head.

11

Louise

"Hey there, Louise. Where you off to?" MinLee yelled my way as she and Carrie stood on her front porch running they mouth.

"I'm coming from work."

"Everything all right? You look madder than a rattlesnake tangled in a hornets nest. Don't she, Carrie?"

"Sho do," Carrie chimed in. "What's wrong with you on this beautiful day?"

Plenty was wrong, but ain't no way was I gone tell them two anything.

"Just hot is all. Ya'll have a good day."

I'd just left the McLands. On Monday, Wednesday, Thursday and sometimes on Saturday, I clean and iron for them. Occasionally, like last week, when I gets real busy, I'll send Pearline over to help me. She ain't thrilled about going over there, except she does like Mr. McLand. He always giving her a book to read and is always kind toward her, unlike that woman.

Words can't tell you how excited I was to get this job. Even before me and Edga got here, I prayed to the good Lawd that I'd find work and soon at that. *"Got's chilluns to feed, not to mention me and Edga needs to eat too,"* I'd remind the Lawd in my prayers every night. So, when Mr. McLand told Buster, who told Addie, who then told Honey, who told me, that his wife was looking to hire a maid, I was so happy. Then I got sick on the stomach. My nerves got the best of me 'cause was no guarantee they was gone hire me. I just didn't want no mo disappointment.

William "Bill" and Harriet McLand were real important people and socialites of Columbus. He was a handsome, well-known, and respected lawyer with his very own law practice. And well from what I heard, she had the pleasure of sitting at home sipping bourbon with a little tea. They hobnobbed with everyone, it seemed, and their pictures were always in the *Columbus Ledger* newspaper.

The day finally came for my interview—Lawd, I was nervous. As I walked up the long driveway, the strangely colored house was the first to catch my attention. It was painted a funny color of blue. I say funny 'cause it ain't the pretty blue you see in the sky, and it ain't the dark blue like in a man's Sunday church pants. That house is a blue sadly stuck somewhere 'tween green and yella. Unsightly was the first thang that popped in my head, but what did I care? I was 'bout to interview and, God's will, get this here job. As I got closer, I noticed a woman peeping through some lace curtains in the front of the house. I just minded my business like I didn't see her, and kept walking. Once I got up to the house, I passed the front door but stopped at the side door. Before I could even knock, I heard a woman holla, "Use the back door."

"Yes, ma'am."

The back door was cracked open as I approached it, not enough to walk right through, so I knocked.

"Come on in, Louise," a man said as he pulled the door open and greeted me with a wide smile and an extended hand. "I'm Bill, pleasure to meet you. Sorry I didn't get to the door sooner, my hands were full. Any-who, come on in. How you doing today? Would you like some iced tea?"

"Huh, no suh. But thank you, though," I said confused at his pleasantness. Nice white man, I thought.

"Forgive my manners, have a seat." He pulled out a chair for me to sit.

"Thank you," I said with caution. See, I ain't never had no white man to open a door, step out of my way, much less pull a chair out for me.

"Bill, tell Louise I'll be right there," a woman yelled from somewhere in the house. It was the same voice I just heard.

I sat in the kitchen, very uncomfortable, even though this seemingly kind man attempted to settle my nerves.

"Buster told me a good friend of his was in need of employment. After speaking with my wife, we decided the timing was perfect. Our last maid quit unexpectedly, so we could really use the help right now. I think you'll do great. Buster and Jim speak really high of you."

"Thank you, suh."

"Oh, look at the time. I got to get out of here, get back to the office, but I wanted to meet you. My wife, Harriett, is going to interview you. She most likely will ask you several questions, but don't worry," he whispered, "you got the job."

"Suh?" I said a bit confused.

He leaned down and said real low, "You got the job."

"Hello, I'm Mrs. McLand, Bill's wife." This pale woman wearing heavy red lipstick entered the room. She was so busy looking down at the polish on her fingernails that she barely looked at me.

"I think she figured that out, Harriett," Mr. McLand said with a chuckle, remembering to kiss her on the cheek as he grabbed his jacket before leaving the house.

"How do, ma'am. I'm Louise Scott. Pleasure to meet you." I stood up and extended my hand toward her, only for her to pretend not to see it.

I could tell right off that this woman ain't gone be friendly, not at all. Mrs. McLand ain't too tall or too short, she somewhere in the middle, I guess. She skinny too. The black dress she wearing ain't offering much help for that li'l body of hers. It just make her look mo skinny. What she need is to eat. I can tell she ain't doing much of that. Some of my fried chicken with biscuits and gravy would do her skinny behind some good.

"Well, I'll keep this short and to the point. I have several meetings today and my time is very limited."

"Yes ma'am," I said, still standing.

"Gone ahead and sit back down," she said to me, as though I had forgotten to do so myself. "Well, looks like my husband has already made the decision for me, so today's your lucky day. However, there are some rules and expectations of the help. I would be remiss if I did not take this opportunity to tell you just how fortunate you are to work for us. I don't know if you know this or not, but my husband is a prominent attorney in Muscogee County, and he's sought out by many throughout this fine state of Georgia including the mayor and the governor."

"Yes, ma'am."

"We are a very busy family. As members of the United Baptist Church, the Rotary Club, and the Country Club of Muscogee, it's very rare that we aren't having an event or at one. You must keep that in mind. There will be days when I'll need you outside of your regular schedule."

"Yes, ma'am."

"Oh, and how could I forget this? I am also the president of the White Linens Ladies Auxiliary Club. We are always in the Sunday paper's society column. And our children, Dick and Jane, are just as busy. Dick is a troop leader with the Cub Scouts. And Jane is in Home Makers of America. I'm preparing them both to be good citizens of these United States."

"Yes, ma'am. 'Scuse, ma'am. Are they here?"

"Who?"

"Your chilluns. I'd like to meet them too if possible."

"Oh, why, of course."

Next thang, she start yelling, "Dick and Jane, come in here."

"What?" the boy yelled first. Then "Huh?" from the girl. Them two chilluns come dragging in the kitchen, like they was bothered. It was clear they was spoiled.

"Say hello to Louise. She's our new maid."

"Hey" from the boy, then "Hello" from the girl.

"Is that it?" asked the girl.

"Can we go back to bed?" asked the boy.

Annoyed with them that they couldn't care less, she shooed them on out of the kitchen. After they left, I sat and listened to that woman for at least an hour, though it felt like ten. She went down a list of everybody they knew, what her husband do, what she do, then gave me the do's and don'ts.

For example, I should never use the side door. It was too close to the front one. When her lady friends is over, I should always greet them with a smile but absolutely no talking to them unless of course they ask me a question. Otherwise, I can stay busy elsewhere. Then she went on about her chilluns. They rooms should always be clean. That Dick gets diarrhea when he eats too much peanut butter. And since Jane is a little plump, I should watch her portions. After all of that, she even pulled out a what-to and what-not-to-do list. You'd think a do and don't list was the same as a what-to and what-not- to list, but for her, two different list was required. After showing me around the house, finally, thank you Lawd, she was finished, and said I could start Monday.

"Oh, one more thing, Louise," she said as I turned to leave.

"Ma'am'?" I said, disappointed that there was more still to come.

She pushed back from the table and walked over to the cupboard near the icebox. Not sure what she was about to do, I stood near the back door and hoped whatever it was, she'd be finished soon. After reaching up into the cupboard, that woman pulled down an old chipped plate that had a fork, spoon, and knife on it, even a napkin. Then she pulled down a drinking glass and set everything on the kitchen table. I still was not sure what it all meant.

"These are yours."

"Ma'am'?"

"These are yours. We don't share our plates, eating utensils, or drinking glasses with the help. And we certainly don't share the bathroom. You'll find yours right next to the washing machine downstairs. I'm sure it needs cleaning, but you can do that when you get here Monday. Any questions."

"No ma'am. There ain't."

"Good. See you Monday, bright and early."

"I quit today if I could," I said, entering my house.

"Louise, what in the world is wrong with you?" Edga asked as I nearly tore the door from the hinges.

"That woman. She just the devil, I tell you. Got my pressure boiling."

"What she do this time?" Edga asked me.

"Guess it don't make no difference what she did and she know it. She just plain evil. I hate when Mr. McLand ain't there. Like she sit and wait on him to walk out that door so she can start. When I got there this morning, Mr. McLand was reading the newspaper and finishing up his breakfast. He spoke like he always do and made a little small talk, then told me to have a good day and left. Them bad chilluns was gone, but left they room like a storm went through it, dirty clothes was everywhere. Don't know how they make that kind of mess in such a short time. I got started with my work, washing clothes, sweeping, dusting, you know, everything I do. Then here she comes. I said to myself, there go my decent day. I was already busy, which she could see, but that wasn't good enough for her. She pulled out her usual long list of to-do's. That don't bother me none 'cause I'm used to them list now. After going over everything I had already started doing anyway, she come telling me about a story she read in one of her magazines about keeping ants and bugs out yo house. Didn't think much about it 'cause ain't no bugs and ain't no ants in they house. I keep they house real clean. Well, all the while she talking, I notice she standing at the sink pouring water, soap powder, and Clorox in a li'l bucket . Said that if you dip the toothbrush in the concoction she was holding and brush the doorways, the bugs will go to running. Next thang I know she tapping a toothbrush on they countertop. I just stood there 'cause I knowed what was coming next. That woman expected me to get on my hands and knees and scrub them doorways with a toothbrush."

"Something wrong with that woman," Edga said.

"She held her hands out with the toothbrush and bucket until I took it. Before I knew it, my eyes welled up with tears. I took a deep breath and got down on the floor and started to brush the door way like it had teeth. I guess that satisfied her, 'cause before she sashayed her tail out the room, she stood there with a smile as wide as her head. I must have been down there at least twenty minutes for I heard Mr. McLand coming through the other door."

"Louise, you okay?"

"Yes suh."

"What are you doing on the floor?" he asked me.

"Suh?"

"I said, what are you doing on the floor? And is that a toothbrush?"

"Ah, yes suh. Mrs. McLand told me to scrub the doorways to keeps the ants and—"

"Before I could finish the sentence, he reached down to help me up. He apologized, handed me a napkin to wipe my tears, and said that they'd see me tomorrow. My face must have shown him that I was worried 'bout my pay for today and my job. He just shook his head, handed me this twenty-dollar bill and said that he was sorry again, not to worry, and that

they'd see me tomorrow. I grabbed my handbag and turned
to leave. That's when that Harriett made her way back and
asked me where I was going. Mr. McLand answered for me
and his voice alone scared her 'cause she didn't know he had
come back home. I didn't get out the door good before he
lit into her. Told her she ought to be ashamed and that I
would not be scrubbing the floors with no damn toothbrush.
She come back with what she read in her magazine and that
she makes decisions for the house too. Next I hear him tell
her that's one decision that won't be made and that was just
ridicu-lous. He know she ain't shame. None at all. That's the
only woman I know that takes so much pleasure from other
folks' pain."

Edga sat there biting on his tongue like he do when he lost
in thought. I knew it hurt him for me to be treated that way,
and it hurt him more that I had to go back the next day.

12

Pearline

Uncle Simee Scott strolled into Columbus like a mist right before a storm. No one saw him coming, but his presence was undeniable. He was quite a handsome man. Women, men and children alike would stop and stare at him. Looking up at him made the sun compete for his attention, he was just that demanding. His skin was a smooth brown just like dark honey straight from a beehive. His legs had a little bow in them which added rhythm to his strut. Those eyes of his sat back in his head like almonds and were clear of any concerns. And his smile was wide, white, and positioned quite nicely between those two deep dimples. He was simply an Adonis, a fine specimen of a man. Even as his niece I could see that.

"Ya'll seen him yet? My Gawd, my Gawd, my Gawd. They don't make them like that no mo, I tell ya. Now, that's one fine ass man. 'Scuse me, Lawd. I know it ain't right to use yo name in the same talking with some cussing, but damn. Oops, there I go again." Looking up toward the heavens, she continued, "Sorry, Lawd. But you yo-self know, we ain't seen nothing like that in a month of Sundays, Mondays or Tuesdays, for that matter," Miss Carrie said, laughing as she and MinLee, Addie, and Spudnick watched him from a distance.

As usual, my presence is forgotten. I feel like I become a part of whatever scenery there is. The wall, carpet, wood, even trees, it just doesn't seem to matter, I become a part of it, unless Momma is around, of course. I'm trying not to get offended but come on. I consider myself noticeable even if I'm the only one who does. My smooth chocolate skin, thick lips, round clear eyes, and coarse hair reminiscent of tribal women from the royal blood line of a Nigerian tribe, not to mention my intelligence, which beams attractive all day long. How could they or anyone else miss all that? Goodness, I thought as I stood on the porch waiting for acknowledgment and directions.

"Hey there, Pearline."

"Hi, Miss Carrie," I said, relieved in some odd sense that finally she noticed me. The women and Mr. Spudnick met at Miss Carrie's as they normally did each Friday evening. Miss Wilhelmina would often be late, as she had business to tend to at her place, but nevertheless, she'd make it over.

"Momma told me that you had a few errands for me to run for you."

"And I do. Got twenty cents waiting on you once you done."

"Yes, ma'am."

"Gone in the back and get them three packages on the kitchen table."

This Saturday I had the displeasure of walking over to the sisters Miss Cutie Pie and Miss May Alice, Deaconess Lois, and

Sister Kate for my errands. They all lived in The Quarters, but Deaconess Lois was working in town over at the Springer Opry House, which meant I had a longer walk. I wasn't too happy about that, but if I wanted that twenty cents, I'd get happy.

"I tell you one thang, he is beautiful, pure de beau-ti-ful. Is that a proper thang to call a man?" Miss MinLee asked.

"Why, sho it is. It's fitting, ain't it? Just look at him," Mr. Spudnick said.

"In my opinion, he can give that Duke a run for his money. Better yet, I say he better-looking than that Duke Ellington. And such a fine dresser he is. Clothes look like they straight from the department store. What you thank, Addie?' Miss Carrie asked

"Can't say!"

"Yes, you can, Addie. Stop being so stuffy. Well, if you can'ts, I's be happy to say it for you. He is delicious," Spudnick chimed in.

All three looked at Spudnick and jointly said, "Delicious?"

"That's right, delicious."

The ladies or, as Daddy liked to call them, the Hens, had already done an informal background check on him. He was in town no more than two days before they collected as much information on him as they could. It was hard to miss them bustling back and forth to each other's home, comparing notes on their new subject. In no time at all, they'd found out that he had moved from Chicago. He was widowed three times, had served in the U.S. military with the 92nd Infantry Division, was some type of businessman, had three children, two in Chicago and one in Detroit, wore a size fourteen shoe, extra-large shirts and pants, and enjoyed liquor, preferably whiskey, but would settle on anything that had been fermented.

"Here he comes. Look at him, walking round like that. Ought to be shame of his-self," Miss Addie said.

"Walking like what, Addie?" Wilhelmina chimed in with as she walked up and joined the chatter. "How else he pose to walk? Crooked with a bent leg? I thanks he walks quite nicely myself."

"You would," Addie said right before she yelled at one of the neighborhood children to stop running in her grass. "Boy, you want a wuppin?"

"Addie, yo ass crazy. You always asking these chillun if they want a wuppin. Have you heard one say yes yet? Why yes, Miss Addie, I'd love to get my ass beat," Miss MinLee said as they all laughed.

"Well, as I was saying, look here, I called him first. So, ya'll stay back. He a taken man and don't even know it yet!" Wilhelmina said, laughing to herself.

"You call what first, Wilhelmina? We ain't in grade school no mo, you know. Next, you gone say tag. Crazy ass! Talkin bout you called him first. And ain't you got enough mens already? From the looks of the comings and goings at yo house, you do!" Carrie said.

"And anyway, MinLee, you and Carrie is married and Addie, you is too damn ornery, and Spudnick, well you, you know."

"No, I don't know. What you tryin to say, Wilhelmina?" Spudnick asked while standing with one hand on his hip, adjusting the trademark flower he wore in his hair, which he felt made him look like Billie Holiday, all while shooing away a fly.

"Well, you, you, ain't exactly...."

"Naw, exactly what?" he asked.

They'd gotten so caught up in their conversation, neither of them noticed that Uncle Simee had walked right up to the porch. Next thing they heard was his deep yet raspy voice.

"How ya'll ladies and well," he stopped, noticing Spudnick, and cleared his throat, "ladies doing today? Simee asked. Spudnick always caught people unfamiliar with him off guard. This was no exception.

"We doings fine," Wilhelmina answered for everyone as she stepped in front of the group and extended her hand his way.

"And you is?" Spudnick asked, clearly already knowing the answer.

"How do? My name is Simee, Simee Scott. I noticed ya'll out here and thought I'd introduce myself. I just moved in a couple of days ago."

"Naw, the pleasure is all mines—I means ours," Wilhelmina said as Addie rolled her eyes.

"Scuse me, did you say Scott? Some other Scotts moved up here from Preston. Edga and Louise. You some kin?" Carrie asked.

"Why, I sho am. I's Edga's younger brother."

"Big head Edga yo brother?" Addie said, with a look of confusion on her face. "Ya'll got to have different mommas or daddies for sho."

"Addie. Would you be quiet? Crazy ol' fool," Spudnick said. "You got to 'scuse her. She hadn't taken her spell medicine yet."

"I was only saying what ya'll was thankin," Addie said.

"Hmmm. Didn't know Edga had kin, specially someone as handsome as you," Wilhelmina said.

"You got's chilluns?" Addie asked.

"Scuse me?" Simee asked.

"I said, you got's chilluns?"

Everyone collectively shook their heads, expressing irritation with Addie's policing duties.

"Yes ma'am, I do, but they live elsewhere."

"Just letting you know, if you did, and they was here of course, I helps out watching all the chilluns round here," Addie said.

"Well, he don't have none here, Addie! Goodness," Wilhelmina let out and then added, "If there's anything I—I mean, we—can do to help you get settled in, just let us know."

"Sho will and thank you." As he turned to leave he said, "Oh, which way to a May Alice and a Cutie Pie, I believe that's their names?"

"Just go right down to the corner and turns left. They house is bright orange, with brown shutters. It's quite unsightly, I should add. But you can't miss it," Spudnick said.

As Uncle Simee walked off, he turned and waved goodbye. He must have felt them watching his backside, so much so that he hurried his pace and shyly waved again.

"See, look at him. He already making his way to Cutie Pie and May Alice," Miss Addie said. "Ain't been here nothing but a day or so, done already found the liquor house."

"Good, a little shine ain't neva hurt no body," Miss Wilhelmina said, smiling.

"Did ya'll hear what I heard?" MinLee said.

"We heard," Spudnick said

"Said he Edga brother? How we miss that? Well, do tell."

"Who cares? He so good-looking he could be Spudnick's brother for alls I care," Miss Wilhelmina said.

"Scuse you!" Spudnick said as he shot a glance over at Wilhelmina.

"Well, he done found May Alice and Cutie Pie. Wonder if he gone fine yo house next, Wilhelmina?" Miss MinLee said, looking sideways.

Laughing, Mr. Spudnick said, "He will if Wilhelmina got anythangs to do with it."

"Wait a minute. Louise gone have a fit," Miss MinLee said.

"She sho is." Mr. Spudnick said. "Yeah, she gone be surprised for sho."

"Pearline?" Miss MinLee yelled.

"Ma'am'?" I said from the house.

"Maybe she didn't hear," Miss Wilhemina whispered to everyone.

"Of course she did," Mr. Spudnick said. "She was standing right behind the screen door."

I made my way to Miss May Alice and Miss Cute Pie before Uncle Simee, since I knew a shortcut. Plus, I had to hurry to get back to Momma with this news. This was the beginning of a busy weekend for The Sisters. A pair of identical twin sisters, who still dressed alike and were the younger sisters of Deacon Buster Carter. The Carters were a well-established family in The Quarters. They were plump, fair-skinned people with fire red curly hair. All of them, including Mr. Buster, his two brothers, Earl and Hollis, had an unusual birthmark. It appeared to be the same size and color, and it was stamped right on the left side of their necks. I wouldn't make mention of it, but it was hard not to since every last Carter I knew had that mark in the same place.

The sisters were moonshiners, although they took offense to that designation. Miss May Alice said once, with a hint of air, *Moonshining is what our daddy did, and that's certainly not what we do.* Both felt their daddy was of the criminal element, which was quite contrary to their business enterprise.

Those two considered themselves reputable, legitimate business owners, and they had set up their refinery, Spirits, to reflect that. They insisted that all products be poured in specially ordered jars from the Sears and Roebuck catalog. The jars came two for a nickel, which was quite a deal, as Miss May Alice noted. Each jar was labeled with the name Spirits and right underneath that, it said, *Let the Spirit Move You.* The saying was quite fitting, actually awfully smart, since that's exactly what their liquor was known to do to those who indulged. All monies were due upon exchange for the alcohol; however, credit was extended with a finance charge of one percent for good measure.

"Come on in, sweetie. How you today?" Miss May Alice asked me.

"I'm well and you?" I responded.

"We good, baby. You got our package from Carrie?"

"Yes ma'am. Here it is."

"All right. Give me a minute and I got something for you too."

"Yes ma'am." I stood in their kitchen and watched the wonder of their enterprise. Spirits lined the countertops in an assortment of colors and flavors. The aroma in the kitchen hailed from a collision of fruits, berries, grains and other untold ingredients which created their famous elixirs. Eager customers bustled in and out of the house with a rapid step. Miss Cutie Pie and Miss May Alice managed each calculation without the need of a pencil, piece of paper, or one of them fancy calculators I read about. Momma said they kept everything in their head, including what was paid and what was owed. The only thing they seemed to not be able to manage was Mr. Turnerd.

"Ain't nothing like shine from May Alice and Cutie Pie, I tell you. Them two sho can make some good drank. The Corn, White Lightning, Apple, even the Blackberry is sueperb. They must be putting they's foot in it," Mr. Turnerd said, grinning as he and a few of his friends sat on the porch outside.

"Don't know what it is 'bout this concoction, but my Gawd, it sho is good. Don't know which is better, a ripe young virgin, untouched, lying still waiting just for me, or this here brew. Cutie Pie, I frankly am conflicted."

"Look like you don't know a lot today, Turnerd," Miss Cutie Pie responded

"My beautiful butter-cream fine ladies. How ya'll womens today?"

"Turnerd, don't come in here with them syrupy words of yours. You got a balance with us."

"Now, now, May Alice, how you gone treat me like that?"

"Easy. Where's yo dollar? You know you's short, Turnerd, and I ain't talking bout how high you stand. That'll be one dollar from last week and one dollar today. I'm doing yo behind a favor. I didn't even ask for my other money or the interest you done got!"

"Interest? Is this the bank or what? Well, damn." He reached into his pocket to collect their money.

"Watch yo mouth. You see dis her chile standing here?" Miss May Alice said to him as I continued to wait.

"Here it is, all two hundred."

"Two hundred? Two hundred what?" Miss Cuite Pie asked.

"Pennies," he said as most of them spilled to the floor and the rest tumbled onto the kitchen table. "What you thank? They spends just the same."

"Cutie Pie, this here fool done brought two hundred pennies over here. Lawd Jesus."

"I tell you, since I'm here every week, looks like somebody would be a little bit mo kinder to this here good gentleman customer of ya'lls."

"Humph! Also look like you woulda growed taller too, but you didn't. Just give me my damn two dollars, Turnerd, and git the hell on," Miss Cutie Pie said.

"Gurl, you's mean," Mr. Turnerd said, "but you pretty, though. And did I say fine as dis here wine. Look at them hips on both of them. Ump, ump, ump," he said, nodding his head from side to side, while gaping in the direction of Miss May Alice. "Cutie Pie, I just got one mo thang to say for I leave this her lovely place? Is you listening to me?"

Narrowing her eyes, she said, "What is it, Turnerd?"

Slyly he asked, "When ya'll two old asses gone stop dressing alike? Don't ya'll thank it's time?"

The men on the back porch heard the question and broke into hearty laughter. I held mine in or at least tried too. A quick snicker slipped through.

"I'll tell you when, Turnerd." Miss May Alice pointed a wooden spoon at him, "It gone be as soon as yo ass get two feet taller and pay yo bills on time."

More laughter erupted from the back porch, this time louder.

Miss May Alice and Miss Cutie Pie's irritation with Mr. Turnerd went away almost as quickly as it came when they both looked up and saw Uncle Simee enter the back door. After all, he had that effect on people.

"How do, ma'am? My name is Simee and I was told I can get some shine here."

"You was told co-rectly, but it's called Spirits here. Why, come on in, yo name is what?" Miss Cutie Pie asked.

"It's Simee."

"Well, welcome, Simee. I'm May Alice, and this here is my sistah Cutie Pie." She said

"And I'm Turnerd," Mr. Turnerd abruptly added, while giving Uncle Simee a once-over.

"Well, nice to meet you. Now, what can we do for you?" May Alice asked.

"Well, I'll take two jars of shine—'scuse me, I mean spirits, please. One white and one peach if you got's that."

"We do and that'll be one dollar," Miss May Alice said.

"Here you go and thank ya." Uncle Simee pulled two dollars from his pocket and handed it to her.

"Suh, it's only a dollar," she said

"Keep the change."

"Why, thank you, Simee. We don't get much extra round here," Miss May Alice said looking over at Turnerd.

"You welcome."

"Come again now," Miss Cutie Pie said

"Be sho to do so," Uncle Simee said.

"Ol' pretty boy show-off. That's what he is," Mr. Turnerd yelled in the direction of Uncle Simee as he walked down the porch.

Once Uncle Simee departed, Miss Cutie Pie said to Mr. Turnerd, "See, that's how real customers pose to do. We give them the merchandise and they's gives us the money. Was you watching him? I'ma say it slowly for you. We hands ova the merchandise and the customer give us the money. Not half, not part of the money, but alls of the money."

It was almost impossible for them to stay bothered by Mr. Turnerd too long. He was as funny as he was short. Upon his departure, he pinched Miss Cutie Pie's bottom and stood on a chair, kissed Miss May Alice on the cheek, and winked at me. Each gesture caused all three of us to hesitantly smile.

"See ya'll good peoples tomorrow now. Bout to go and finds somebody that 'preciates my company."

"Good luck," Miss May Alice said.

"Bye, Turnerd," both said while smiling and shaking their heads.

13

Honey

"Need some help with that?" this stranger asked me as I was making my way home.

My arms was tired from walking and holding them clothes I got from the McDunkins, and it must have shown. "Naw, I sho don't."

I could tell my reaction was fairly unsettling to him. Seem like he quite used to women fawning over him. Maybe, but not me. Them fancy clothes he wearing must make him feel like he special or something. It ain't even Sunday and he dress like that. If you ask me, he acting like an ol' yard bird, clacking for attention. I'm just gone igno him, like I barely see him.

"What's yo name, girl?"

"Why?"

"Cause I'd likes to know. Didn't think it was a crime to ask a beautiful woman her name."

"Betty Jean, but they call me Honey."

"Honey, huh? My, ain't that fitting, you look like Honey," he said, smiling. "Wonder if you taste like Honey too?"

"Scuse me!"

"Now, don't get all offended. I'm just saying, for someone to look as pretty as you, I bet those lips taste just the same."

"You ain't gone eva know. Now 'scuse me!"

"Okay, I'm sorry. Just trying to be friendly is all. I done met some unusual folks in the last day or so. Kinda nice to meet a regular person."

"Yeah, these is some different folks living here in The Quarters. But overall, they good people."

"Who are you anyway?

"Oh." Remembering he had not introduced himself yet. "My name is Simee."

"Simee, huh?

"Yep."

Look to me like yo name should be Trouble. Got trouble written all over you for sho, nothing but. I can see it a mile away, I thought as I made sho to avoid eye contact with him. I'd already noticed him before he noticed me. It was hard not to since his looks were as wicked as they were wonderful.

"You ain't from round here is you? This is my first time seeing you."

"Naw, I ain't. I just come in from Chicago. But I am familiar with these parts. I was raised in Preston."

"How you get from Preston, Georgia, all the way to Chicago?"

"Well, I left and joined the army and was eventually stationed outside Chicago. When my duty was over, I just stayed on in Chicago. I recently decided to move on back closer to home."

"Can't say I blame you for leaving that Preston. Not much of nothing going on down there but cotton and drinking shine. And since I do not pick cotton and I do not drink shine, not much for me, I'd say. I left there years ago when I was a young gurl. Yeah, my sistah and her family moved here from there too. They couldn't get away fast enough."

"Well, I can't say much is down there myself."

"Yeah, Louise and even that Edga said it had to be more to life than Preston."

His face lit up with interest. "What's them names you say?"

"I said Edga and Louise. Is you hard of hearing too? Our daddy still down there. He bout the only family we still got down there. Well, him and witch Jean, 'scuse me, I mean Miss Jean."

He began to laugh, which further added to his appeal. "Gurl, I knows it was a reason I met you today. Edga my brotha."

"Yo brotha? I ain't never heard Edga talk of no brother," I said, surprised.

"That's what I said. And you his wife sistah?

"I am, her older sistah."

"Well, damn. He be a lucky man if you two favor."

And we did. Louise was a little bit shorter than me. We were both told to be pretty, with small frames, with the same dark brown complexion. We both wore our hair twisted and up. Wearing it that way helped with the heat in the summer and was convenient in the winter. We even had the same narrow hips and, to our disappointment, the same skinny legs.

With my defenses rising by the second, I was without dispute attracted to him, although I was not quite ready to admit that even to myself. His good looks didn't escape me, nor did his charm. A blind man could see just how good-looking he was and that smile of his was awful sinful. But I did notice he was a li'l uppity and I didn't like that none. Heck, I never wanted a man that stayed in the mirror more than I did.

Simee stood there staring at me without any notion of turning away. Just looking at me seemed to make him happy. Maybe he liked my spunk and or my "smart mouth," as he called it. It wasn't my intention to make him laugh. I just did.

"Well, take care," I said, hoping to escape his spellbinding hold. "Got plenty to do."

I started walking so fast that I stumbled a bit and almost dropped my basket. This caused Simee to laugh just enough to piss me off.

"Now, you be careful girl. I'd hate to have to carry you all the way home if you hurt them pretty little ankles of yours." Then he caught himself. "Come to think of it, that might not be such a bad idea, after all."

"In your dreams!" I said, walking away. All the while I was wondering, who is this here Simee?

14

Louise

Edga was in the bathroom, "taking care of business," as he put it, when a hard knock on the front door interrupted his concentration. I knew that a disturbance like this brought about great annoyance to him. He always felt the toilet was his special retreat, so to speak. He said it was the only place in the house he was guaranteed some peace. I had my hands up to my elbows in dishes, and I just waited for it to go away. After noticing that the knocking continued without any intervention from anyone else, he finished his business and headed for the door. Fearing it was the Jehovah Witnesses again, he tiptoed his way to the front window instead of the door. He was grumbling all along the way.

"Man, can't even sit on his throne without being bothered. Shoot, the next time they come a calling, I'm gone answer that do' butt naked. Come to thank of it, I'm gone be naked and holding an open umbrella. Bet that take care of them showing up here every Saturday morning. Look like after the last hundred times I didn't answer, they'd get the message."

As he carefully moved the curtain aside, he whispered with dread, "Lawd, have mercy, that can't be who I's thank it is? What in the hell is he doing here?" I was finishing up and I drew to the kitchen door, wondering why he was so shocked. "Well, I'll be damn. It is him. He the last somebody I wants to see. What in the world is he doing back down here?" Edga continued to stand with his back sealed against the wall, still not moving to answer the door.

After several knocks continued, I walked through the room to address the knocking. As I approached the door, I commented, "What you holding that wall up for, Edga? Answer the door."

As I made my way to the door, he scooted over and blocked it.

"Edga, what on earth is you doing? What is wrong with you? Move so I's can see who at the door. Move, ol' fool." I said as I pushed him away from the door.

"Can I help you, suh?" I said as I opened the door. Immediately I was staring at this beautiful man standing in my doorway.

"Why, yes you can. I's looking for Edga. I was told he resides here."

"You was told right, he does. And may I ask who calling?"

"Course you can, pretty lady. My name is Simee, Simee Scott. I's Edga brother. Bay brotha, to be exact."

"His brother?" I asked in a tone revealing that I was confused. Especially since my husband had never told me of any living relatives, other than a few cousins, much less a brother.

"Well, okay now. Why, come on in, Sim –ee? Say yo name one mo time."

"It's Simee. Simee Thomas Jefferson Scott."

"Yeah, you his brother, al' right." I thought, hearing his middle name. Both he and Simee had dead presidents for middle names.

"I'm Louise, Edga wife." I pushed the front screen door open and motioned for him to enter our home.

As he crossed the threshold, he took off his hat and said, "What a fine, fine place ya'll got."

Edga finally came out from behind the door with a different posture than I had seen before. His shoulders drooped and for the first time, his eyes didn't make contact with me. Nor did they meet his brother's.

"Well, I'll be. There you is, hey there. Boy, come here and let me look at cha," Simee said as he pulled him closer for a hug. "It's been a month of Sunday's then some since I last saw this here boy."

I had seen Edga friendlier with a rattlesnake than he was with his own brother. But I just chalked it off to his quirkiness and decided to ignore his behavior.

Finally, Edga said with the driest tone he could muster, "What you doing down here in these parts, Simee?

"Well, it's good to see you too," Simee said, not losing his smile. "At least yo pretty wife Louise glad to see me."

Flattered and giggling a bit, I said, "Why, thank you. Sho he glad to see you. Come on in and sit a spell."

"Thank you, kind lady, I believes I will. I just moved down here a couple of days ago from Chicago."

"Scuse me, Simee."

"Why, sho."

"Edga, is Pearline in back?" I yelled from the front room.

He just shrugged his shoulders as if I spoke Mexican or something.

"Pearline, is you back there? Well, I guess she ain't. Simee, would you like some iced tea?" I asked him.

"Why, yes. Be real good with this here heat."

I walked in the kitchen confused, but in time I'd have Edga to myself and hopefully gather an explanation. I could hear the conversation 'tween them, which only created more mystery.

"When I pulled in the filling station, the good Rev told me where to find ya'll after I explained who I was," Simee said as I approached him with the tall glass of tea.

"We's be sho to thank him for that," Edga said sarcastically.

As we all stood in the front room, Pearline raced in through the front door and stopped dead in her tracks.

"Hi, Uncle Simee," Pearline said.

"Uncle Simee. How you know him, Pearline?" Edga asked with the same curiosity as me.

"I actually don't, Daddy. I saw him over to Miss MinLee's and then Miss Cutie Pie's," she said, out of breath as she extended her hand toward Simee. "Hi, I'm Pearline."

"Hey there, young lady." Simee said. "Nice to meet you."

I took the liberty to stop the talking 'tween them. They back and forth didn't settle right with me. "All right, Pearline. Say good-bye now. Just us grown folks in here now."

"Yes ma'am." As she left the room I noticed that Edga was uncomfortable with Simee, and it strangely began to make me uncomfortable too.

"Seems I bout met everybody that lives round here already. I was getting a lay of the land, talk to a bunch of womens outside, just down the street, and a, er, strange wo-man sorta."

"Spudnick," me and Edga said in unison.

"Oh, and best of all I already found Miss May Alice and Miss Cutie Pie," he said, slapping his knee.

"Oh, that's good. Ain't it, Edga?' I said, hoping to get a response from him.

"Yeah. Well, good to see you. When you leaving?"

"Edga . . ." I said.

Simee put on a bright and shiny face. "Oh, that's all right. Edga been a jokester since we was boys. Who said anythang bout leaving? Done found me a place already. The good Rev also sent me to this nice man on my way in. Told me he rents his houses. Yep, got a place with a Mr. Carter, I believe. Though he told me to call him Buster."

Edga sat straight up and said, "Buster?"

"Yeah, Buster," Simee said as if he knew his relationship with Mr. Buster was a concern of his brother's.

"Well, you must be tired and hungry for some home cooking."

"Might say I am, Louise"

"Well, gone down to Wilhelmina's," Edga put in quickly. "You probably done met her already. She sell plates and other thangs. Be right up yo alley."

"You gone do no such thing. You can eat with us. I was just simmering some turnips with mustard greens and corn bread."

"That sounds mighty good, I tell you, Louise. I's 'preciates it, but I's gone make my way on home." All the while he had his eye on Edga's sour face. "Pretty tired. But I's take you up on it next time for sho."

"Won't be no next time," Edga said.

"Oh, my goodness, Edga. Just 'scuse him please," I said

As he stood to leave, he stopped and said to Edga, "Oh, how could I have forgotten? I met this beautiful lady named Honey."

Turning toward me, he asked "You some kin to her, Louise? Ya'lls favor each other."

"Why, yes. That's my sistah."

That last comment from Simee seemed to sicken Edga. The uneasiness and tension that was already simmering came right out. "Simee, I'm telling you, don't come here with...."

Quickly interrupting him, Simee said, smiling, "Yep, I was walking along just yesterday, leaving Miss May Alice and Miss Cutie Pie, and lo and behold, I walked right into this lovely lady. Kinda feisty, though."

I was now even more confused than I was when Simee first introduced himself, but I tried to ease the tension in the room. "That would be Honey for sho. Feisty ain't the word."

I had a bad habit of wringing my hands together when I was nervous. I had rubbed my hands together so much this morning, they could have sparked a flame.

"Well, it's time to leave ya'll good people, but I's be sho to take you up on supper next time, Louise."

As he walked to the door, Edga just sat with his head rested against his hand and watch Simee cheerfully hug me and leave. He didn't get up nor did he say goodbye to him either. He just watched. I had never seen him in such a state. Before I could begin to lay into him about this clear secret he'd been keeping, along with this peculiar behavior I just witnessed, that man was up already walking toward the back door.

"You do got a brother," I yelled. "What in the world is going on round here? Edga! You hear me?"

He stopped for a brief moment as if he was going to answer me. However, that wasn't going to happen. Shaking his head, he kept walking. Determined to get something from him, I kept yelling and walking behind him. That is, until the snap from the back door slamming shut in my face made me jump.

15

Louise

"Momma?"

"Yes, Pearline," I said as I folded a load of the Petersons' laundry. Me and Honey had picked up another family for washing, and they was all keeping us both quite busy.

"Daddy's been acting awfully strange since Uncle Simee moved here."

"Um-hum, Pearline."

"Have you noticed that he hasn't made one bad joke lately, not one? Not that I'm a fan of his jokes, by any means, but he almost seems sad."

"Yes, I noticed."

"And have you noticed that it's been over a month and he hasn't invited him over for supper or anything?"

"Noticed that too, chile."

"And have you—" she said before I interrupted her.

"What I noticed is that you got a lot of thangs you noticing, my goodness. What have I told you 'bout tending to grown folks business? And anyway, this ain't nothing for you to worry 'bout. Yo daddy and uncle gone be fine."

"Momma, can I share one more thing that I've noticed?" she asked me, hoping the answer would be yes.

"What is it, chile?"

"Well, the other day when I was walking home from school I passed Mr. RaShay's vegetable stand. And guess who was standing there buying fruits and vegetables?"

"Who?" I asked, entirely uninterested.

"Mr. Buster and Mr. McLand. All three were talking up a storm."

"And what's wrong with that? Mr. McLand ain't nothing like that Harriett. He a decent man. She a ... well, I best not say. Wouldn't be Christian like if I did."

"Humph. Well, if you ask me—"

"Don't recall doing that."

"Momma, listen, please. It was just odd how they seemed to talk like you know Daddy does with his friends. Laughing and all. He even slapped Mr. Buster on his back. They were too friendly with each other. If I didn't know better, I'd say they were friends."

"Well, you don't know any better. Be quiet and mind your own business."

"Yes ma'am."

Knowing Pearline, she read right through me. Probably 'specting she was on to something, she'd temporarily stop with the questions and just watch. There were a number of times in our comings and goings, me and Edga would comment on the relationship 'tween Buster and Mr. McLand. It was no secret that whites and Coloreds did not socialize on any level other than work, and sometimes not even then. So seeing Mr. McLand interact with Mr. Buster as he did stirred up curiosity among everyone.

"Hey, look like Uncle Simee done taking a liken to yo Aunt Honey?" I said, hoping to change the subject.

"Maybe so, Momma, but she doesn't seem a bit interested in him. She bristles every time he's around, or even if she hears his name."

"Bristles? There you go again with them big words of yours."

"She gets annoyed, or irritated."

"Oh, that. Don't pay that no 'tention. She does that because she likes him."

"Huh? Well, she has a funny way of showing it. That's for sure."

"She been like that since we was chilluns. It's two times Honey won't look at you. If she likes you and if she really pissed off at you. I guess you gotta know her to know what's really going on in her head."

"Well, I sure hope Daddy and Uncle Simee can be friends. After all, they are brothers."

"Well, that they is. Can't argue that. I will say, though, this whole thang mighty strange. For as long as I known yo daddy, he ain't neva mentioned no brother. With both his momma and daddy dead and no other kin ever mentioned, I guess I just thought it was him left. I know he got a few cousins scattered down in Preston, but not one of them ever mentioned Simee either. Matter of fact, all I really know 'bout yo daddy's people is his daddy and granddaddy. Can't stop him from telling how he learned butchering from them two, but that's 'bout all."

"Yeah, Momma, even at church Daddy walks right pass him."

"That kind of foolishness embarrass me. Folks pose to speak in the house of the Lawd, specially to yo own people. Edga know better. I know other folks whispering 'bout it. After all, yo daddy a deacon, and they is brothers. Not speaking like that is a shame and a pity. But, like I said, ain't nothing for you to worry 'bout. They be fine."

Pearline recognized my tone quite well. She knew I was trying to convince myself also that there wasn't nothing to worry about. We both knew I was wrong.

16

Pearline

Bernice and Rufus Jones were owners and operators of Heavenly Rest Funeral Homes. They started using Momma and Aunt Honey to wash and fold for them when Mr. Rufus noticed how white my daddy's shirts were. One day he made the mistake of asking Miss Bernice in front of the church women why she didn't get his shirts just as white. That was a big mistake. She cursed him out and told him Louise would be washing all his shirts and everything else from now on.

I had come around enough to know that they had grown accustomed to Miss Jenkins' morning calls. Although the calls were routine, they were still met with great annoyance. Both would often just sit and look at the phone when it rung and with much disdain. Business calls were one thing, but a call from Miss Jenkins was another. Each week without fail, they would debate over who'd answer her morning call.

"You answer it. I know it's her. Ain't nobody but her calling this early in the morning."

"Naw, you answer it, it's yo turn," Bernice snapped back at Rufus.

"If I's remember correctly, and I normally do, I answered it the last time."

"Well, you must not be remembering co-rectly. Now answer that dang-gone phone, Rufus."

"Hello."

"Yez, Miss Jenkins. I's just fine and you? Why, that's good to hear. Uh-huh, uh- huh. I'm glad yo bursitis done settled down. Yez ma'am. Uh-huh. Sho can be painful, specially when it rains. Uh-huh." Rufus said while watching Bernice roll her eyes, shake her head, and tap the table as she always did when she was annoyed. I just hung back, trying to listen without being noticed.

"Naw, nigh, we ain't got no new visitors this week. You know, thangs been kinda slow round here. But sho 'preciate you's checking in, though. Yez, ma'am, will do. Bye now," Rufus said before he hung up the phone.

"Tell me one thing, Bernice. Does this look like a damn motel to you? Last I checked, the sign outside said funeral home on it. She calls here like it say the Holiday Inn or something. Act like dead folks just stroll on in looking for a night's rest. They come in the front door, introduce they's self, *Hi, I'm Mr. Dead and I'm on my way to hell. Any rooms 'vailable tonight?*"

"Lawd, have mercy, that woman something. Did I tell you she stopped me last Sunday and offered her services?" Bernice said.

"Services?"

"Uh-huh. That's what I said. But before she could explain exactly what she offered, I's quickly, and I means quickly, 'scused myself. I had no desire to hear 'bout any of her services. Whatever they may be."

"Good. I'll stick with the quiet dead folks. The talking ones is asking a bit too much."

"Ain't that the truth. Now, Rufus, what time you say Simee coming by?

My ears pricked up. I was always hankering for news about my mysterious uncle that my daddy never said as much as boo to.

"I believe he said bout two o'clock. Bout another thirty minutes or so."

"Oh, okay. I must say, I was quite surprised when he stopped me after the deacon's meeting and said he like to speak with us bout a business opportunity."

"Yeah, me too. Specially since we already got a business. You know, I ain't good with juggling. This place keep us plenty busy," Bernice said

"I know, but I didn't want to be rude, so I said for him to stop on by. Wouldn't be no harm in listening to what he got to say."

That was mighty strange to me. From what I could tell, Simee didn't like to do much of anything except for sit around and drink moonshine.

"What you thanking it is?"

"Well, I don't rightly know. He was real funny about sharing it at the church. All I's know is it got something to do with the church and a railroad. Guess we find out pretty soon. He did say, the church gone make a whole lot mo money if we, ah, how he said it now"—Rufus tried to properly remember this new word he'd just heard—"de-ver-cee-fy" the church's business. Said it was something real popular up there in Chicago."

"De-ver-cee-fy? What, pray tell, is that?" Bernice said.

"Something about adding other business to the one we got."

"He been hanging round Pearline? De-ver-cee-fy. That sound like something that chile a say," Bernice said, not aware that I was hanging back right outside the door to grab what else, laundry.

"Well, as long as he don't talk 'bout no cremation. That's what I first thought he wanted to talk about. Remember at the conference last fall, that was all the talk. Them folks from What a Way to Go did that meeting on that new burial service," Rufus said.

"Talking 'bout that cremation? Is you crazy? Down here in The Quarters? That ain't gone happen," Bernice said.

"I know, I know, but I sho didn't know nothing else he'd want to talk about."

Shaking her head, Bernice said, "Rufus, some of these folks round here already know they goings straight to hell, and I do believe they ain't interested in burning twice."

"You got a point, huh?"

"Look at the time. That bell ringing got to be Simee. It must be bout two," Mr. Rufus said when he heard a ring from the door. As he pushed himself away from his desk, I decided I'd better get going. I had been pushing my luck by eavesdropping this long.

Simee

I anxiously stood at the door of Heavenly Rest several minutes before I reached to ring the doorbell. Standing there, I could feel the beads of sweat gather on my forehead and trickle down to my nose. This display of nervousness surprised me. I never knew myself to be edgy about much of anything, especially a simple con like this one. After all, this scheme had proven to be quite successful and quite profitable. Churches, land, and deeds; generally one didn't come without the other. I learned the best way to a man's wallet was through the church, and I took this route every time I could. Heck, it worked very well in Arkansas with Holy Spirit Church, in Chicago with Antioch United Baptist Church, in Mississippi with the Good Samaritans Baptist Church, and almost in Birmingham with the Believers Baptist Church.

Ruby, sweet Ruby, as I fondly remembered her, was a beautiful young parishioner at Believers. I noticed her and that red dress she wore as she switched in and sat on the front row during my presentation. Our unspoken lustful connection was immediate. After I completed my speech, she approached me and discreetly suggested that we meet behind the old water shed. It was the one right behind the church. I didn't ask her why, I knew. The invitation itself was enough needed to accommodate her request. That girl and me took good care of each other as we nestled in transgression behind that shed. Unfortunately for us, her husband, the Pastor Lyons himself had the same plans for Beatrice, another young sweet church-goer. The collision that occurred among us four created a stir that only God himself could untangle. Since he wasn't available, distance and speed would have to do. I escaped, although barely. I didn't leave alone, though. Two black eyes and a couple of broken ribs went right along with me.

What I got's to be worried 'bout? Just do what I do best. Won't take too long in this podunk town. These simple folks likely to bite any bait I dangle in front of them. It is all about timing. And this, I do believe, is the right time.

I took out my handkerchief, wiped my entire face, tucked it back in my front pocket and rang the doorbell.

"Boy, you ranging that doorbell like yo finger done got stuck. Come on in, Simee. Good to see you, good to see you," Rufus said as he extended his hand to shake mine.

"Why, thank you. How ya'll good people doing today?"

"We doing mighty fine and how you?" Bernice asked.

"I's good. Thank ya."

"Would you care for some lemonade? I just made some," Bernice asked

"Yes ma'am, that sounds nice on a day like this. May I have a seat, ma'am?"

"Sho you can."

"Now, I knew from the first time I laid eyes on you and yo pretty wife, ya'll was decent people, not only decent but smart business people. Matter of fact, I told Buster, them two seem like they real good people. And he agreed with me. Now, I know ya'll some busy people with a lot to do, so I's get right to the point."

"Uh-huh. Well, let's get to it," Rufus said.

"I done lived a many decent places, but I can't say I eva lived in a better place than rights here."

"Why, thank you, Simee. That's awfully nice of you to say. Yes, we proud of The Quarters too," Bernice said.

"I ain't being nice, ma'am, it's the truth," I said, knowing that flattery would get me anywhere. "Well, being the good church folks ya'll is, I thought it only fitting to start with you two. See, once I trick"—I cleared my throat—I mean, treat you two wonderful people to this opportunity, I'd ask both of you to join me before the church and the board and share how we all can benefit. I believe it's Proverbs 11:25 that says: A generous man will prosper; he who refreshes others will himself be refreshed. Now I don't know bouts you two, but I wants to be refreshed."

Leaning in to listen, both Bernice and Rufus said, "Amen. That's right, that's right."

"It is my purpose in life to see others prosperous. Ain't no fun being at the top by yo self. Proverbs also says in 13:21: Misfortune pursues the sinner, but prosperity is the reward of the righteous. And ya'll two look mighty righteous to me."

Looking at each other and smiling, Bernice and Rufus clung to every word I said. I learned long ago that church folk love to be reminded of just how good a church folk they is. I also learned that they were a thieving man's dream. Memorizing scriptures and anything else from the Bible generally guaranteed acceptance and credibility.

"Now, ya'll know where Macon Road meets up with Taylor Drive up north from here?"

"Uh-huh, we do. Funny you ask. We own about forty plus acres up that way. Heading on up to LaGrange."

"Rufus," Bernice said, in a manner to refresh Rufus's memory.

"Well, to tell the truth, it's the church that's own it. But me, Bernice, Wilhelmina, Buster and the Rev, we all on sits on the church board that controls it. All of us has got's to vote and agree in order to do anything with it. That's how Job set it up."

"Job and Wilhelmina?"

"Yeah, Job. Gawd bless his soul. He was a good one. He obtained that land many, many years ago. I believe his granddaddy, who was a freed slave, bought it acre by acre. Said his granddaddy gave it to his momma and she passed it on to him. Since Job neva had any chilluns, he left all the land for the church. Before he died, he sat down with Mr. McLand and drawed up a will to make sho it was done co-rectly and could not be mistaken for gov-ment land. He said he saw that many times the gov-ment would come and steal land from us Coloreds left and right. Specially handpicked, me, Rufus, the Reverend, Buster and even included that Wilhelmina to take care of it. Don't know why he chose her, though , but he did."

"I do," Rufus said.

"Oh, hush up with all that nonsense," Bernice said.

"Wilhelmina too huh?" I asked as I pondered my next move.

"Yes, suh," Rufus said. "The church been thanking bout building a bigger church up that way and even putting a business and a new school up there too."

"Well, that's what I's here to talk to ya'll bout. Figured I'd start with you and yo wife first, and then maybe we could all gets together and discuss it further."

"Discuss what? Bernice asked, concerned.

Here goes the pitch. "I'm just gone say it straight. Ya'll sitting on a gold mine right here in Columbus. Who knew they had gold mines in Georgia?" I said, laughing

"Gold mine? What you talking 'bout, Simee? Last I heard, you had to have a mine for you could find gold in one," Rufus said.

"That piece of land right up there that is worth a lot of money. Way more than what Job's granddaddy bought it for. Nobody know 'bout it 'cause the gov-ment don't won't nobody to know bouts it. My sources tells me the United States gov-ment itself is planning on running a railroad track right through there to connect with Atlanta and on up to New York City. I got a hold of what is a called a land survey which lays it all out for you."

"A land survey?" Rufus asked with skepticism. "Really, now and how you get that?"

"Like I said, my sources done gave it to me."

"So how much money is the land worth, how much you talking?"

"That piece of land been sitting up there and nobody, I mean nobody, but the three people in this room gone know. You ready?"

"Ready as we gone eva be." Rufus said leaning in towards me.

"That piece of land is worth over two hundred thousand dollars."

"What you say?" Bernice asked, choking on her lemonade.

"I said, two hundred thousand dollars."

"Boy hush, yo mouth," Rufus said.

"Lawd have mercy. Hand me one of those fans, Rufus, and get me a wet rag. It done got awfully hot in here."

"You mean to tell me, them few acres worth two hundred thousand dollars?"

"Yes suh, and maybe more."

"Well, I'll be."

"Look like to me you gone be rich," I said

Nervously Rufus said, "Now wait a minute. This here a lot to take in. All that money? That's a whole lot of money for forty acres. And this would have to be something everybody agreed on. Everybody. Meaning, Buster, Wilhelmina, the Reverend, and us. That's a whole lotta yes's, you know."

"Yeah, I know, but that's why I's here with you two first. I need ya'lls' understanding and agreement first, than we can take it to the others. In this here briefcase, I got the survey, the contracts, and the permission to buy it from ya'll, but before I sho ya'll this here information, I need yo word, this go no farther than this here room. Just us, at least for now."

"You got's our word." Rufus said, more intrigued now than ever. "Me and Bernice known to keep a secret or two round here."

Actually, those two couldn't keep a secret if their lives depended on it, and that's exactly what I was counting on.

So far, all seemed to be working according to my plan. The rippling effect of talking to Bernice and Rufus seemed to pay off. By the end of the week, everyone in The Quarters knew of the big money deal that was gone make the church rich. "Sources" that key word always worked. Swindling these folks out of their land was gone be a piece of cake for Simee.

I stood in front of the mirror, carefully trimming my beard while also admiring myself and that hundred-dollar suit I was about to put on. While standing there, I began to reflect on the task ahead of me.

All I got's to do is get my hand on that damn deed and I'm outta here. I'm sho Lucy and her "sons" probably looking for me. Just need to gets that deed. Man, I cannot get that fine Honey off my mind. Look like she gone be harder to get into than a rusty lock with oily hands. But, they don't call me Mr. Magic for nothing.

17

Honey

My front porch was the meeting place for shelling peas, sipping coffee and most importantly, gossip. On most Saturday mornings, me, Louise, my niece, along with a few other ladies from the church would meet up for our weekly ritual of shelling, cleaning and canning a bushel of something. Anything from pole beans, black eye peas, butter beans, speckled peas, even tomatoes was up for canning. All of us sit with a big basket of peas set right next to us with a bowl held still by our thighs and knees. This left our hands free for the real work. Although my darling niece loved to eat peas, she dreaded shelling them. She fussed more than a time or two that shelling peas was a wearisome and quite honestly *painful and tedious process.* She was right.

> *Step 1. Look at basket with well over two hundred unshelled peas.*
>
> *Step 2. Recover from the immediate shock of having to shell two hundred plus peas,*

Step 3. Pick up pea from basket.
Step 4. Snap both ends.
Step 5. Split pea with thumbs,
Step 6. Slide peas down from top with both thumbs,
Step 7. Say "Ouch, Ouch, Ouch,"
Step 8. Repeat Steps 1 through 7.

These steps, though necessary, always caused the inside of our nails to turn green and our hands and thumbs to become strained, cramped, and sore. Po Pearline, that child knew complaining was useless. Louise made it clear that *as long as you eat them, yo behind gone shell them.*

"Honey, you know he sweet on you," my sistah said as we all sat out front shelling away. She knew exactly how to get Jim and Maybell started.

"I think he is too, Auntie. Plus, Uncle Simee is really good-looking for an older man. He kinda remind me of Langston Hughes but much taller."

"Old?" I said as I looked at the other ladies.

"Yes ma'am. He's at least twenty-five."

"Lord, she probably thank I'm two shakes away from dead, then," Jim said.

"Well, ain't-cha?" I said, laughing.

"Well?" Jim asked, looking in my direction.

"Well, what?"

"Honey, gurl, you know what I'm talking 'bout."

"Yes, he is handsome, but . . ."

"But what? I remember a time when all that was needed was a hairy chest and a big—"

"Watch yo mouth, Jim, done forgot this child out here."

"She don't know what um talking 'bout anyway, Louise. Calm yo self. This here sistah of yours gets on my last nerve.

I ain't like these others folks round here, I say it to your face. Like I said, you gets on my nerves, woman. Look like you be a li'l bit mo interested in the man if for nothing but to look at him, with his pretty self. Although I'd do more than look at him, if I weren't married, of course."

"Course," I said with a slight smile. "He all right, I guess. Just so ya'll old busy bodies know, I done stood outside the house and talked to him a few times."

"Oh, really?" Francine said, leaning in.

"Yes I have, but um, it's something about him that's just not right. Can't put my finger on it. Sides, that Wilhelmina got her eye on him anyway. I hear she makes her rounds to him, or she sends one of her girls to take him a plate of food. Don't matter what time of day, she got a 'scuse to see him." Mocking Wilhelmina, I went on: *"Mawning, Mr. Simee, here is yo breakfast. Whew, lunch time got here so quick like, Mr. Simee, you's a working man and you need yo trition. Mr. Simee, shame a man like you got's no hot food waiting on you, so I's figured, I'd brang you some. No bother at all.* And if I know Wilhelmina, he getting more than just food, some desserts in there too, if you know what I mean." Laughter erupted all around. "Plus, I ain't in the mood to battle Wilhelmina. You know how she is. One day she speaking, the next day she ain't. And I ain't got no time for her foolishness. Ya'll know she evil too. No telling what she might do if she suspects somebody tipping in what she consider her territory. Remember when Rochelle took a liking to Buford, Wilhelmina's old ass won't having none of it. We all know the mystery bout Rochelle's shed burning down ain't no mystery at all. Even burned it down knowing Roscoe was in it. That po dog. Shame she did that, just a shame. I just ain't in the mood to look over my shoulder every minute. Specially ova no man."

"Humph, I took a good look at him again the other day and you might reconsider. Hell, for him, I get to looking ova my shoulder so much, ya'll a need a crank to turn my head back straight. Goodness. What size shoe you thanks that boy wear?"

"What? Why in the world you worried 'bout his shoe size?"

"You know that saying" the bigger the feet, the bigger the...."

"Francine!" Louise said.

"Looks mighty tempting," Francine said, laughing.

"You heard?" Jim put in.

"Heard what and pass me some more of them peas?" I asked.

Leaning in, Jim said, "You ain't heard it from me, but I heard Simee done been over to Bernice and Rufus talking 'bout some business deal. It got something to do with the land the church owns up in north Columbus. Bernice told MinLee and of course MinLee told Carrie, and then Carrie told Spudnick. I ran into Spudnick over at the Walgreens yesterday while he was shopping for lipstick and barrettes for his hair. You know how he likes to change up the colors for the seasons. I told him red was very becoming on him with his yellow com-plex-sion and all, plus I told him Billie Holiday was on the cover of *Jet* magazine with some of that same red on. He almost lost his mind since he thanks he looks like Miss Holiday—"

"Gurl, would yo ass stick to the point? What the hell is you talking 'bout? Damn Billie Holiday. Heard what bout Simee?" I interrupted.

"Seem like he looking for the church to sell that land up there. It's something 'bout a railroad track suppose to run from here northbound. Now, if I heard it right, it's suppose to run from Columbus to Atlanta and all the way up to New York. He said it's worth a lot of money."

"North Columbus, talking 'bout them forty acres?"

"Yeah, Honey, that's exactly where I's talking 'bout," Jim said.

"Momma?" Pearline said.

"Yeah baby?"

"Next he going to ask for a mule too," Pearline added.

"Huh? What is this chile talking 'bout, a mule?" Jim said.

"Never mind." Pearline said, annoyed that none of them connected forty acres and a mule.

"Never-you-mind, li'l gurl. Keep shelling," Louise told Pearline.

"Now, how that's pose to work anyway? If the Rev got any say, they ain't selling nothing. And how he know 'bout that land anyhow? He just moved here," I asked.

"See, that's exactly what I said to Buster. First I asked him if he knew anythang 'bout it yet. With his smart mouth he said, what you thank? Told me, Rufus told him. Said Bernice and Rufus can't hold their water, much less keep a secret. Then he said, Simee told them about some sources of his. Not sho who they were, though," Jim said.

Pearline sat there listening to them as intensely as she could. She knew at any moment, her momma could decide this conversation was a little too much for her. Then she'd be shooed right off that porch.

"Well, I just don't know 'bout all this. Louise, you gone talk to Edga 'bout it?"

"Honey, he probably already know, if Buster know. I'll try, but talking to him 'bout that brother of his usually go nowhere fast."

"Well, once Rev. Evans hear bouts it, he probably gone call a meeting at the church. You know how he always calling a church meeting for one thang or the other. I promise you this ain't gone be no different."

"Well, Honey, look like yo new beau not only good-looking but just might have some money too."

"Jim, who said anythang 'bout him being my beau?"

"He will, might even end up being yo husband," Jim said.

"Chile, please," I said. If truth be told, I was secretly hoping Simee would be something. Though I knew for him to be anything, there would be a battle with that Wilhelmina.

18

"Um coming, baby. My, you got here fast. Yo momma just told me you was on yo way. You musta ran over here," I said as I opened the front door. I was completely surprised at who stood before me. "Oh. It's you."

"Hey gurl. How you doing?"

"Fine, Wilhelmina. Everythang OK? I was thanking you Pearline."

"Sho is. I was out for my nightly stroll and thought I'd stop by for a spell. You ain't busy, is you?

"Well, not really, I guess. I am 'specting Pearline any minute, then I thanks I'm gone call it a night." I barely opened the front door without stepping all the way out of the house. Wilhelmina wasn't a welcomed guest and I wanted to make it obvious.

"Uh Huh. I see. Well, I's just get straight to the point with you."

"Bout?"

"Well, word round here in The Quarters is that you is sweet on Simee."

"Simee?"

"Yes, Simee. Folks saying that you been courting him or trying to ever since he got's here. I just thought it was only fitting that I stop and ask you personally, you know, since it's the Christian thang to do. Besides, me and him is going together. You know me, I don't like no gossip, so I'm here to get it straight from the horse's mouth."

"The horse's mouth, huh?"

I stepped completely back into the house, behind the screen door, narrowed my eyes, folded my arms, took a deep breath and said, "Wilhelmina, hear me clearly and hear me good. Do I look like a damn horse to you?"

"Bam" was the next sound Wilhelmina heard from me slamming the door shut.

"Well," she said in frustration and shock that a door had been slammed in her face.

As she hurriedly made her way down my four narrow porch steps, almost slipping along the way, I yelled from behind the door, "Well, hell, Wilhelmina, and gets off my damn porch."

She made her way from the front porch huffing, puffing, and mumbling along the way, then yelled, "This ain't over."

I walked back to the kitchen to stir some simmering poke salad, grumbling to myself, "The nerve. I can't, well, yes I can, believe that crazy woman just did that. Talking 'bout she want to get something from the horse's mouth. The last time I looked at a horse, the damn thang didn't look a thang like me, the nerve. And who said I owe her an explanation for anythang I do or decides to do? Gets on my nerve."

Before I could lift the lid of the pot or pick up the wooden spoon to stir the turnips, another knock came from the front door.

"This woman gone piss me off. What she want now? What, Wilhelmina?" I said as I snatched the front door open.

"I been called a lot of thangs, but Wilhelmina was never one of them," Simee said, smiling widely.

"Oh… I thought you were that crazy woman again," I said, standing behind the screen door. I couldn't help but notice his cologne. The smell of it was just as powerful as his looks. A hint of oak and musk, all wrapped in charm.

"What brings you here, Simee Scott? I don't recall sending out an invitation."

"My, my, my. Look at you. Gawd must have woke up in a good mood the day he made you. Shame you this pretty."

"Uh-huh. And how you know where I live?"

"How I know where you live? Easy, I just ask." He made a motion with his hand. "You gone make me stand out here talking to you through this screen door?"

"It's a thought."

"Well, can you thank again? Goodness, why you so mean? May I please enter yo lovely home?"

It did seem silly to be talking this way. "Come in, Simee. What can I help you with?" I asked, still bothered by my unexpected guest.

As he crossed my threshold, he removed his hat and coat and began to look around, taking note of my orderly home and those simmering turnips. Silenced dwelled as he stood awkwardly at the entrance, holding his hat.

"My, my, my, sho smell good in here. How you? I haven't seen you in a while. Been a few weeks since you talked to me."

"Well, I'm fine, Simee. Just been a bit busy is all."

"Where you been?"

"Here, working, and at church. I'm there every Sunday. Real easy to see me there."

"Gurl, you sho got a mouth on you. May I have a seat, please?"

"For a minute, Simee. My niece is on her way over and I got business to take care of with her."

I finally unfolded my arms and motioned for him to come into the house.

"Why, thanks you," he said as he made his way inside. "Yeah, you right 'bout that. I been gone a few Sundays. Got a lot going on, some big plans."

"I done heard 'bout your big plans. That land deal. Folks can't keep from talking 'bout it."

"What? This whole thang pose to be confidential. I tell you, I thought Rufus and Bernice was good to keep quiet till I talked to the Rev and the church."

"You what? Those two, please? You might as well had put it on the front page of the newspaper. Seem like you got several hands in that deal. Way too many for one man or even two to make a decision. You gone have to convince all them people including the Rev to sell that land, even if a lot of money can be made. I hope you know that land hold a lot of history for these parts. Mr. Job, left the church all that land. They's good memories attached to him."

"Memories, good or bad, ain't neva fed nobody, bought no clothes, or paid a bill."

"Oh, really? That smart mouth of yours gone work real good. See how far that get cha with the board."

"I'm just saying, the church can make some money and benefit real good from this. Everybody in this here Quarters, be better for it, everybody, including you."

"Now, how's that gone work? I ain't a part of the board. Sides, the church owns it and that means the church will benefit, not separate people."

"You part of the church, ain't you? Yo vote count too, right?"

"Not really. I'm telling you, it's the board's decision. "You ain't got to convince me, you got to convince Buster, Rev, Wilhelmina, Bernice and Rufus. Looks like you already started with Bernice and Rufus, and let's not foget that Wilhelmina."

"What is you talking 'bout, woman? I ain't got to forget Wilhelmina. I got to remember her first."

"So, that's what you creeping round here for? Needing my help to talk these folks out of they land?"

"Naw! You the one who brung the land up. I'm just telling you like I know." He seemed very offended. "I came here 'cause I like you. "

"Huh? Like me? What grade you in?" I asked with my usual sarcasm. "You sound crazy. You don't even know me. Humph, ain't got no time for no courting anyway."

"Well, I ain't one to beat round the bush, so I thought I'd just come right out with it. I know you said you ain't interested, but I tell you, I is awfully interested in you. Don't seem quite right that a woman such as yo-self all lonesome and by herself. You need someone round here to protect you, take care of you. Keep you warm at night." He stood up and attempted to swing his arm around my shoulder.

I shook it off. "What in da world is going on tonight? First, I'm a horse, now I'm lonesome and don't forget cold. And who said I'm lonesome anyway? I ain't no mo lonesome than anybody else round here. I's getting right tired of folks telling me that. And I got plenty of quilts and wood for a fire when the frost comes. Goodness."

"All right, calm down. I didn't mean no harm, Honey. All I's saying is I like to officially court you. That's all."

"Really? Now, how you gone do that? Almost impossible to court two women round here without the other knowing. Listen here, I ain't interested in sharing clothes, much less a man. Yeah, I done heard 'bout you and Wilhelmina, with her crazy ass. Uh-huh, sho have. She just left here right for you came to inform me of her position with you."

"Her position? With who?"

"With you. Seem to me ya'll more than just friends. Folks round here say she show up all times of the day at you house wit yo breakfast, yo lunch, and especially yo dinner. And whatever she seem fit to brang."

"I done told Wilhelmina the best I know, I ain't interested," he said, out of patience with her. "We can only be friends. She just don't seem to listen, I guess."

"Well, I guess she ain't listening to something that ain't being said."

"Lawd have mercy, woman."

He seemed so put out that I decided to take him at his word. He couldn't be blamed for liking free home-cooked meals. "Look, Simee, with all honesty. I 'preciates your interest, I really do, but."

"But what?"

"I just thank it's best we be friends and that's it."

"Well, I find that contrary to what I want. I'm a determined man, and I goes for what I want." Simee came closer and gently embraced my shoulders. I stood there hating to admit it to myself that his touch was appreciated and a touch I enjoyed.

"Just been a crazy night is all. Shouldn't be taking it all out on you, I guess," I said, surprising me and Simee. "First that nut Wilhelmina comes by unexpected with her foolishness, then you come knocking. Not to mention got plenty of work to take care of. So I guess I'm just a bit fussy."

"A bit?"

"Yeah, just a bit. Don't push it," I said as I eased away from him. I was trying to shield my attraction.

"How 'bout you let me take you over to Tullulah tonight and buy you a big steak dinner? I hear that place got the best steak dinners down this way."

"No, but I 'preciate you asking. I'm simmering some dinner for me now and sides, Pearline on her way over. Guess we stuck here talking."

Looking at me with curiosity, he said, "Can't believe you not taken. Can't believe that one bit. As fine as you is, look like men be lined up outside to spend a li'l time with you."

"Well, they ain't. What 'bout you? You ain't' married, got no woman, other than Wilhelmina," I said with a laugh. "Hard to believe that. I tell you, if you ain't seeing Wilhelmina, her plan is that you do real soon."

"Don't care what her plan is. I'm right where I want to be."

Simee got up from his chair and nervously paced around the small room. After shoring up his nerve, he approached me again and knelt down before me and gently kissed my lips. Before I could protest, we were in a passionate kiss. So passionate that I could feel his manhood begin to rise and press against me. I pulled away, only to be pulled back by him. He

took his hands and removed the clamp that held my hair together, then nibbled on my neck. As my hair dropped, his fingers roamed through my hair, causing a sensation that made
me tremble. I found myself moving his hands from my head
directly to my breast, hoping and praying he'd squeezed them
as I so desired. After fulfilling my wish, he moved to unbutton
my dress, exposing my hard nipples. As only Simee could, he
took his tongue and playfully circled them. His breath was
warm and sweet, only adding to my lust for him. I couldn't
resist him anymore. I stepped back and began to remove my
own clothing. My dress was first to fall, then my brassiere, my
stockings, and finally with his help, I stepped out of my pant-
ies. I reached for his hand and we walked to my bedroom. He
laid me down and began to remove his clothing. I watched
with curiosity and delight, since he was more tempting naked than with his clothes on. He leaned over me, spread my
legs, and even kissed me down on my private. I'd heard about
people doing that, but I thought never in a million years that
I'd participate in an act such as that. I was wrong. I moaned
in delight from that alone. Once he finally entered me, his
thickness was intoxicating. We both groaned as he thrust
back and forth with no intention of stopping. Finally, he released and I did too.

As we both lay in my bed, silence hung in the room. I
could only think on the huge mistake I'd just made. At best,
he'd keep it 'tween us two. At worst, the entire Quarters would
know by tomorrow morning.

"You okay?" he asked me.

"Not really. Lawd, I don't know what I was thanking."

"Humph, I ain't sure, but whatever it was, I'm glad you did."

"Scuse me?"

"I didn't stutter. I'm glad you did. Been liking you since the day I saw you walking with them clothes. Ain't nothing changed."

"I-I think, uh, you want, well, I have some lemonade. Would you like a glass?" I nervously asked while awkwardly getting out of the bed and putting my dress back on. As he pondered on his decision, I tied a knot in my dress belt that only a pair of scissors could unlock. Making sure that something other than hope would keep me from him.

"Lemonade? Naw, but I can think of something else I'd like."

Watching me hurry into the kitchen away from him seem to bring him more pleasure. He smiled as he pulled a cigarette from his pants pocket and lit it. I said nothing. That cigarette was the least of my problems.

After hanging out in the kitchen for as long as I could get away with, I emerged composed or at least I hoped to give that impression. I had no intention of allowing what just happened to move beyond tonight regardless.

"Where's that lemonade you ran off to get sweet Honey"

"Lemonade?" I asked, having for a moment forgotten what I'd gone in there for. "Oh, I drank it all. Oh, well. Look at the time. Bout time you get up and head on outta here."

"Well, can't say I'm ready to go. Was hoping to lay little longer. Maybe we could go for seconds, if you know what I mean."

My voice got harder. "Not a good idea, Simee. You best be getting out of here."

"You sho?"

"Yeah, I am."

Simee got up and clothed himself just as smoothly as he'd disrobed. For a minute I was tempted to grant his request, but I knew better. I learned long ago that loneliness plays tricks on you. Besides, something about this man was more than I could handle.

As I ushered him to the door, every thought that could run through my mind did. I stopped cold in my tracks right before I turned the handle on the door for him to leave. For some reason I can't explain, I could only ask him one question.

"Mind if I ask you a personal question?"

"Woman, you can ask me anything you want to right now."

"Not trying to get in yo business, but I been thanking on it for a while now."

"What is it?"

"Well, how 'bout you tell me what's going on 'tween you and Edga?"

He blinked in shock. "Edga?"

"Yeah."

"Me and you just finished making the hottest love I done had in, I'll say ever, and you want to ask me 'bout damn Edga?"

"As crazy as it sounds, yes. I want to know. You heard me, Simee Scott. Now, let's be clear, Edga ain't neva been one of my favorites, mostly gets on my nerves, but I tolerates him for my sistah and them chilluns. He ain't a bad man, just being Edga, I suppose. You probably don't know this and you may not care, but it hurt Louise's heart that Edga will pass right by you, no talking, no speaking, no nothing. He is yo brotha, ain't he? Just don't seem right for kin folks to do what ya'll two is doing."

This question caught Simee off guard. Heck, it even caught me off guard and I asked the question. Instead of me

189

drowning in concern of what I'd just done in my bedroom, I was more caught up on those two. I'd convinced myself that Simee would forget about what just happened to us as soon I as I did—and that would be immediately.

"It's a long story. Besides, you was just putting me out a minute ago."

"I know, but thangs easy to change round here. I'll make the time."

Simee took a seat on the couch and began to make himself real comfortable. He crossed his legs, pulled out his cigarette and even lit it. Although smoking was normally not allowed in my house, I made this an exception. I was determined to hear his story. *Hmm, he a bit too relaxed,* I thought, *ain't frazzled one bit.* This response was quite contrary to Edga's whenever the subject came up. But I sat in silence waiting to hear a story I was entirely unprepared for.

"To tell you the truth, that boy ain't neva liked me. Act like everything that happened was my fault."

"What you talking 'bout, Simee? Everything like what?"

"You see, Edga and I was born from the same daddy but different mommas. His momma was named Helen and my momma was named Willie Jean. Now see, our daddy, Delmar kept two houses, one in Preston with Helen, and one in Guthbert with my momma. I sho miss my momma, she was a good Christian lady. Always working at the church, trying to help somebody. I tell you."

"I don't mean to be rude, but you was saying . . ."

"Well, after my brother Junius was born, Daddy started spending less and less time down in Guthbert with us. He all of a sudden stopped branging food like he used to and doing other thangs. At first Momma didn't pay it much attention.

She just blew it off and made 'scuses for him. She'd say he had to work, he was sick or "that woman" kept him tied up. Then everything started to change, she started to change. I could see the anger grow in her. Every night that he didn't come home, her anger seemed to boil to a new place. Then she started doing strange thangs."

"Strange thangs like what?"

"For one, she started talking to herself. And she had a thang for pinching and twisting her hair, so much that she pinched a whole heap of it from her head. Folks started saying her mind was getting bad. At night, she would look out the window for him and stand there for hours at a time, just waiting. Sometimes she would even take to the old rocking chair and sit there all day rocking, back and forth, back and forth, like she was in a trance or something. See, Daddy couldn't decide what he wanted to do and strung Momma along as long as he could. I'll never forget the night her mind just snapped like an old twig. She said she was tired of playing seconds to that bitch and that she'd had just about enough. All of a sudden she grabbed my hand and off to Preston we went. It was a terrible rainstorm that night, hard to see past your hand. The rain came crashing down like the devil himself was pouring it. I'll never forget them trees waving in the wind like they did. Even with all that, she kept walking. Finally, we got to his other house and I was a scared something, I tell you. Momma marched up to the door and got to banging and kicking it too. With all that banging Daddy pulled the door open fire mad and said, *Woman, is you crazy? What you doing here?* Well, when he said that, Momma hauled off and slapped that man so hard he lost his footing. She looked like Joe Louis taking out that ol' German, Max. Didn't know she had that in her to box like that. Don't think Daddy knowed either. Now Momma was a big woman and tall too, she wasn't no fri-gil li'l thang at all, no suh. I remember real clear what happened 'cause me and Edga was standing right there, too scared to move. After he fell, Momma walked up to Rose and started punching her and screaming, like something had taken ova her. With all that hitting, Rose slipped and fell. And before she could get up, Momma walked over to the stove, grabbed a iron skillet and smashed that po woman in the head. Blood went everywhere. Daddy got up stumbling and yelled, *"Woman, what you done did? Lawd have mercy, you done kilt her."* After that, Momma just walked out the house and kept going. I think she forgot I was with her, 'cause this time she didn't grab me. Everybody, including the sheriff, got to looking for her for days. That was a bad week, 'cause it stormed hard every day and it was still hard to see anything. Finally, they found her dead in the woods bout three days later."

"My Lord, that's horrible."

Laughing and slapping his knee, he looked over at me and said with a twisted delight, "To this day, that was the quickest kill I done seen yet. Been born a man, coulda been a boxer."

Shocked at his last comment, I asked without hesitation. "What did you just say?

"Oh nothing," he said after taking note that I was looking at him with disgust.

Watching him closely, I was hooked on the way he told such a horrible story. I couldn't help but think, *What the hell? Quickest kill? What kind of crazy shit is this? Who in they right mind takes pleasure in a memory of this nature, seeing someone die and all like that? Specially with his momma being involved. Shoot, I got*

*enough death behind me, don't need to add no mo. And Lawd Jesus,
I just slept with this fool.*

At that moment I knew three things for sho: there was a
God, after winter comes spring, and the very last person on
this earth that I should have ever gone to bed with was crazy
Simee Scott.

19

Pearline

"All I do is work and for free at that. Well, at least when it concerns Momma," I said to myself as I walked over to the McLands to pick up clothes and then head to Aunt Honey's for another errand. "Unlike me, the McLand children actually get paid for doing chores and the simplest ones at that. Both their kids, Dick and Jane get a dollar a week for doing what they should do anyway. Things like, making up their beds, taking out the trash, and even picking up their dumb dog Spot's poop. You know, it is their dog. By the way, I never took a liking to that old mangy dog, and frankly I believe it's mutual. Whenever I'm at the McLands', Spot follows me throughout the house, gazing at me like he's a security guard on duty or something. When I walk, he walks, when I stop, he stops. He growls at me at all the time and will sometimes even poop right in front of me. The first time he did it, I thought it was accidental, but not after the second, third, and fourth time, I concluded this was quite intentional. Whenever it happens, Mrs. McLand gets into a frenzy, running and yelling for him "to stop that right now," "What on earth is wrong with you?" She'll ask that mutt, as if an answer is soon to follow. Regardless of her command, he continues until his task is completed. I have thought about kicking him a few times, actually more than a few times, but so far I haven't. I did bump him once, not enough to hurt him, but enough for my liking. By the way, who names a dog Spot anyway? Silly me. Probably the same people who'd named their children Dick and Jane. I can't wait to grow up and not suffer these chores or that mutt anymore. As soon as I graduate from high school and move, the only chores I'm doing are my own. Come to think of it, I might be rich enough to hire my own maid. Who knows, maybe I'll call Mrs. McLand and offer her the position.

Mr. McLand must have seen me walking up the driveway because he opened the door before I could knock. "Hey there, Pearline," he said, appearing surprised to see me here on a Sunday.

"Hi, Mr. McLand. How are you?"

"I'm great, young lady, and you?"

"I'm well, thank you. Momma told me to bring this basket to Miss McLand to pick up a few things. May I see her, please?"

"She's actually not here, but come on in. Hmmm, not sure why she couldn't wait, but that's Harriet for you. Sorry to be a bother."

"No bother, sir." I said, although it was clearly a bother.

"Make sure you tell your momma that Harriet appreciates her doing this. Would you like some water or iced tea? I see it's hot out there today."

"No, thank you. Oh, thank you so much for this book." I handed it back to him. "I thoroughly enjoyed every bit of it."

"You're welcome young lady. Hey, hang tight. I've got another one for you. Grab a chair. Be right back."

"That's okay, I'll stand." I said tensely, having never been offered a chair at that house before. Also understanding it was not acceptable for me to sit in their lavish dining room.

"Young lady, have a seat. You're always welcome to sit at our table."

"Hmmmm, but . . ."

"No buts, have a seat."

"Yes sir." I pulled a chair from the dining table and sat down.

I sat there uncomfortable, more on the edge of the seat than fully on it. A minute had not passed before Mrs. McLand walked in. Temporarily distracted by the clothes basket I'd placed on the kitchen table, she did not see me. As a matter of fact, she walked right past the doorway to the dining room. Then she backed up.

"Excuse me?" she screamed at me. "What in tarnation are you doing?"

"I-I was waiting on Mr. McLand to bring me a—"

"The nerve. Get your Nigger ass up from my table. Right now!"

"Yes ma'am."

Tears began to flow from my eyes before I could restrain them. The pain which accompanied being called a Nigger was something I had not yet experienced. I quickly pushed back from the table but stumbled and fell to the floor.

"What's going on in here?" Mr. McLand asked as he quickly entered the room. Seeing I had fallen, he reached to help me stand up.

"This gal was sitting at my dining room table, Bill. Now, she knows better than that. I just can't believe this. What if the Ladies Auxiliary finds out about this? I'll never have another club meeting here. You bout to make your mammy lose her job, gal."

"I'm sorry, Miss Harriett," I said, terrified. "I apologize. Please don't fire my Momma."

Then Mr. McLand thundered, "Harriett, shut up. Pearline, it's okay. No one is firing anyone."

"What did you say?"

"I said, shut the hell up. What's wrong with you? Can't you see that's a child you're speaking to like that? God damn it Harriett," he said, hurling the book he held against the wall. The thwack it made caused both me and Miss Harriet to jump.

"What I see is a Nigger sitting at my table. I'm not sure what you see, but that's exactly what I see," she said, seething.

I could not believe my ears. I wiped away my tears, apologized again and ran out the back door. Both Mr. and Mrs. McLand were both so engaged in their argument, neither bothered to acknowledge my departure. So, I wiped my eyes and I decided to stick around, out of sight, to see what they said.

"You're a piece of work, Harriet."

"Call me what you will. I don't care. She had no business sitting there. What if I'd walked in with someone? Next you're going to let her eat off my fine china or invite her over to the country club. You know what, things are going to change around here."

"Really now?"

"Things have gotten plumb out of hand. That gal reading your books, smiling in your face like she does, taking French,

197

walking in here like she's more than the help. And you, yes, you hanging around those Coloreds or whatever they calling themselves these days. Every weekend you find a reason to go down to The Quarters. Enough is enough. I'm tired of explaining to my friends, club members and all the other decent whites around here about your behavior. Whether you know it or not, there's always talk about you and them. Behind my back and in front of my face, chatting it up about the famous attorney at law Bill McLand and his Nigger friends. It's humiliating."

Mr. McLand stood there and listened to her entire diatribe of anger and venom spewed in his direction. "My, my, my. Harriet. You said a mouthful. Humph. Now you tell me, how you can stand there like that knowing what you know?"

"And that would be?"

"Ha. Your memory fails you once again. Hopefully a fainting spell isn't soon to follow," he said sarcastically. "Well, Harriett, let me refresh your memory."

"I'm not listening. I'm not listening," she said as she covered both her ears and turned away as if she was a child cowering from a thunderstorm.

That's when she saw me by the back door and yelled again, "I said, get."

"No need to yell at me again," I mumbled. I gained my composure, walked away and headed to my Aunt Honey's.

As I got closer to her home, I noticed my Uncle Simee's car sitting in front. *Oh good,* I thought. *Whenever he sees me, I get at least fifty cents.* As I approached his car, I also noticed that Miss Wilhelmina was oddly bent over, kinda stooping right next to his car. *Hmmm maybe she'd dropped something,* I thought. Then it occurred to me that she was actually creeping around his car and peering over his hood, attempting to look into my Aunt's house. Miss Wilhelmina was so consumed with her snooping that she didn't notice when I walked up behind her and tapped her on her shoulder.

"Everything okay, Miss Wilhelmina?"

"Arrgh!" she yelled, being startled. When she stood up, she had to catch herself on the car to keep from falling. I must have really frightened her because she was out of breath and had to pat her chest and then swiped her hair back in place, since she'd become a bit disheveled.

"Whew, chile, where you come from?" She said, looking all around. Didn't yo momma and daddy teach you bout sneaking up on grown folks like that?"

"Yes ma'am, but I wasn't sneaking. Did you lose something? I can help you find it."

Miss Wilhelmina's yell was loud enough for a few folks to look out of their own windows, including Aunt Honey.

"What's going on out here?" Aunt Honey asked when she and Uncle Simee stepped on the front porch.

"Nothing. We're fine," I said, embarrassed.

"Whose we?" she asked me in a tone that clearly expressed agitation.

"Me and Miss Wilhelmina. I think she must have lost something."

Miss Wilhelmina quickly placed her finger over her lips and said *Shh.*

"I'm helping her look for it on the other side of Uncle Simee's car." I said happily, especially now that I recognized Miss Wilhelmina was snooping.

Aunt Honey shifted her head around to get a closer look. Uncle Simee had no trouble seeing her at all. He let out a deep breath, raised his hand, and shook his head along with Aunt Honey.

"Anythang I can help you with, Wilhelmina?" she asked.

"Oh, no. How ya'll doing? Whew... I was just passing through, is all. Fraid I dropped my keys by this car. Forgive me for disturbing you. Whew-we. Oh, is that you, Simee Scott? Funny seeing you here, ain't it?"

"Yeah, it's me Wilhelmina," Uncle Simee said, sounding disappointed.

An awkward stillness lingered among all of them for what felt like an eternity, although it was only a few seconds. Miss Harris from next door heard the commotion and also stepped out to see what was going on.

"What's all this fuss out here? Folks yelling like theys crazy. It's late and us working people got's to work. Humph! Ya'll chilluns should be in the house by now anyway. "

"We's fine, Addie. Looks like Wilhelmina done lost something," Aunt Honey said.

We all stood, gazing at Miss Wilhelmina. Finally my Aunt broke the crippling silence and said to me, "Come on up here, baby, and get this package. Yo Momma gone be looking and waiting for you."

As I skipped up the steps, I heard my frustrated aunt say to Uncle Simee, "I tell you, Wilhelmina ass is crazy. Tiptoeing round yo car like some teenage gurl. And after she done called me a horse. Nothing but foolishness. She crazy and you crazy if you thank I'm gone be bothered with this here mess."

"A horse?" Uncle Simee said confused. "What horse? You keep talking 'bout some horse."

As Aunt Honey guided me in her house, she reached in and gave Simee his hat and coat then said, "Good evening, Addie, Simee, and you too, Wilhelmina."

"You okay, Auntie?" I asked as we made our way to the rear of the house.

"Yes, baby, I'm fine, don't you worry none. Why yo eyes red? You been crying? Did that Wilhelmina say something mean to you?"

"Oh no, ma'am. It's probably the pollen. It makes my eyes red sometimes," I said, lying. The last thing I wanted her to know was what happened at the McLands'. "I wasn't sneaking, I promise. I was just walking up and saw Miss Wilhelmina stooping behind Uncle Simee's car and I guess I scared her when I tapped her shoulder."

That brought a smile to her face. "You scared her, all right. Wish I coulda seen that. Not a thing for you to worry about. That woman is nuts, always been and always will be. I know you wasn't sneaking, baby. Now, grab them clothes and then you go straight home. Getting late in the evening now and your Momma will be mad at me if you take too long getting home."

"Yes ma'am," I said while watching Aunt Honey with heightened curiosity. I can't explain it but she was different. If I had to describe it, I'd say that she was reluctantly relaxed if that makes any sense. I guess Uncle Simee had that effect on her.

20

"Y a'll heard 'bout Wilhelmina's crazy self tipping over at Honey's Sunday night?" Turnerd asked as he sipped on his favorite spirit along with his fellow drinkers on the ladies' porch.

"Yeah, I heard 'bout it. But for you gets started, remember they's two sides to every story, Turnerd," Spudnick said as he touched up his blush and round his lips with his new Revlon Rouge lipstick.

"Naw, they's three, his, hers and as my momma used to say, the truth," May Alice yelled from inside the house.

"And the truth is, something ain't right 'bout that Simee Scott. I'm telling ya'll, he ain't right, he ain't right. I can tell," Mr. Turnerd added.

"How can you tell anythang, Turnerd? Folks round here say you ain't right and I tends to agree with them," Miss Cutie Pie said.

"Look here, woman. Just 'cause he one of them flashy pretty boys—with that straight Crisco grease hair, I might add—causing ya'll to miss everythang else 'bout him."

"Like?" Mr. Spudnick asked.

"Like, where he come from anyway. My cousin Govner lives right up there in Chicago. He told us he used to live there and he know everybody. I asked him about Simee and he said he ain't never heard of him. He even asked a few other folks and nothing. And answer this, why won't his own brother even talk to him? That's strange enough. Why he ain't working but got all this money and them fine clothes of his? And mo important than anything, when the last time you heard of any white man, near or far, calling anybody that look like you or me to help him make some money? Yeah, like Mr. White Man woke up one day and said, *I thank I'm gone call this here special Negra and tell him where he can make a lot of money. Why? 'Cause, I just love Negras.* Uh-huh, bet ya'll ain't got one answer for that. I tell you, that boy is a liar and the truth ain't in him. He ain't got no money. I tell you he ain't got nothing but elbows and ass."

Those were actually great questions, I thought as I sat in the kitchen with the other children. We were all sent over to help the ladies on a makeshift assembly line. Rosa, my new friend Bunkee, Roosevelt, Tyrone and me all lined up in the hallway peeling, cutting, and batching peaches. It was fun for us, since we did more eating than anything. Plus, Miss May Alice promised each of us something special for helping. For me, I always got a roll of S & H Green Stamps to fill up my book. Everyone else got a nickel. So far I've been able to fill up 10 pages with only 14 more pages to go for a full book. I am determined to order my first complete set of encyclopedias from the catalog. I've grown irritated with reading the same old four encyclopedias Miss Rochelle gave me. I do appreciate them, but I do believe

Q, W, U, and Z have got to be the four most boring letters in the alphabet.

Although I was there last night and witnessed the entire debacle, I dared not to chime in. Not unless I wanted a pinch from Miss Cutie Pie and then a whooping when I got home. After learning that the hard way, I keep my mouth shut and my ears open. This set of grown folks didn't practice the same care that my momma did when children were present. Once she noticed us, she would shoo us out of the room, but not this bunch.

"Turnerd, mind yo own business and leave his alone," Mr. Spudnick said

"Anythang that's got to do with these here Quarters, that land up yonder and these two fine ladies right here is my business."

"Turnerd, that land belongs to the church anyway and since the church ain't seen you in a month, rather a year or two of Sundays, you probably don't have much of a say," Miss May Alice said.

"That's a lie you tell. I'm still on the church roll as a bona fide member. I make sho I pay my fifty cents to the church every Easter." He began singing, *"He arose, He arose from the dead . . ."*

"Yo ass is crazy." Miss Cutie Pie said

"Yeah, I'm crazy, all right. Uh-huh, crazy like a fox," Mr. Turnerd said. "And by the way, Spuddy, go and grease up them ankles of yours. Look like you been kicking flour. And please, please, for the love of Gawd and all that is holy, cut that cone off that big toe of yours. That thang look like a turtle done climb up on yo foot and fell asleep. Jesus."

"Go to hell, Turnerd."

"And May Alice, look like you may need to take a break."

"What? A break from what, Turnerd?"

"Eating. That behind of yours is starting to spread like honeysuckles. But I like it."

"You's just a damn fool."

"But a fool in love," Mr. Turnerd said.

21

Simee

"This right here is plumb ridic-lous," Wilhelmina said to Bessie, one of her girls, as she scolded her for leaving her room in such disarray. "You gone make me late fooling with you. What man you thank gone wanna lay in here with all this mess, Bessie? Bed ain't made, dirty water still in the pan, you looking a mess, just look at cha. I frankly don't see why it's taking you so long to make up a bed, throw out some dirty water, and clean yourself up. You know the Bible say cleanliness is next to Godliness, and from what I see, you ain't near nor next to anythang close to that. You need to make this here quick and in a hurry. I got thangs to do, bout to get over to the church right now for Sunday school. Though they ain't likely to start without me. Girl, it's almost nine o'clock and you gone make me late. That Lois been eyeballing my poe-sition. Gotta watch that one. Shouldn't have had to come up here to help you anyway. You know what?"

"No ma'am, what?" Bessey said.

"I thanks I'm gone dock you a dollar for this."

"A whole dollar?"

"That's what I said."

"But, Miss Wilhelmina," she said with disappointment ringing in her voice, "I make sho not to do that again."

"I know you ain't. That's right. Part of you com-pen-sation is cleaning this here room and yo-self. And by the looks of it, you ain't did either. Got lots going on today. I ain't got time for this. My sweetie Simee is gone tell the church bout this big opportunity and I gots to be there to support him, you know. I'm sho that Honey gone be there too. She ain't slick, I know what she up to. Now, I'm gone, but I tell you, if you don't want to lose two dollars, better get yo self right. You hear me?"

"Yes ma'am." Bessie said, as she quickly scrambled to address each of Wilhelmina's demands.

I learned not too long after my arrival in The Quarters that Wilhelmina's, or as some would call her Madame Wilhelmina's, house was the stopping point for most of shenanigans in the community. She had one of the largest homes in The Quarters and the busiest. Folks, mostly men and young women, bustled in and out of her home. It was well known that debauchery resided at her place like a paying tenant. Seek and ye shall find all the trouble you were looking for right at 1901 Sheffield Drive. Gambling, women, liquor, and the hottest fried fish and chicken sandwiches you could find. All were plentiful and readily available, for a fee, of course.

Her scolding Bessie woke me up. Last night I'd been feeling so good that I walked upstairs and fell right onto a bed. But if it was as late as she was saying, I had to hurry on over to the church.

I made tracks and arrived just in time. Wilhelmina and it seemed the entire community packed the church this special Sunday morning. Everyone, including those who had not been to church in quite some time, came to hear me, Simee Scott, they's ticket to good fortune.

Gaw-awd, be with you. Gaw-awd be with you, Gaw-awd be with you, until we meet again. Gaw-awd, be with you. Gaw-awd be with you, Gaw-awd be with you, until we meet again.

As the singing and benediction concluded the service, I noticed that none of the parishioners motioned to leave, they all remained seated. Chatter, speculation, and clear excitement filled the church. Today was the much anticipated day. I could finally present my scheme to the church and hopefully get my hands on that deed. To my delight, the news of the land deal had swelled in The Quarters. Everyone in earshot was anxious to learn more about this opportunity which some felt was delivered straight from heaven. And it was my intention to keep it that way. There were still two very influential people, however, who would not be so easily persuaded. Those two would be Rev. Evans and Buster. Bernice and Rufus, and that Wilhelmina, I had concluded, probably would not be as tricky, but only time would tell.

"We come to order," Rev. Evans said as he settled the chatter amongst the church members. "Amen?"

"Amen."

"Today, I want to introduce to some and bring back to others Mr. Simee Scott. Most of you know him as the newcomer here, but he ain't so new no mo, and he also the brother of Deacon Edga Scott. Well, today is the day we all been, I guess I can say, waiting on. It's the day Simee gone explain why we should sell our land and allow him to negotiate this deal on our behalf. Now, I must say, I come before you all—and I'll speak for the board too—with much concern. This here is a big thang for us, and especially this here church. Mr. Job, Gawd rest his soul, left that land to our church. He entrusted us to keep good will over it and use it *to further the kingdom*, as he used to say. And I's determined to do that. Them forty acres took a long time to gather and we gone be very deliberate with our decision. Now, from what Simee says, the government is anxious to run a railroad track through there on up to Atlanta, then to New York and bout willing to pay anythang to make that happen. So we asked Simee to come before the church, talk to us as one, and then we can make our decision from that."

"Amens" and "Yes Suh's" flooded the church. Fans were waving and heads were nodding as Rev. Evans continued to speak. Louise, Edgar, and Honey all sat together. Didn't take much to notice that all three of them seemed annoyed and leery of my proposition. Edgar shuffled so much in his seat, I caught Louise elbowing him to settle down. Honey rolled her eyes and smacked her lips one too many times for her sistah. The last lip smack caused her to reach over and pinch her along with a look that only her chillun generally got.

Rev. Evans continued, "Now, I'm gone let Simee up here in a minute to explain exactly what this is and how it's pose to work for our community. I ask that you all listen with an open mind, but a thanking one too. Amen?"

"Amen," hailed collectively from the church.

I sat in silence for several seconds, almost an entire minute. I'd learn a long time ago that a little thought-provoking delay created more anticipation and more excitement, so there I sat and sat. Finally, I rose slowly to approach the front of the members. Instead of standing behind the podium, I found standing among them especially in the aisle was more effective. Made them feel like I was one of them. As I stood in front of everyone, I began to whisper ever so softly to myself. Just loud enough for them to hear, but low enough that they couldn't make out what I was saying. As I anticipated, this action caused them to begin scooting to the edge of their seats as if they'd be better positioned to hear me. No matter how close they leaned in, I made sho they were still unable to interpret exactly what I was saying. *So far, so good.* Then I began to cry, pushing as many tears from my face as dramatically as I could. As the tears began to stream down, I lifted my arms to the heavens and began to speak louder but this time in tongues. Didn't quite know exactly what tongues was, but as long as I talked real fast and used *la, ba, and sha* at the beginning and end of whatever I said, seemed to cast the spell I hoped for. And without fail, both *Oh hallelujah,* and *Thank you Jesus* always found its way in my delivery. After it was clear that I accomplished exactly what I set out to do, I settled down and began to speak directly to this mesmerized crowd.

"First, giving honor to Gawd, the head of my life. I wants to thank the good Reverend and the board for 'lowing me to stand here amongst you good people today. Um here to tell you, ya'll some blessed folks. Why I say that? I'll tell you why. 'Cause it takes people of courage and strength to try something or even listen to something that is different and new. *Oooh Sha ba la.* And this here church is governed by leaders that both strong and wit courage. Let's give a hand clap to Rev and the board. Now, if ya'll don't mind, I'd like to start off with a few favorite scriptures of mine."

"*Go right ahead. Yes suh. We don't mind none,*" clamored from the congregation.

"Proverbs 13:21 says: Misfortune pursues the sinner, but prosperity is the reward of the righteous. Now, I believe I see some righteous folks here today. Can I get an Amen?"

"Amen."

"Joshua 1:9 says: Have not I commanded thee? Be strong and of a good courage; be not afraid, neither be thou dismayed: for the Lord thy God is with thee whithersoever thou goest. Now tell me, what ya'll got to be afraid of?"

"Amen, Amen."

"That boy pretty good, ain't he? Mr. Thee said as he leaned over to Turnerd.

"Humph. Good at what? Lying and thieving?" Turnerd said.

I heard them, but I didn't pay them any mind. "Now I'm here today to bring some good news and for others, some bad news. Hear me now. I say bad news for some, 'cause it's sad to say, but some folks just don't want to do better or ever have nothing. So for those of you in the room who this applies too, you can get up and leave now."

Rumblings and discord flowed through the congregation. None of those present had ever heard of anyone being told to leave the house of the Lawd and I knew that.

"Now hold on, Simee," Rev. Evans stood up and interrupted. "Never in all my days have I ever asked nobody to leave this here sanctuary and I ain't starting now."

"Yeah, who the hell he thank he is?" shouted Turnerd from the back.

Turnerd's input caused the congregation to momentarily turn in his direction. Most thinking, did he just curse in this church?

"Turnerd, watch yo mouth. We in church," Cutie Pie said.

"Yeah, you right. 'Scuse me."

"Folks, calm down, calm down please. Now Rev, I said that for a reason. If you look around, not one person stood up to leave. Everybody in here wants something better for they family and theyselves, and this here experiment proves it."

Clapping and agreements roared through the church.

"That boy good," Buster said.

"I still say he full of it," Edga said.

I hurried on, "Now, the only reason I'm here is 'cause the good Lawd sent me here. That's the only reason. I can't tell you the number of times our people—that's right, us Colored folks—get left behind, 'cause we either scared, ignorant, or both. Now, don't gets mad that I used the word ignorant. That word just means uninformed, without knowledge. Well, today I'm here to give you knowledge and to inform you. Come on now and shake the devil off. I'm shaking off both fear and ignorance. I wants something different for ya'll 'cause, as Jeremiah said in 29:11: For I know the plans I have for you," declares the Lord, "plans to prosper you and not to harm you, plans to give you hope and a future."

I watched Edga as much as I could without it being too obvious. Peering from the side of my eyes was quite taxing, but I managed the challenge. I knew to this very day, Edga still had not shared with his wife—or anyone else, for that matter—what was really going on with me and him. His body remained stiff and his lips kept together, determined to hold in what he desperately never wanted to share. He continued to shake his head in disagreement and even motioned to stand and leave the church until Louise pulled him back down in his seat and pinched his arm, causing him irritation.

"Now, I know I have some nonbelievers in the crowd. Some that don't believe in what I'm presenting today, but that's okay. Thomas doubted Jesus too. And if anybody can doubt Jesus, shorly, they gone doubt me. Now, what I'm 'bout to show ya'll is a official legal document with a stamp from the federal government office of Railroad Services. By showing you this, I'm placing my trust in each of you being that this here is top secret, since this is something I'm not pose to share, but we all family here right?"

"Right," hailed from the congregation.

"See, I am what they call a secret official representative from the United States government, sent directly by the department of Railroad and Transportation," I said. "I'm what is called the liaison."

"Leeann's son? Who the devil is Lee Ann and what her son got to do with this?" Turnerd asked Spudnick.

"Stop being so ignant, Turnerd. He said liaison, fool. It means a go-between person. If you picked up a book now and then, you'd know these thangs."

"Did he just say 'official'?" Edga asked Louise.

"That's what I heard."

"Official? Official what? O-ffi-cially crazy. Man, please. What in the world is he talking 'bout?" Edga said. "I'm leaving and I'm taking my family with me. Ya'll come on now."

Before Louise could protest, he and his family were in the aisle, making they way outside the church. He brushed by me so quickly, he almost knocked me over. Rev. Evans rushed behind them and asked Edga to come back and hear me out, but to no avail. That was it for Edga. His exit caused a stir and it looked as if a few families considered joining him. As it turned out, it was only a consideration.

"Look, Reverend. No disrespect to you or the church," Edga said with a look that reflected pain and discontentment, "but I promise you if I don't get away from here and that lying bastard, I just might hurt somebody today. And I strongly advise you to get away from him too."

"Calm down, Edga. It's all right, everything all right. You and I can talk later. Just calm down." Rev. Evans looked over at Louise, clearly confused and saddened by his friend's behavior.

While they stood outside of earshot, without missing a beat, I continued to cast my spell over the worshippers. I was clear that all was taken in by my showmanship, my smarts, my delivery and I knew it.

"Brothers and sistahs, it's okay. My brother and I have always had a hard time seeing eye to eye, but I tell you, all is well. I love him as Jesus loves me. Now, what I have in addition to the gov-ment letter is what is called a land survey. It shows the current layout of the land and you'll see where this one also shows you where this train gone go through. I'm gone lay out these documents and anyone who wants to see it can once I finish. Now, I'm guessing ya'll want to know more than anything what money is involved in this here transaction, and what does all this mean to you, yo family and this here church? I would ask you all to sit down first, but looks like you already doing that."

As planned, that comment drew laughter from the crowd and a few smiles and head nods from the women. I found that a joke or two always worked in my favor.

"Well, if you ready to be blessed by the hearing of my words, then I'm ready to bless ya'll good folks. The good Lawd done shined on me and it's only right that I returns the favor amongst his cherished flock. Now let us pray. Father, I ask that as I present your glory before these righteous peoples, you direct my footsteps, my mind, and my tongue so that I talk with the wisdom that can only come from you. In yo name I pray. Amen."

"Amen"

"It means two hundred thousand dollars, that's what it means."

"Did he say two hundred thousand dollars?" May Alice asked.

"I do believe he did," Carrie replied with hesitation.

"Once I get that deed properly signed over to the government in an official financial transaction, it means two hundred thousand dollars, to be exact, for the church. You can build a better school, a bigger church, yo own stores to shop in. Keeping yo money right here in The Quarters. What can't you do? The sky's the limit. Hallelujah."

It was hard to contain the excitement in the church. Two hundred thousand dollars was an amount most had never heard, much less thought they'd ever have access to. I watched as those in the crowd began to swell with dreams of better for theyselves and they chilluns. Before I could end my presentation, I was once again disrupted. This time by that Jamaican, Rashay.

"Well, excuse me, sir. I have a question."

"Go right ahead, suh."

"As everyone around here knows, I consider myself a businessman. Sell fruit, papers, clean some of the buildings downtown, and I'm a connoisseur of the ganja."

"Ganja?" Turnerd quietly asked Spudnick.

"He talking 'bout them funny cigarettes he always smoking."

"Oh."

"With all due respect, what's in this for you? You've given us all this information on how this will work in our favor, but my man, there must be something in this for you."

I noticed that his calm question begin to make others in the congregation nod their heads and agree with his line of questioning. I needed to think fast. Of course, I couldn't say, the money is what's in it for me. So I quickly decided to say:

"As a Christian man, my first duty is to the Lawd. And all my steps is directed by him. As the good Lawd said to me, give a man a fish, he eats for a day, but if you teach a man to fish, he eat for a lifetime."

"Didn't he say that to everybody?" Turnerd whispered to Miss May Alice.

"Shut up."

"I'm just saying."

"Well, that's what I'm doing, I'm teaching mens to fish. I will only get a mere two percent, which is only four thousand dollars for all my time. Now, that money gone be used to travel around this here United States of America and work with other churches so that they can be as prosperous as this here one."

"That sound good enough for me," Wilhelmina blurted out.

"Us too," the sistahs chimed in, as everyone in the church seemed content with that answer.

I decided to close in prayer. The impression necessary to gain their trust, and more importantly get that deed, was accomplished. As I began to walk down the aisle, it dawned on me that one more thang I needed to do before I left this captive audience. *Must be getting soft, Simee, sholy you ain't walking away from here empty-handed.* Rev. Evans was sitting a bit distracted from my presentation. I could tell he wasn't entirely sold but hopefully getting there. I motioned Rev. Evans over and whispered in his ear for permission to request an offering.

"Now it's time for the offering. Can a man rob Gawd? Yes. How may you ask? Well, I'll tell you. Through his tithes and offering. Don't thank none of ya'll interested in going to jail in the high heavens."

"Did this fool just ask for some mo money?"

"Yeah, Turnerd, he sho did," Spudnick replied.

22

Louise

As we pulled the car away from the church to drive home, we all sat in silence. That is, until I grabbed the stirring wheel and almost made us crash. Edga pushed my hand away, pulled the car over and parked us safely on the side of the road.

"Woman, what in the world is wrong with you? Bout made me drive into that tree. Just bout hit it?"

"That tree ain't the only thang gone be hit. You know what's wrong with me, Edga. You know exactly what is wrong with me."

"And me too," Honey chimed in.

"Look-a-here, enough is enough. Bout time you tell me what in the hell is going on round here with you and that brother of yours."

They all stared in shock at me for a couple of seconds. I never cursed, that was Edga's and Honey's job.

"That's right. I'm so tired of this cat and mouse mystery game 'tween you and that Simee. Make no sense I find out you got's a brother from some fool at the county fair. Make no sense you treating him like you do, not even speaking to the man, even in church. Now, you bouts to tell me and Honey what's what. You hear me, Edga?"

He let out a deep breath. Then slouched in the front seat and rested his head against the seat's head rest.

"He kilt Momma," he said at last.

"He did what?" we all responded.

"I said, he kilt my momma."

"Oh, my Gawd. He killed yo momma?" Honey repeated almost in a whisper.

"Now, hold on, Edga. Wait a minute. My head is spinning now. You say he killed yo momma? You never told me yo momma was killed. Look-a- here, Edga, you fixing to sit here, right here and tell me the truth, from start to finish. Now I'm telling you, and I swear for Gawd, you better tell me everthang or I-I . . . Lawd have mercy, you don't want to know what I might do."

"All right, woman. Just don't 'xaclty know where to start."

"The beginning," Honey said.

We all sat there for what felt like a long time. My nerves was bad and getting worse. Still, I could tell it had been a long while since he had to bring those memories of his momma's death to the surface. I believe he'd buried them long ago.

"Well, my daddy wasn't a bad man, but he did some bad thangs, and one of those was living a double life. Like some men—not me, of course," he made certain to add, "he had a wife at home and a woman on the side. As a matter of fact, from what I know, he was seeing Miss Helen way for he met Momma. I heard them two met over in Guthbert at a juke joint. Wasn't long before he met Momma, though, and decided to marry her. Nothing stopped Daddy from doing what he did, so he kept seeing Miss Helen and got her pregnant with Simee. Not too long after he was born, I came. Now even though Daddy done married on her, she still wanted him. She thought 'cause she had a baby wit him, he was gone leave my momma for her. Well, that just wasn't the case. Years passed but he stayed with his wife. I remember like yesterday the day Momma woke up and told Daddy if he went back one mo time, he best to stay there. Well, he decided he wanted his family and was moving on for good. That didn't sit well with Helen but specially her boy, Simee. At twelve, he was already six feet tall and strong. Folks say he started acting crazy round Guthbert. So crazy, even his own momma started to get worried. They said he felt his daddy used his momma and he wasn't gone stand for that. It was a cold, stormy night when everything just went crazy. Me and Daddy was home with Momma. She was making supper and Daddy had me helping him fix a leak in the roof. All of a sudden, somebody was banging—I mean banging hard—on the front door, almost like kicking it. Me and Daddy looked at each other, and Daddy motioned for me to go over to Momma. He grabbed his shotgun and went and opened the door. As soon as he did, Bam! Simee knocked Daddy down. Daddy didn't have a chance to do nothing for he was on the floor. Once Daddy was down, Simee turned his 'tention on Momma. I tried to stop him, but he was just too big for me. Momma got to running from him and screaming. She ran but slipped and fell, then hit her head. The knock made her a scramble getting up. She wasn't fast enough. While she was trying to stand,

Simee calmly walked over to the stove and grabbed the frying pan. Next thang you know, he hit my momma in the head. The blow seemed to kill her right there. To this day, it still feels like it happened just yesterday," he shared through a few tears.

"Lord have mercy," Louise said

"Edga, I'm so sorry," Honey said.

"Me too, Daddy."

"His momma was running behind him, but by time she got to the door, he'd already done what he did. That woman just started screaming when she saw Momma. It was like he was in a trance or something. He pushed past Daddy and walked into the woods. The next day, the sheriff and his deputies came out looking for him. They found him hiding in an old shed. They said when they put the handcuffs on him, he just broke out laughing. Laughing like a madman. They locked him up in one of those crazy houses for boys for 'bout five years. His momma went to a crazy house too, for she died. I guess something was wrong with both of them, crazy, that is. I always felt specially bad 'cause I couldn't save my own momma."

"Edga, you was just a boy. None of that was yo fault," I said.

"I knew he was crazy, but not this crazy," Honey said.

"I been trying to tell ya'll, he nothing but bad news, nothing but. As soon I could, I put Simee out of my mind. Before Daddy died, he 'pologized for what he had caused and told me to stay as far from Simee as I could. Death circled back to our house one more time and took my younger brother. He died from the pneumonia when he was five. After all that killing and dying, I had to shake them memories and I did—well, at least I tried to. Remember Elroy from the county fair in Columbus, Louise?"

"Yeah."

"He knew everything and was just trying to 'cause trouble. That's why I walked away as soon as possible. Him and Simee cut from the same raggedy cloth."

Honey was disturbed by this news, and she said, "Edga and Louise, I-I just got to tell ya'll something."

"Okay," Louise said.

"Well, bout two nights ago, Simee came over. I was gone rush him out, but then I decided to ask him what was wrong 'tween you two. I figured that was as good a time to ask him as any, so I did. Lawd, Edga, he told me the biggest lie. I mean, he told me 'bout everything, 'cept he switched it all around. Ooo, Lawd, my head spinning," Honey said while wringing her hands together so hard, she could have started a fire.

"What you mean, he turned everything round?" I asked right before Edga could ask the same.

"He said his momma was the crazy one and that she killed your momma."

"What?" I said.

"Yeah, he said, his momma killed her."

"He said what? His momma kilt my momma? That lying bastard, lie on his own dead momma."

"Yeah, the way he told the story made me leery of it anyway. The way he was looking and sitting there. It was like he thought the whole thing was funny or something. I couldn't put my finger on it, but I knew something wasn't right. My goodness."

"I tell you one thing, Louise. He ain't nothing but trouble. You mark my word, what he selling the church ain't nothing but a scam and ain't nobody gone tell me different. I can't tell you how he doing it, but I can tell you it ain't right and nor is he."

We finally pulled up to our house, and I told Pearline and Felton to go on inside.

"You two get ready for supper. Wash yo hands, Pearline, and turn them pots on low."

"Yes, ma'am."

Edga got out of the car also and walked behind the house. I knew what that meant. He was headed for a swig or two of that brown liquor he kept out back. The secret he thought he'd created was no secret at all.

"C'mon, Honey."

"Where?"

"Back here with Edga."

We walked up just in time for what appeared to be the second sip. He nearly dropped the bottle when he opened his eyes and saw us two standing right in front of him.

"What the—?"

"Make room for two more, Edga. "

I took a quick sip and nearly choked. It was my first time drinking and it was far from tasty. It tasted like what I thought gasoline would taste like, strong and rusty. After choking and coughing from the burning sensation it left me with, I passed the bottle on to Honey. She took a sip and quickly took a second one.

"Damn, I hate that I slept with him," she said.

"Honey, what you say?" I asked.

"Ya'll heard me. That s-e-x you talked about. Well."

"Girl, give me that bottle back," I said as I bout snatched it from her hands.

23

Pearline

I woke up this morning a little confused. I knew it was Sunday, fourth Sunday to be exact, except this day, we weren't in church. On a normal Sunday morning, we were up by now, finishing up breakfast and out the door headed to Sunday school. But not today. I overslept and for some odd reason, looks like everyone else did too.

"Momma?"

"Yes, Pearline."

"Where's everybody? And what happened to church this morning? Are you okay? Where is Daddy?"

"Can I answer the first question before you fire off another one?'

"Yes ma'am."

"Your brothers went with your daddy fishing."

"Fishing?" I said in disbelief. "It's Sunday." I must be talking to somebody eles's momma, I thought, puzzled. This one certainly isn't mine. Before I could make my way out of the kitchen,

I heard Aunt Honey approach the back door. She didn't get a chance to enter before Momma walked out back herself.

"Ooo, my head hurts," Aunt Honey said.

"Mine too." Momma replied. "I just couldn't bring myself to go and worship the Lawd with this liquor on me from last night."

"What in the world was I thinking, swinging that demon juice back like that last night."

"Don't think you was thinking. I only had a tiny bit and it still gave me a headache. I sent Edga off with the chilluns and let Pearline sleep a little late. We'll be back next Sunday."

"You know them tongues a waggin, wondering where ya'll at."

"They'll have to keep wagging. Sides, I shouldn't be drinking no way."

"Why? You pregnant again, Louise?"

Momma was slow to respond. I had suspected that she was, although I dared not to ask. The throwing up, moodiness, leaning her body on whatever would support her, and that short temper was always a sign that another one of us was coming.

"Looks like it," Momma said.

"Lawd, ain't you tired?

"Of?"

"Making babies. My. Look to me like you need to sit with an aspirin 'tween yo legs or something. Shoot, I thank if he look at you, it's over. Now looking at Edga, you'd neva thank he was capable of such feats, but miracles do happen, I suppose."

"Honey, best you watch what you say. You know that chile of mine listen bout as much as she reads, she always somewhere tuning in, like a dang-gone radio."

"What child? You got bout fifteen of them."

"You know um talking 'bout, Pearline."

Momma was right. When they were out hanging clothes, I could hear everything they whispered about by leaning against the back wall in the kitchen just beside the door frame. I found listening in on them was the only time I considered a rest from my book. Occasionally, the stuff in The Quarters was just as, if not more, entertaining than Ernest Hemingway could ever be.

"And what feats you talking about, Honey?"

"Making babies like he do. Shoot, one come right after the other. Frankly, I never thought he had it in him. And they even come out pretty and smart. Shocking, simply shocking."

"Chile, please. You better stop while you ahead, Honey. He is my husband, you know."

"Yeah, I know," she said, twisting her lips in disappointment.

"What about you? Talking all that mess. Bout time you had some of yo own."

"Now, why on earth would I want to do that when I can come by and borrow yours whenever need be? And when I'm finished being the good aunt that I am, I can send them right on home."

"Well, ain't nothing like having yo own, Honey."

"Uh-huh."

"I guess you right. I'll leave that alone. You need to marry first anyway. And as mean as you is, take a special man to make that happen."

"Don't thank I'll be getting married. You know my luck with courting. It always ends, and not in the best way, mind you."

"That's in the past, Honey. No need in you branging that up anyway."

Humph, in the past. And bringing what up? I thought. This conversation was a first for me.

"You know if them hens at church had it they way, I'd be married now. Drive me crazy how they act like if you ain't married around here, something got's to be wrong with you. I tell you one thing, if one mo of them busybodies try and corner me after church bout my personal affairs, I just might have to draw a line."

"You still drawing lines with your ol' behind."

"Ain't never gone be too ol' for that."

"So you plan on fighting at church now?"

"Will if I have to. I get tired of them same ol' dumb questions by them same ol' dumb women. They start with, *How you today?* Like they really care, then *Chile, when's you's gone get married? You do wonts to get married, dont's you?* Looking at me sideways, then here comes, *You do know you ain't getting no younga. Don't go too old, now. Know this, old men's makes old babies. But then again, Sarah, you know Abraham's wife from the Bible. Well, she had her baby at ninety, so I guess it is possible.* MinLee and Carrie done cornered me for the last time. Them two love to stand and gossip 'bout you, like you don't know it's you they talking 'bout. I swear they look at me like I got two heads growing from my neck. I told both of them that I'd get married just as soon as they husbands left them, and from the looks of it, it won't be long. That shut both of them up. Hadn't had a whisper from either since. As a matter of fact, they switched pews at the church. Humph, works for me"

"Pearline?" Momma unexpectantly yelled from outside.

"Yes ma'am." I was so startled by her call that I dropped the apple I was chomping on.

"We know you standing back there, missy. Get yo little nosy tail from behind that door."

I sheepishly wandered out from behind the door, picked up my apple, and stood in the entry watching them. Aunt Honey smiled and shook her head at me, almost telling me silently that I should hide better than that.

"Need you to run over to the McLands for us."

"But it's Sunday."

"Do tell. This ain't Wednesday?" she said mockingly.

"Momma."

"I know what day it is. That Harriet told me that she needed me to wash a load for them before next week. Claim she needed some table linen sooner than me coming over Wednesday. That party she having ain't until next Friday, but you know how she is. Always want to show that she the boss and can change thangs with a snap of her little pointy fingers. One day I'm gone be free of that woman."

"You and me both," I mumbled.

"Louise, I forgot to tell you something. How on earth could I forget to?"

"What? Do I need to sit down for this one? Can't take to many more of your surprises."

"Naw, you can stay standing. Well, last Tuesday I went down to Woolworths like I do every Tuesday. This time I saw that Harriet in there. She ain't see me. When she went over to the counter to check out, I noticed her and Louella got real close to each other, like they was talking 'bout somebody. "

"And I'm sure them two was."

"I took the liberty to mosey right on over where they was and pretend to be reading one of them magazines. Being that she only seem to notice me is when I'm cleaning her nasty house, she paid me no attention. And that's when I heard what they planning on doing to Ms. Agatha."

"What now? What they plan on doing to Ms. Agatha? That woman don't bother nobody."

"I heard her say out of her mouth that on the agenda for the next Ladies Auxiliary meeting is Ms. Agatha. Said it was due time that Agatha stop this nonsense with the Negras. Why on earth a Negra would need to learn French was beyond anyone's understanding. And if she was gone teach anybody anything, it should be the good Christian whites of Muscogee County, much less a Negra. And if she don't cooperate, they will be consequences. "

"Like what?"

"Like running her out of Columbus."

"What? How they gone do that? Last I heard, we was free, and if you and me is free, then for certain Ms. Agatha is. Make me sick. Lawd, they need to leave that po woman alone. She ain't bothered nobody. Them white folks can't stand to see somebody getting one step ahead of them, even if it's something as simple as a lesson from an old French woman."

"That ain't all. Even said, how can she go to our chuch? Said she ought to be shamed to go to that Negra church with them Negras. Just not Christian like."

"Ooo, don't tell me no mo. I can't stand that woman. Always causing trouble for somebody. Like the good Lawd only see fit to stop by they church. Humph."

They both stood there shaking their heads at one another. Probably praying that nothing bad would happen to Ms. Agatha.

I was hoping the same. Ms. Agatha had become one of my favorites. She was no-nonsense and funny at the same time. How she was able to mesh the two distinctions was something I'd never figure out. Speaking of French, Mr. McLand had loaned me *The Count of Monte Cristo* by Alexandre Dumas and I needed to return it. I lifted the ever waiting basket of clothes and grabbed the book on my way out. I told Momma, "Will you please tell your children *pour rester hors de mes choses?*"

"Why sho, Pearline. Won't mind telling them at all, once you tell me what I'm telling them."

"Please tell them to stay out of my stuff. Last night Jr. spilled some juice on my notebook and ruined my report. Now I've got to rewrite everything."

"I sure will. Now, hurry on so you can get back for supper."

"Yes, ma'am."

24

Honey

"I ain't inter-rested no mo, Simee. Thangs done changed. Can't you get that in yo head? And stop following me. Goodness."

I sounded like a scratched-up record that kept jumping to the same part of the song ova and ova. No matter what I said or how I said it, he would not listen. Seem like everywhere I went, there he was. I was in the checkout line at Woolworth's, lo and behold, there is Simee. I'm leaving the McDunkins, who live way cross the tracks and who do I bump into, Simee? Once, I even stepped on the city bus to ride to town and that fool was already on it. When I saw him, I told the driver to let me off. Nothing I say seem to sway him. Done thought about asking one of the mens from the church to say something to him. Then I changed my mind. That would require sharing too much of Louise and Edga's business, not to mention my own.

Me and Louise sat outside on her porch and watched Edga drive away with a car load of chilluns. All of them except Pearline. She was over to Miss Agatha's for her fancy French lessons. Just me and my sistah today, at least for a while. Having her to myself was something that hardly ever happened, so I was gone take full advantage of it. I neva say it, but I. She my best friend. Ever since Momma died, she has always been there for me. Yeah, I fuss and complain 'bout her bossing me and trying to run my business, but if I stop, that will bother her more than my fussing and complaining.

Sitting out here on the porch rocking, fanning and sipping lemonade was normally something we both looked forward to, specially on a beautiful day like it was today. 'Cept right now, we just trying to find a way to lose me of that man.

"I believe they got laws against what he doing, Honey," Louise said. "Ain't right for him to keep to chasing you like he do."

"Girl, who you telling?"

"Just don't make no sense, him carrying on the way he do. Like he gone make you be with him. Ain't seen nothing like it."

"I know."

"He got these folks in this here town so fooled, but not me. Edga don't know what to do. He just say he gone stay out of everything. He don't want nobody else to know 'bout him and Simee as chilluns. I guess I can't blame him. Something like that will keep most men quiet. What we gone do?" she said, shaking her head.

"This ain't yo problem, Louise."

"And when has that eva mattered?" she said with a big laugh.

"Well, looks like our time is up."

"Why you say that?

"Here comes Pearline."

"Oh, well I guess it is."

"*Bonjour, Madames. Comment allez-vous?*" Pearline asked as she walked up to the porch.

"I'm good, baby," Momma said.

"You know what she said?" I asked.

"Uh-huh. You live with her long enough, you will too," Louise said, laughing.

"So, what good news do you got for me today?" I asked.

"Other than having received all A's on my report card—for the sixth consecutive time, I might add—and being elected as class president, and progressing quite nicely with my French, I guess not much."

"Humble, humble, humble," I said. "We gone start calling you Humbline instead of Pearline," I said with a laugh.

"Oh, guess who I just saw?"

"Who?" Momma asked.

"You didn't guess," Pearline said in a teasing manner which only annoyed Momma.

"Girl, who you saw?" Louise said.

"Uncle Simee."

"You did?" I said.

"Yes, and guess what else?"

"What?" I said.

"He gave me a whole dollar."

"For what?" Louise asked

"Well, he asked if I could keep a secret, since I saw what he was doing and when I said yes, he gave me a dollar."

"What he was doing?" I asked, not sho what she meant.

"Yep."

"What was he doing? Louise then asked.

"*Maman! C'est un secret,*" Pearline said.

I just looked over at Louise, still confused.

"Um gone secret yo behind, chile. What was he doing?" Louise asked again.

"Okay, Momma, but don't tell him. You two have to act surprised or else he'll know I told. Plus, he may ask for his dollar back."

"Chile, I'm losing my patience. For the last time, for I gets my switch."

"Okay, okay… Well, just now when I was leaving Miss Agatha's house, I saw him coming out of your house, right out your front door."

"My—my front door?" I said.

"Yes. He looked really surprised when he turned around and saw me standing in the yard looking at him. I spoke and asked what was he doing 'cause I knew you weren't home. That's when he told me he had left you a big surprise in your house, so I needed to make sure not to tell."

"Lawd. That man been in and out of my house while I ain't even there. Jesus."

"Then he told me to look through your window and I could see what he left."

"What did you see?" Louise asked.

"Flowers. Flowers everywhere."

"Flowers?"

"Yes and they are beautiful."

"He probably stole them," I blurted out. "Chile, let me get home lock my door. Ain't neva had to lock my door neva."

"Yeah, that's 'xactly what you need to do. You want me to walk with you?" Louise asked.

"Naw, I'll be all right. Gone go throw all that mess away."

As I walked back to my house, anger was rising up in me like heat coming from a furnace. "He best be gone by time I turn this corner," I thought. I kept walking and picked up my pace. I was walking so fast, I walked right pass that fool trying to get to my door. He was leaning on that big old tree next to Carrie's house.

"Where you going so fast?" he asked.

"Don't ask me no damn questions. What the hell you doing in my house, Simee Scott? That's what I wants to know."

"You know already. Aw, that niece of mine can't keep no secrets. That's all right, though. I'll let her keep the dollar."

"To hell with that damn dollar, Simee. Now, this getting plumb crazy. It's against the law for you to go in my house without my permission. Flowers or no flowers."

"See, here I am trying to be a good man to you. Trying to surprise you, make you feel good and this what I get?"

"Look, would you please just leave me alone? It's ova," I said with frustration and fear tangled together.

"Can't do that," he said, walking closer to me. "Keep telling you that."

Before I could step back from him, he grabbed me and planted the wettest kiss I'd eva felt on my lips. He even grabbed my behind and squeezed my breast. All while we stood outside for everybody to see. I pushed him away and told him to stop.

"What in the world is wrong with you, Simee Scott?"

"You. You is what's wrong with me, but I plan on making it right. I'll see you soon."

25

Pearline

As I walked down the street I saw my old friend RaShay. He was loading his truck like normal. Since my time was limited, I only waved and said hello. He returned the same pleasantries and kept moving. I was anxious to finish this so I could hurry home. The thought of Momma's fried chicken, corn pudding, and my aunt's chocolate pecan cake were enough to hurry my trip.

This walk seemed to be getting longer and longer. I had other things to do. Hopefully, today, Mrs. McLand wouldn't play peek-a-boo through the curtains, pretending she don't see me.

I knock once, then twice. No answer. "Hello?" I yelled as I opened the door and stepped in. I was nervous doing so, but I needed to go.

"Hello, Mrs. McLand, Mr. McLand? Anybody home?"

"Come on in," I heard Mr. McLand say from the sitting room. "How are you today, young lady?"

"I'm fine, sir. You all right?" Regardless of his response, I knew he wasn't. The smell of what he was drinking told the truth.

"I'm as right as I'm going to be, young lady, at least as long as I live in this house."

"Sir?"

He grandly patted the chair opposite his desk. "Are you good at keeping secrets?"

"Of course," I said, knowing that answer really depended on who you asked.

"Good. Make yourself comfortable."

I sat down with more curiosity than I'd experienced before. My heart sped up, but I held my composure. What was I about to hear?

"I'm Colored, Pearline. Been this way all my life," Mr. McLand said as he poured more brown liquor into his glass.

"Excuse me, sir?"

"Yep. You heard right."

"Well, not all of you," I said, unable to think of anything else to say.

Ignoring me, he continued. "I was born one and I shall die as one."

He must have been awfully distressed, or he'd had a big head start on that drinking before I came, because as I sat there, he told me the whole story:

The fact that William "Bill" McLand was not white was something Miss Harriett was well aware of, he confided. She learned of his true identity many years ago after meeting him on the campus of the University of Georgia. Back then they were college students: he a junior political science major, she a sophomore with a major in home economics. He'd noticed her a few times on campus. She was pretty enough and definitely a southern girl, all prim and proper. Like clockwork, they seemed to bump into each other exactly at six-thirty every Wednesday evening for study hall. They'd also pass each other in the dining hall, where he bussed tables. Being the sorority girl and former debutante she was, Bill felt approaching her for anything other than to ask, *May I take your plate?* was out of the question. Although, on a few occasions, he sensed that she may have an interest as well. He caught her stealing a glance at him a time or two.

One rainy afternoon he finally gathered the nerve to approach her and ask her for a date. He was so nervous that when he spoke, everything that came out of his mouth was jumbled.

"Hi, I'm William, I'm mean Bill. You can call me McLand."

"Excuse me?" she said, confused.

"I mean, I'm Bill McLand. Would you like to float chocolate grab?"

"What?" she said, laughing.

Taking his time, he slowed down and asked, "Would you like to grab a chocolate float with me this Saturday?"

"Yes," she said without any hesitation.

From that day forward, conversations over chili dogs and chocolate floats, for him, and for her, a garden salad and Coca-Cola, became their Saturday night ritual. He'd save every dime he made from bussing tables and working in the print shop to pay for his tuition and afford his newfound love a simple Saturday night treat.

It would be a year to the date that he would summon up the courage to share everything with her. He'd already told her of his aspiration to one day become an attorney and own his own law firm. In addition to that, he expressed his desire to become a father of at least three children, two boys and a little girl, have a dog and of course marry the woman of his dreams. After meeting her, he felt those aspirations were in arm's reach. With his grades being exceptional, scholarships to prestigious law schools rolled in. He had his choice of Columbia, University of Virginia, Duke, even Georgetown to attend. But none of those locations would suffice; he couldn't leave Harriet. She'd made it clear her roots were where she stood, and she was going nowhere. So, he sacrificed attending one of the top schools in the country for Harriett and eventually entered law school at the University of Georgia.

"Have a seat," Bill said to Harriett one Sunday morning as they sat out on the main campus lawn. "I have something I need to tell you. I guess now is as good a time as any."

"What is it? You seem bothered. Everything okay?" she asked, concerned.

"Not exactly. I have something to tell you that may end our relationship."

"What could possibly do that?"

Bill took a deep breath. "I haven't told you everything about me."

"Yes, you have, silly. What could possibly be left? My goodness, you're only twenty."

"Remember when I told you my Aunt Sarah raised me in Alabama because my parents died?"

"Yes."

"Well, that's kinda true. My aunt did raise me, but not because my parents died."

Harriet sat silent and listened.

"My father was a very prominent man. He ran the city of Columbus and basically controlled everything and everybody. He chose not to marry my mother. Actually, he was already married. My mother was his mistress." She continued to look totally lost, and he frowned. "How do I say this?"

"Just say it, Bill."

"He fathered me by a Colored woman."

He looked away, ashamed and embarrassed, but continued. "After my birth, he shipped me off to Alabama, where I was raised by my aunt. She wasn't actually my aunt, but that's what I called her. He provided money for us to live off and paid for my college tuition, but any extra I'd have to earn myself. That's why I work so hard bussing tables and working in the print shop." Finally, he dared to raise his head. "Harriet?"

She sat there with a nauseated look on her face.

"Are you okay?" he asked.

"What did you say? A Co-lored woman? Is that what I heard you say?" she asked, discounting everything else he shared.

"Yes, my birth mother was Colored. I never met her, but I was told of her. She had other children, so that means I have sisters and brothers out there. I never met them but they do exist. Sometimes I dream about them. What they might be like. Do I look like them. All kinds of thoughts go through my head."

Not hearing a word other than Colored, Harriet said, "That means you're a Nig."

"A what, Harriett?"

"Well, it means you're not white. All white, that is," she said, oblivious to the pain in his face.

"No, I'm not, Harriett," he said, sighing. "I'm sure you're not interested in continuing to see me now. I thought I'd tell you. Probably was a mistake. I was hoping maybe you'd be different."

Harriet abruptly stood up. After standing for several moments and peering down at Bill, she walked away.

"Humph. I guess not," Bill said as he began to clear up the area in which they sat.

She walked maybe twenty yards away. All of a sudden she turned and walked rapidly back toward him. Once she reached him, she lifted her hand and slapped him as hard as she could.

The blow stung, but it didn't really hurt. "What the hell is wrong with you, Harriett?"

"You listen to me, Bill McLand. I never, ever want to hear tell of this again. Ever."

"Huh? I mean, okay," he said, not sure where she was going with this.

"Now, are we going to the dance tonight or what?"

He gathered his composure the best he could. His head was swimming with pain and confusion. After all, he had just shared a deep secret with the woman he loved, been slapped almost into next week—then was reminded about the dance tonight.

"Huh, why, huh, of course we're still going to the dance."

"Good. See you tonight around seven. And don't be late."

Bill honored her wishes to the best of his ability. It would be years before the topic would surface again.

Bill and Harriett married shortly after his graduation with all the fanfare of a southern wedding. Although he was uncomfortable with the selection of venue, he tolerated her wishes and married her on the old Shaw Plantation. She made sure to have all the accoutrements of the pre Civil War era very visible. All of the help was suited up in white coats with black bow ties and the women in white dresses, available at every guest's beck and call. She even made the women curt-sey as they walked around with cocktails and hors d'oeuvres. Bill finally put his foot down when she requested part of the entertainment be a young Colored boy, reminiscent of an old Bojangles. She felt it would be quite entertaining for him to tap dance for coins.

"What the . . . ?" Miss McLand screamed as she entered the room. Her face was so red, I thought she might drop dead right in that room.

"Bye, Mr. McLand," I said as I quickly exited the room to leave the house. Before I walked through the door, though, I decided to take my chances and listen to as much as I could.

"I don't want to hear anymore, I tell you. Talking to them like you do outside this home is one thing, but the nerve of you to allow her black behind back on my furniture. That's is simply unacceptable."

"So, is there a problem when I sit my black behind here?"

"That's different."

"No, it's not. I'm a Colored, Harriet. My momma was a Colored woman. You know the story already. She was basi-cally raped by my lovely white daddy until she submitted and became his . . . never mind. This is pointless."

"Now is good a time as any to discuss everything Bill."

"Oh, there's more you're unhappy with?"

"You're always somewhere talking with that Buster. Or heading over to May Alice and Cutie Pie's. Do you have to be so obvious? I can't take it anymore, Bill."

"Oh, so now I can't even talk to my own brother and sisters, really? They've held this secret as close to their vest as possible, but now you're telling me not to acknowledge them, much less talk with them." I could hear his voice getting louder. "That shit ain't gone happen. Buster has always been there for me—and you, for that matter. Who do you think help paid for our wedding or bought me my first car that you so happily rode in? Oh, and my sisters—the Nigger bitches, you so eloquently refer to them as. Where do you think the food we ate when I had no money came from? Them. Those people."

"Well, it's not even definite they are your siblings. That red birth mark means nothing. Just because you all have them could be condensal."

"You mean coincidental?"

"Whatever."

"Yeah, right. Me and three other people that actually look alike with red hair and a red birthmark on the left side of our necks, by the way, in the exact same place, is by *condensal*."

"You're horrible, just plain horrible. Now you're making fun of me."

"No, Harriett, you're doing just fine all by yourself."

The two of them fell into an ominous silence, and outside, on the back side of the house, my mind was whirling with all the things I'd heard. "What? He's Colored? Like me? And Mr. Buster, Miss May Alice and Miss Cutie Pie are his sistahs and brother? Wow. Wait till I tell Momma." I thought as I stood there frozen unable to move. "Now everything makes sense. That's why he's always in The Quarters. Always with Mr. Buster. Well, do tell."

As I stood there thinking, Mr. McLand abruptly walked through the side door still yelling. He didn't notice me, hidden around the corner.

"Harriet, I'll be back to get my things."

She ran behind him, yelling right back, "And where are you going?"

"I don't know, but what I do know is, I can't do this anymore. I am who I am. I've lived a lie for long enough. Denying myself, my family, my brother, my sisters. This lie has affected me in every facet of my life. We don't even make love anymore. We barely talk. Well, I barely talk. I do more listening than anything. We're not a family anymore. We just cohabitate."

"We what?"

"Just live together, Harriett. I'm away more than I'm here. And I do that on purpose, to avoid scenes like this. The arguments and comments are enough already. And for my children to have no idea of their father's true identity kills me. But I know with all the foolishness you've loaded them with, it's probably best they don't." His voice changed, becoming more thoughtful. "I can stay at Buster's for a while."

"Buster's? Are you crazy? You have a thriving law practice. How will you possibly explain to your clients that you've moved in with a Nig, a family down in The Quarters? We could lose everything, Bill. You're not thinking clearly. They could disown me. Kick me out of the bridge club, the ladies auxiliary club, even church. What will me and the children do?"

"As usual, it's all about you Harriett. All about you. You and the children will be fine. The house is paid for. You can have it and everything in it. You can have the car, and I'll make sure the lights stay on and food is in the house. Dick and Jane will stay in private school. But you will get a job."

"A what?"

"A job. It's a place people go to work and earn income."

I decided I had better scoot. If Mrs. McLand caught me now, she'd never forgive me. I hurried away from the house, headed down the driveway. I was afraid she'd see me, but she just stood in the doorway. Tears were streaming from her eyes. This was the beginning of the end of her marriage, her life as she knew it.

As I reached the street, Mr. McLand came out of the house with a suitcase in hand. He popped open the back trunk and threw it in. I started running, to create the proper amount of distance, so I only heard, rather than saw, his car starting up and then roaring down the driveway.

26

"Pearline, where is my basket?" Momma asked me as I walked in the house without it.

I'd contemplated on my way home how I would share this incident with her or if I would share anything at all. One thing about Louise Scott, she loved her *chilluns*, as she called us. At a minimum, the information would hurt her. At the maximum, she just might march straight over to the McLands and slap Miss Harriet.

"Momma, you're not going to believe this."

I began my tale by asking her to take a sit. At first, my request was met with a "why," then an "ain't got no time for that," and finally a flat "no." Each response rattled out before I could answer her "why." My swollen eyes and bubbling nose from crying was noticed on third glance.

She walked to the chair with an unsteady gait. I knew she feared the worst: *Lawd, what this chile branging home?*

I began to share with her everything that just happened to me and everything that I'd witnessed. I detailed every bit of it. From being called a Nigger to learning of Mr. McLand's true identity to watching Miss McLand stand at the door with the most empty look I'd ever seen. Momma listened initially with anger and disappointment, then began to soften and listened with sadness and compassion.

"And that's it, Momma. Can you believe, Mr. McLand is one of us? I knew it was something. Always with Mr. Buster. Sometimes I'd see him leaving Miss May Alice and Miss Cutie Pie's. And come to think of it, he looks just like them. They all look alike. How could I have missed that?"

Momma sat very quietly as I continued to talk. She had a great ability to listen with her full attention. So much so that occasionally I'd ask, *"Are you listening, Momma?"* She'd always respond with *"Can't listen and talk at the same time, chile."*

Finally she began to speak. "Well, to tell you the truth, I always thought he was one of them. That red hair and funny white-looking skin, they all tall and lanky, but one day he proved it to me. Didn't mean to, but he did. I just didn't think it was right for me gossiping 'bout something that I wasn't certain of. And even if I was, just wasn't right to repeat, not even to yo aunt.

"A few months back, I was over to the McLands' working and he walked in, smiling and polite like always. This was the first time I'd seen him without his button-down white shirt and tie. He had one of them cotton shirts he always plays tennis in. I know 'cause I'm always washing them. On this particular day, I believe it was the blue one. He got 'bout a hundred of them shirts, it seems. Yeah, that was it, 'cause that blue one got a gold patch in the shape of two C's for country club on it. So it happen me and him was standing in the kitchen talking a li'l bit. He told me them greens I was cooking for they supper smelled so good and he'd like a taste if I didn't mind. I said, Mr. McLand, I'm cooking them for you. Course I don't mind. That Harriet always complained about the smell, but he loved them, so she had me cook them.

"While we was standing there, she yelled out to him to ask a question. He turned to answer her and just at that moment, I turned too. And there it was. Baby, that mark might as well had some lights shining on it, cause that's how it lit up in my eyes. I saw it and had to catch my breath. I turned back round real quick, for he saw me staring. When he did turn around, he threw a towel over his shoulder , trying to make certain I couldn't see it no more. I think he know I saw it. He asked if I was all right, guess I didn't look like I was. Sweetie, I never breathed a word of it. But that mark was on him. And I saw it."

"Momma, you mean to tell me you've known about this the entire time?"

"Chile, that ain't none of my business and nobody else's, including yours. That kind of information can do a lot damage to folks. Bring on a lot of hurt and pain. Shoot, I'm busy enough worried 'bout ya'll and your aunt. Sides, you know I ain't never like that Harriett McLand. Not one bit. I worked for her 'cause we need the money. Ain't no co-reer pro-gress-shun with her, for sho. Didn't know I knew them words did you—co-reer pro-gress-shun. Uh-huh. Know way more than you thank."

"Momma, you're one of the smartest people in the word. A large vocabulary doesn't mean much coming from a small mind and an even smaller heart. And nothing is small about your mind or heart."

"Well, thank ya, baby. You sho got a way of putting words together. I tell you. Don't mean you ain't got to finish up your chores, but I thank you."

"Easy when it comes to you, Momma."

"I feels sorry for that Harriett right now, she quite pitiful. Here she is a grown woman, done lived a good life. Had all the thangs most women—men too, for that matter—could eva ask for. She done got away with treating me, your aunt, and anybody else she felt was beneath her awful with her words and her deeds. Said we had to use them old dingy cups to drink from, couldn't use the house toilet, only the one out back near the pool. No plates, silverware of hers would eva be touched by the lips of ours. And on top of all that, she done even called my baby, my child a Nigger. But yet behind all that, she marries the very thang she claims to hate. Ain't life something. Humph, humph, humph. Life something I tell you. Well, looks like my last day with the McLands' was today."

"Noooo, Momma, you can't lose your job." Tears immediately started piling up in my eyes. "Aunt will probably quit too if you do. I'm so sorry. I should have kept my big mouth shut. Momma, you can go back."

"Baby, ain't that much money in this world or beyond it for me to eva go back and work for that woman. We'll be fine. I'll find something else to do. Plenty folks needs they house clean. Don't you worry none. Thangs gone be fine. Maybe one day me and your Aunt Honey will start something of our own, who knows? Now, gone and wash up and get your sistah and brothers ready too."

"Yes ma'am."

I walked from the kitchen, relieved. Everything was going to be okay, I knew it for sure.

"Oh, Pearline."

"Ma'am?" I yelled from down the hall.

"Come here. One mo thang."

I walked back to the kitchen, wondering what that thing was. I entered the space where she stood. Although she never turned in my direction, her message was loud and clear.

"Didn't raise no pot that's likely to spill over?" she asked me.

"No ma'am, you didn't."

"Good. Didn't thank I did."

27

Simee

*I*t's been well over two months now. What's taking them so damn
long? Ain't a Quick Deed supposed to be quick? One meeting
after the other with them—how much meeting they got's to do?
I began to count on my fingers to make sho I'd covered the
usual highlights of this con. *Let's see, I covered the scriptures, the
money, and schooling for these country ass bumpkins. Don't thank
I missed nothing. Hell, I got to get outta here. Fo long, Tight Lucy
and her sons gone figure out I'm down here and come looking for that
money. Damn. Somebody gone tell me something – today!*

Just as I moved to grab my coat and head over to Buster's,
a knock at the door stopped me short.

"Who is it?" I yelled

"Why, it's me, silly. Did you forget about us and our day
together?"

"Shit," I whispered as I recognized her voice. "Ain't got no
time for Wilhelmina today."

"Hold on a second. Give me a minute."

"Sho thang," she replied. I could imagine her out there primping her hair and touching up her lipstick.

Wilhelmina was the very last person I was interested in seeing today. With all that was on my mind, even sex free of charge wasn't enticing.

"Hey there. How you? I asked as I open the door a bit disheveled, an unusual appearance considering my normally dapper self.

"Fine, and you, handsome? You all right? Look like you might not be feeling good. Musta forgot bout today huh?" She sashayed into my home, looking around, no doubt for another woman.

"Well, not exactly, but something done came up. You know, I was thanking you and the rest of the board would have by now signed over that deed to me. I must say, I'm quite surprised and disappointed it's taking this long. After all, I've provided the proper paperwork for the transaction, even handed over a quick deed form for ya'll to sign. Plain and simple."

"It ain't me," she protested. "I told them, they taking way too long and if we don't hurry up, we might lose out. They just looked at me all tight face when I say that, since they know I'm your girlfriend and all. Thinking it's me being smitten with you instead of bout business. I told them they was wrong, but you know how mens is, you one of them. And that Bernice do whatever Rufus tells her too. Sides, I like having you around. The quicker we sign, the quicker you gone leave."

"What did you say? The quicker I'm gone leave?"

"Yeah, as soon as we hand over that deed, I-I mean, we won't see you no more."

It's this damn Wilhelmina that's holding this thang up, I realized. *It ain't them, it's her. She dead set on me staying here and trying everythang she can to delay my exit from this place. I should have known this.* I had to come up with a remedy to Wilhelmina's scheming. Then the answer came to me. Of course. Nice and easy.

"What make you thank that, baby? I told you I love this place, and you got to know I love you too. All that rolling and rocking we been doing should count for something."

"It do," she said, but I could tell she was still doubtful.

"Hadn't told you yet, but been thanking bout settling down here. I'm still a marrying man and looks like you'll make a fine wife."

"Wife?" she repeated, motioning to clean her ears in disbelief of what she'd just heard. "Did you say wife, Simee Scott?"

"You heard right. That's exactly what I said. Now, don't tell me that's the first time you heard somebody say you'll make a good wife," I said as I pulled her close and softly kissed her cheek.

Giggling and clearly flattered, she made a beeline from my arms to the door.

"Where you going?"

"Down to the church, of course. They taking way too long to get that deed signed. Gone make sho it happens today. It's Wednesday and we meet every Wednesday."

"We?"

"The board. Right after Bible class, we get together and discuss church business."

Well, well, well. "Shoot, don't let me hold you up. Gurl, you betta gone outta her. Be waiting for you when you come back tonight."

I smiled and waved goodbye to her as I opened my front door for her exit. Couldn't help but to think, *Yeah, you'll make a good wife—for some other fool.*" I lit my cigarette, leaned against the door and puffed real hard.

Then it occurred to me that I better make sure things turned out my way. I wasn't invited to the meeting, but I could make a special appearance if they needed any more convincing.

Following Wilhelmina to the church was no easy task. Being the nosy ass woman she is, seems like she turned around looking over her shoulder more than anything. The last thing I needed was for her to mess up things mo than she had.

I arrived at the church and stepped in the back near the shed. This way nobody would see me. I was hoping for dismissal of Bible study already. *How many amens does it take to wrap this up, goodness, Deacon Jones,* I thought as I anxiously waited by the stairs. It was now 8:15 and he was still talking. I'd forgotten that was the fourth Wednesday of the month, which meant it could be a while before Deacon Jones wrapped up the 6:00 to 7:30 session. Wilhelmina had told me that he'd become quite determined in his later years to do exactly what he wanted to do, how he wanted to do it, and the length of time it took to do it. After being asked, then told, on many occasions by the deacon board, and even the Pastor, to please watch his time when he led Bible class, he'd snapped back, "I don't wear no watch, so I don't keep no time." Luckily, Wilhelmina decided not to tolerate his behavior tonight.

"Jones," Wilhelmina whispered to him after she tiptoed up to the front of the church with her index finger up.

"Yeah?" he said, surprised to be interrupted by her.

She smiled and leaned toward him. "Look, ain't got time for you today. Gone and close this right now. Got business to take care of."

"What?"

"You heard me, old fool. Lessen you want me to tell everybody in here 'bout you, Deka and them so-called herbal weeds you always buying from RaShay. Best you shut this down."

He was shocked that she not only disrupted him, but that she knew about his little inclination. However, he apparently knew it was best not to cross her on this one. So, he followed her instructions.

"Well, my good Christians, bout time we said good evening. May grace and mercy follow us all through our day and our lives. Amen."

"Amen."

The church finally cleared of everyone. Now the board meeting could begin.

Finally, everyone was gone, so I eased my way from the rear of the church to the side of it. Them big windows was never closed 'cause it was so hot. I could hear everything.

"I thank we all been going about this all wrong," Wilhelmina said to Buster as she sat with the board to discuss the agenda.

"Going about what the wrong way, Wilhelmina? You know you ain't following the procedures co-rectly. We ain't even opened the meeting up. Par-li-a-mentary procedures requires that you at least have a call to order, roll call of members present, minutes read, and—" Buster said.

"I don't care 'bout no Parlortolaria procedures," she interrupted him. "Time we dealt with that deed once and for all."

"Now, that land deal is on the table, but it ain't first on the list. Got to come up with date for the church anniversary." He said.

"That can wait. This way mo important," she said.

"Just let her go on, Buster," Rev. Evans said, equally annoyed.

"Well, we've all had a chance to look at the survey and read the deed ova and ova again. We even took a trip up there, walked, prayed, and everythang you can think of. I can't thank of one reason we shouldn't move forward with this."

"Scuse me?" Bernice said. "What in the devil done changed yo mind, Wilhelmina? We been wanting to do this pretty much since he spoke at the church almost two months ago. You been the reason it's been taking so long."

"Yeah, Wilhelmina. Why you in such a hurry now?" Rufus asked.

"I ain't in no mo a hurry than before. I just needed to think is all."

"Uh-huh," Buster said.

"Well, since we all seem to be in agreement. All that's needed now is a vote."

I hurried back to the house and pretended to be bored when Wilhelmina knocked on my door.

"It's official, the ayes had it," she announced in triumph. "The board finally voted to sell the land to you. I brought the quick deed over to you and you suppose to act on the church's behalf with the U.S. Office of Transportation." She stopped and smiled at the long word. "Whew-we, that's a mouthful, the U.S. Office of Transportation."

"That's great news," I said. I did some more acting, thinking about what I was going to do next. "So, what we'll do is I'll sell the property, and . . . you and the board will meet me down at the Columbus Bank and Trust on Saturday. Then I'll hand over a certified government check written out to the church for two hundred thousand dollars."

"Oh, my goodness. Can you imagine all that money?" Wilhelmina asked. "I think I'm 'bout to lose my mind."

"Naw, you can't do that," I said. "You gone start planning the wedding."

"Yes!" she almost shouted. "Of course. The wedding!"

28

Louise

I know Rufus regret running that mouth of his. Ever since he shamed Bernice in front of everybody, she ain't lifted one finger to do much of anything round they house but bury folks. Why he choose to mention how she don't wash they clothes so good and how his white shirts could be whiter, all in front of all her lady friends, I'll neva know. That was just plumb foolish. After he said that, I heard Bernice stopped doing more than washing.

All his foolishness turn out to be a good thing for me and Honey. We picked them up as a customer. For only two people, they got plenty of clothes round here.

I decided to give Pearline a break and I came by myself to get they loads. I believe the walls in this place thinner than they is at our house. I can hear everything they saying. I ain't being nosy, but since they was talking, I decided to listen. I'm gone ask if I can go with them to the bank. All they can say is yes or no.

"Scuse me, Bernice. Mind if I ask you a question?" I said.

"Why of course, Louise."

"I know I ain't part of the church board, but I would love to go with ya'll down to the bank. Just the thought of seeing a check with $200,000.00 written on it making my head spin."

"Of course you can. Girl, we just as excited."

"What time the bank open?" Rufus asked Bernice

"The same time it's been opening for the last twenty years, eight o'clock, Rufus. But we not to get there until right after its closing, remember?"

"Yeah, I remember now. Just a li'l nervous is all. I mean, don't you think I got's a right to be? Handing over that deed to Simee without completing the proper paperwork make a man a bit nervous and rightfully so. All of us should be nervous. Be glad when we get over to that bank and everything is official. I saw Simee a few days ago and he said he worked it out with Mr. Kamenski to stay there until six tonight so the other customers is gone and we can do this without all the fanfare. You know, two hundred thousand dollars is a lot of money."

"Yes, it is" Bernice said. "Better get on over to the church to meet everybody."

I stood there waiting on Bernice to give me the okay one more time. She finally did.

"Louise, you coming."

"Right behind you," I said.

"Whew, I'm so nervous, I might wet myself." Wilhelmina said to Buster as everyone met outside the church to drive together to the bank.

"Hopefully, you'll do us all a favor and hold yo self."

"I will, just nervous is all."

"Here he is," Wilhelmina said as Rev. Evans pulled up in his station wagon.

"Well, it took long enough," Bernice said.

As each of them climbed into the Reverend's car, Wilhelmina waited until the last door shut, to share her exciting news.

"Well, now is as good a time as any to tell ya'll."

"Tell us what? I can't take no mo surprises round here," Rufus said.

"I'm pleased to formally announce, me and Simee is marrying."

"Ya'll what?" Bernice asked

"I said, we's getting married."

"Married. You and Simee Scott?" Buster said.

"That's what I said. As soon as we complete this transaction, me and him on our way to sit with you, Reverend, and discuss our impending nuptials."

"Lawd have mercy. So that's why you was in such a hurry to move forward with this," Bernice said. "Wilhelmina, you's something. You done wrapped yo self round this man and this land. And I don't like it one bit, not one bit. But ain't much we can do 'bout it now, is it? You something, I tell you."

"Look, ain't nothing wrong with me marrying Simee. You just jealous is all."

"Jealous?" Bernice snapped back. "Gurl, please, I can't thank of one thang of yours I got to be jealous of."

"That ain't what Rufus said," Wilhelmina said.

"What?" Rufus said, beating Bernice to state the same.

Before Rev. Evans could turn around in hopes of diffusing the rising tide, Bernice had reached over Rufus and grabbed Wilhelmina by the hair and punched her in the eye. For the next five minutes both Buster and Rufus worked diligently to untangle Wilhelmina from Bernice as Rev. Evans wiped his brow, prayed, and continued to drive. Once the battle was settled, the women brushed back misplaced hair, disheveled clothes, and bruised egos. The men sat in silence knowing this was the prelude to some impending doom. The underlining concern they each anticipated had surfaced.

As they pulled closer to the bank, it was apparent that the bank employees had left for the day. The parking lot was completely empty. Even Mr. Kaminski's black Lincoln that always sat in the parking space designated for the President of the bank was gone. The curtains were pulled closed and the metal door that secured the bank had the padlock on it.

"Thought you said Simee was gone meet us here, Wilhelmina?" Rev. Evans asked.

"I did and he is."

"Where is Mr. Kaminski? I don't see him nor do I see that car of his," Buster asked. "Something don't feel quite right, I tell you."

"Ya'll need to calm down. Always thanking somebody up to something. He gone be here and so is Mr. Kaminski. Just running a li'l late is all," Wilhelmina said.

They all sat and watched ten minutes turn into an hour and an hour turn into two hours. Finally, someone pulled up to the bank.

"Here they is. Ya'll was worried for nothing," Wilhelmina said.

The car pulled up next to them and a gentleman rolled his window down. As he did, his face became recognizable to each of them.

"Buford, is that you? Rev. Evans asked.

"Why, yes suh, it is. How ya'll doing?"

"We fine. How you?"

"Fair to middlin and partly cloudy." Laughing, he said, "Thanks for asking. What ya'll doing down here this late?"

"We here for some business."

"What you doing here?"

"Oh, I work here. I clean the place after hours. Mr. Griffin gone meet me and let me in."

"Mr. Griffin?"

"Yes suh, he the new bank president. Been here 'bout a week or so. Came in after Mr. Kaminski left and moved to Boston."

A dread that had its own heartbeat pounded in that car. Everyone sat stone still, just hoping the obvious wasn't so.

"For ya'll gets all crazy and thangs. Maybe Simee meant Mr. Griffin, or maybe he didn't know Mr. Kaminski left and we are to meet up with him and Mr. Griffin," Wilhelmina nervously said.

"Simee? Simee Scott? Is that that tall, pretty boy all the womens like round here?" Buford asked.

"Yeah, that's him," Rufus responded, annoyed.

"Figured so. Interesting fellow he is. You know, the first time I met him, he was beat up pretty bad on the side of the road right up in Atlanta. Just sitting there like he was lost. I pulled over and asked if he was all right. He said not really and asked if he could catch a ride with me wherever I was heading. Felt sorry for him with that black eye and all, so I told him to hop on in," Buford said.

"Black eye, side of the road? What are you talking 'bout, Buford?" Rufus asked. "Simee came here from Chicago."

"Well, must have been by way of Atlanta. For that entire drive, he never mentioned no Chicago one time. Anyway, just saw him 'bout two hours ago over at the filling station, Reverend. Said he had a bus to catch to Philadelphia. Yep, said he couldn't leave though without picking up them RC Cola's, a bags of Lance peanuts, and them banana and vanilla moon pies. Said them foods in particular was hard to find where he was going, so he bought up all of them, every last one. Seemed to be in a bit in a hurry so wasn't much for conversation. I told him to have a safe trip and that was that." As he spoke, he continued leaning from the window, fanning himself with the cap he'd removed from his head.

As he finished sharing his tale, everyone immediately became overwhelmed. Unbeknownst to Buford, he'd just confirmed a fear that had festered in the minds of each of them, even before the truth revealed itself.

"I thank we done been had," Rufus said.

"I thank we better pray," Rev. Evans said.

"Ain't thanking at all," Wilhelmina said. "I'm getting my shotgun."

"Where you going, Louise?" Bernice yelled as I scooted out of the car in a hurry.

"Home. I need to get to Edga for he gets to that lying brother of his."

29

Simee

"**D**amn, these moon pies is good. You want one?" I asked the fellow traveler sitting two chairs over from me. Me and him was both waiting for our bus in the Trailways Bus Station in downtown Columbus.

"No, thank you, suh."

"You sho? Don't know what you missing. Deee-licious. Eva had one before?

"Not that I recall."

"Here, take one. I tell you, they good."

I handed the young man a moon pie and struck up a conversation with him.

"So, what brought you to this here big metropolis, Columbus, GA?" I asked sarcastically.

"Oh, I'm traveling through here. I'm on my way to Washington, D.C."

"D.C.? What you know 'bout D.C., boy?"

"I'm headed to college there. I'm going to Howard University. You heard of it before?"

"Boy, ain't much I ain't heard of. Sho I heard of it. I ain't much for schooling. I'm more a real life man. But good for you. Gone be a educated man, huh?"

"Yes suh."

"That's a good thang. I wish you well."

"Thank you, suh."

"What bus you waiting on?" Before the young man could answer, I continued speaking, "Me, I'm waiting on the number 2009 to Philadelphia, Penn-sy-lvania. Suppose to get here right at eight o'clock. What time you got there?"

"Umm, it's 7:45."

"Damn, they need to come on. Got a feeling I don't have long to get out of this town."

"Everything okay?"

"Depend on who you ask," I answered with a laugh.

"Suh, I do believe bus 2009 just pulled up," the stranger said as he heard an arriving bus enter the bus terminal. "You did say, number 2009? Well, that's it, all right."

"Good, starting to thank I might have to walk on outta here." I grabbed my bag, coat jacket and that moon pie I was eating to head for the bus. I usually travel light, easier to flee that way. "Take care now."

"Yes sir, I will."

Finally, the arriving passengers exited the bus one by one. Then the driver took his sweet time for a smoke break after cleaning the bus out. Once that was all completed, I joyously stepped on the bus and handed the driver my ticket. As I walked to the rear, I noticed the bus would be pretty empty, which was fine with me. I was looking forward to stretching my legs during my northern journey. Once I sat down, I took off my hat and leaned back slowly, at last resting my head on the back of the plump vinyl cushioned seat. With my head nicely positioned, I placed my hat directly over his face, shielding my eyes from the interruption of light, preparing for my journey and for a nap. This was a comfortable position for a man who'd just secured legal documents to some land and big money. The land was worth a lot of money, not exactly the two hundred thousand I exaggerated about before, but still a significant amount, maybe fifty or seventy-five thousand at the most. More importantly, I would be able to sell the deed now, get some cash and get as far away as possible from Columbus, Georgia, that Wilhelmina, and specially that crazy Tight Lucy.

I believe this the easiest money I done ever got my hands on, besides two thousand I earned from Lucy. Hell, dealing with her cause a man to lose his mind. And not in a good way. As soon as I get to the city, I'll sell this deed and get my cold cash like nothing. Easy money, I thought, failing to shield my wide grin.

As the last persons entered the bus and found their seats, the bus driver shifted the bus into gear. The loud whooshing noise from the bus's exhaust pipe was a loud, clear indication the bus was in drive. I shifted uncomfortably in my seat. I just couldn't shake one thing—that Honey.

The last time I saw her, she was still talking that shit, but I know she still want me. Just scared she gone upset her sistah if she with me. Edga still fucking up shit. Humph, I could tell when I kissed her that she still wanted me. Hell, I know I wanted her. My dick was so hard I thought it was gone snap. Too damn feisty, pushing me away so everybody could see. All a front. I could tell she enjoyed every last feeling she got from me with all that moaning and moving. Hell, the look on her face and the grip from her legs said it all. I ain't hardly forgot our night of passion—hell, hot passion. She just playing hard to get is all. I'm gone make this easy for her. I ain't nobody's fool. I know she wants me. *Damn*, I thought to myself. "Shit, stop the damn bus," I yelled as I repositioned my hat on my head. I walked up to the front of the bus, ignoring the groans of irritation from my fellow passengers. I gave the driver a five dollar bill for his inconvenience, pulled the handle, opened the door myself and hopped off.

30

Honey

Early this afternoon I heard some banging on my door.
The noise rattled me some. Knocking is one thang, but
banging gets my pressure up. To my surprise, when I
opened the door, it was Simee.

"Simee Scott, why you banging on my door like that, and
what on earth is you doing here? I asked as I stood behind the
screen door.

"Well, good mawning to you too beautiful," he said with a
crooked, tight smile.

He had some strange gleam in his eye that meant no good.
"What you doing at my doorstep?" I asked while I made sho to
keep the door latched 'tween us.

"You ain't gone let me in, woman?" he asked, standing
there looking mo nervous than anything. "Ain't polite to not
ask yo guest in. You ain't learn that?"

"No. I guess I ain't."

"Damn, Honey, why you think I come here? Ain't gone do
nothing but talk. Sides, be a shame to have to bust this here

door down. Be a lot of work and money for you to have to buy another one, don't you thank?"

Lawd, I stood there stiller than a church mouse. I was getting a li'l scared now. Got to thinking real quick on how he had been following me before making my life pure-de-hell. How sleeping with him done caused me nothing but trouble. I knew if I didn't open door, this fool was gone come in one way or the other. Jesus! I reached for the latch to pull the hook out. As I got close to reaching the latch, my hand seem to have a mind of its own and my fingers closed shut on me. I stood there looking at my own hands, wondering what they was doing. Finally, I reached up again and pull the hook out and pushed the door open. As soon as he crossed over my threshold, I regretted what I just done.

That man walked in my house real different this time. He usually come through here with his chest all puffed out, like he ain't got a worry in the world. Not this time, no suh, he was mo nervous than I done eva seen before.

"I asked you again– what's going on, Simee?"

"You give me a minute, I'll tell you."

He paced my flo back and forth. He asked me for a glass of water, then a glass of shine. I gave him both.

"Look, now, yo minute done turned into ten. You been here long enough to start talking and if you ain't gone do that, ain't no reason for you to be standing here."

"Why you talking to me like that? All I done for you. The only reason I ain't gone is 'cause of you."

"Me? I don't know what the hell you talking 'bout, Simee. All you done for me? Like what? Oh, following me round like a crazy fool, showing up at my work place? Scaring me half to death. Oh, like that." I said, standing with a good bit of distance 'tween us.

"My momma used to have a mouth like yours. Yes suh, she sholl did," he all of sudden said.

"Yo momma?" I asked, thinking of the story Edga told us. "Why in the world would you bring that po woman in this mess?"

"You reminds me of her. Did I eva tell you that?"

"No, you didn't."

"Yeah, she used to talk too much. Just like you do. Yap, yap, yap."

"Simee," I said with as much calmness as I could. He was starting to look angry. "All I know is that you need to tell me why you come here."

"Did I tell you 'bout the time my momma, all by accident of course, walked into my fist? Uh-huh, she was running that mouth like you is doing right now. Telling me everythang I was and everythang I ain't. Don't know how it happened but, wham, she walked right into my fist."

"You hit yo own momma?"

"Course not. It was an accident. You ain't hear me the first time."

"Yeah, I heard you."

"When we was together," he continued, "I felt something 'tween us something deep. You did too. I know you did. I ain't had no other woman like you, Honey, in my entire life and I done had my share of women. Plenty of them and all kinds."

"I'm sho you have."

"Colored womens in all colors," he said, laughing. "Had white, injuns, Ricans and Mexican too. Even a gal all the way from Africa. Lala was her name. She was from Sudan. A real-life African. She was almost as pretty as you. I met her when

I worked on a cargo ship. Shame how she fell ova that damn boat. Then there was Lee. She Chinese. Now them Chinese women, they know they place. Did you know Lee mean plum in Chinese? Yes suh, it sholl do. Come to think of it, she tasted like one. But you, Honey, you got them all beat."

"Thanks."

"You got some good stuff, woman, and I don't plan on sharing that with nobody. Might have to kill a Nigger just for looking at you wrong. That what love do to a man. Make um crazy."

"What? Love?"

"Baby, today is yo lucky day," he said to me as if a new thought had popped in his head. "I'm gone take you with me. Figure we can get married and have a few babies, hell, might even get you a dog. I got enough money for both of us. Just need to grab yo bag and we outta here."

"Is you crazy? Married, babies, dog? Why on earth would I do that?"

"Why would you do that? That moaning and screaming you did when I was inside you should answer that. You was good, Honey, in every way I can thank of. Like when you—"

"Simee."

"Aw, we both know you ain't shy, no, woman, not at all. Even now I feel like I'm gone lose my mind if I don't have you again. But don't worry none bout that, since we in a hurry, we can get to that later tonight. Gone take real good care of you. Come to think of it, you don't need to take nothing. We just gone down to the bus station."

"Simee, I don't want to go anywhere."

"I'll take you right on up to Philadelphia with me. Got plenty of contacts there. Be good change for a woman like you."

"Simee, I'm not going."

After realizing that I had no intentions of going, he started becoming more and more agitated by the second. Both his voice and behavior began to change.

"Look now, I ain't use to repeating myself. Specially when it comes to ya'll womens. I said let's go."

"I ain't going nowhere with you."

"You know, that mouth of yours starting to get on my nerves. I done had bout enough of you talking that shit. Come here," he said, grabbing my arm.

"What? I ain't coming nowhere. Get your hands off me and get out my house. Now!" I said, snatching away from his grip.

"So this how you want me to leave? A broken man without my woman. Okay."

I walked over to the front door and opened it. He picked up his hat and followed me. "Well, before I go, I believe I'm gone take a little something with me. For old times' sakes."

"The only thing you taking out of here is yo behind."

"I have just concluded that I'm tired of yo shit. Tired of yo mouth."

"Simee, get out," I yelled as I backed away from him.

"I'll leave when I'm good and got-damn ready to leave, and that ain't no time soon," he said as he slammed my door shut.

After he said that, I knew it was best to get away from him. Ain't neva been so scared my entire life. The next thing I know, I'm running from him in my own house. I ended up in the kitchen. When I turned around, he was right behind me laughing.

"Girl, what you running for? Making me feel some kind of way. Like you scared of me. All we been through and you treating me like this."

I reached the back door and twisted the knob to get out. Right when I cracked the door open, he slammed it shut. Not knowing what to do next, I looked over and spotted my cutting knives. Seem like they was calling me or something, so I grabbed the biggest one I could, my butcher knife. Thought that might scare him. I started waving it in front of him, thinking he gone back up. He didn't. That demon just kept coming my way, even asked me what I planned on doing with that.

"Gone cut you, Simee, ifin you don't get out."

"Naw, you ain't."

I got round the other side of the table for he could get to me, but he still come after me. When I go left, he go left, I go right, he go right. I felt like a child running from him, only I was running for my life. Finally I made my way out of the kitchen, but I dropped the knife. When I did that, the bastard kicked it.

The first room I come to leaving the kitchen was my bedroom. To get in there, I had to step over Shakespeare. I looked around my room, then noticed the knife along the side of the door. I was shaking like a leaf, but that didn't stop me from bending down as quick as I could and picking up that knife. Was not a moment later, I stood up, turned round, only to see him coming for me.

Like most folks, he forgot about my petunia plant in my doorway. Them big feet of his tripped right over Shakespeare, causing Simee to land chest first on my knife. I didn't know he was stabbed. That is, until he stumbled backward off of me and I saw him gripping the knife sticking out of his body.

I watched Simee fall like a sack of potatoes. For a split second I thought about helping that man. I stooped down next to him, then stood back up. I come to find out that split seconds pass way quicka than I thought.

31

Pearline

Funny, nothing but silence this afternoon as I stepped into Aunt Honey's house. I didn't notice her in her normal spot, the kitchen, so I sashayed through the house on my mission. Langston and John were waiting at the library today and I couldn't wait. I glanced into the back room, the beds were made up and everything was in its rightful place as usual, but no aunt. So, I ventured farther into the house. I approached the last door, the bedroom door; thinking, *She's gotta be in here.* I pushed the door and it slowly creaked open, but not completely. It was one of those old heavy wooden doors that weighed a ton, so I was used to pushing it with some effort. Today, however, for some reason, I had to push harder than usual. Finally, with a hard shove, I opened the door and yelled, "Aunt Honey, where are you?"

As I forced the door backward, I quickly realized why the door felt stuck. There were some legs behind it and my Uncle Simee was attached to them. There he was, laying face up, eyes wide open, dead, right there before my eyes. And there was Aunt, standing over him, bloodied, in a daze.

Walking in and finding a butcher's knife plunged in my uncle's chest was an image that I couldn't shake. The shock of it all held my feet still. Only until my aunt noticed me and shook my shoulder did I have any thought to move.

"Pearline!" she screamed. Her tone was wrenching, loaded with fear and panic. To gain my full attention, she shook my shoulder twice.

"Pearline!"

"Uh-huh, ma'am"

I stayed rooted to the spot. I'd never seen a dead body before outside of a casket. I knew he was dead. He just lay there, looking right at me with a look of shock on his face. Almost like he couldn't believe she actually stabbed him. Knowing Uncle Simee, he couldn't.

"Go get your momma," she whispered to me. Then she yelled, "Now."

Looks like I won't be going to the library after all.

The night brought on an eerie stillness. Even the wind seemed to take a break from disturbing the leaves. Or maybe it just felt that way as I tore through the streets, desperately making my way back to the safety of my home. I ran so fast, I slipped, ripped my dress, and scraped both of my knees. The pain of my own torn flesh hardly stopped me, though. I hopped up just as quickly as I'd fallen. I had to get home.

Although there were several routes to my house, my instincts pointed me in the direction of the church, so that's the route I took. To my surprise, there stood both Momma and Daddy, along with what seemed to be the entire Quarters community. As I approached the crowd, each face had a familiar look. It was that of trouble. Unfortunately, I'd had seen it before mirroring from both my parents. But this was different; the entire community appeared to be stricken. Everyone seemed to have the same disturbed look, including Miss Jim, Mr. Rufus, Miss Bernice, and the Reverend. Mr. Buster was oddly absent.

"How could they already know?" I thought. "It just happened. And what is everybody doing out here anyway? It's not Sunday." As I came closer to the crowd, I could hear the commotion.

"He took the damn deed and is gone," Miss Carrie said.

"Gone?" Miss MinLee said.

"You heard me, gone."

"Look like he set them up right nicely. Meet him over at the bank. Them fools sat out there for hours waiting on his thieving ass. No money, no deed, no Simee," Miss Carrie said.

Right after it became clear that the savior Simee would not be meeting the church board or anyone else at the bank, the news traveled quickly. From one house to the other, the news moved from ear to mouth. With the gravity that this carried, it wasn't long before the entire community had collected outside the doors of the church.

"We gone take care of this. Calm heads has got to prevail or we'll never get that deed back. Ya'll got's to listen to us now," Rev. Evans said to the angry crowd.

"No disrespect, Rev, but listening to ya'll is what got's us in the predicament in the first place," Turnerd said. "I told ya'll he was up to no good. And I was right."

"Be calm, now. Not good to speak to a holy man like that," Mr. RaShay said.

"And ain't no need for the blame game now, Turnerd," a female voice yelled from the crowd.

"Blame game? Who said that? Was it you, Wil-*hell*-mina? 'Cause I got plenty blame to go round, starting with you."

"Hold on there, now," Miss Wilhelmina said. "Now, I was supposed to be his wife."

"Is you crazy? I can thank of plenty thangs you is and wife ain't one of em," he said as he looked in her direction. "Let's see what comes to my mind is . . . let me think a minute. Oh, I know," he said as he tapped each of his fingers, "Mistress, Madame, and misery. Them three come straight to mind."

"Turnerd, leave that woman alone please," Mr. Spudnick said as he held Miss Wilhelmina back from slugging him.

All the commotion amid them created a stir in the crowd. That's when Mr. Turnerd turned to an unfamiliar face.

"Who you?"

"Me?"

"Yeah, you."

"My name is Lucinda, Lucinda Onetha Cromwell."

"You ain't from round here, is you?" Mr. Turnerd said

"Naw, I ain't. I'm from Atlanta. Me and my sons came down here looking for an old friend."

"Uh-huh, well, I know everybody round here. Who might yo friend be?"

"A gentleman by the name of Simee Scott. We heard he may be this way. So here we are," she said with a slight crooked smile. "And you are?"

"My name is Turnerd, but people round here call me Turn-ered."

His distinction was perplexing to her, since there was, in fact, no distinction.

"We saw all ya'll standing out here and thought we'd stop and ask if you or some of these other kind folks might know where we could find him."

"Well, ain't that the question of the day?" Mr. Turnerd said. "Where the hell is that lying, sack of —?

"Turnerd!" Spudnick interrupted. "We still on sacred ground. What is wrong with you? Any minute now, some lighting gone strike you in that pointy head of yours."

"I know where we is, Spudnick." Turning his attention back to Miss Cromwell, he continued, "So, you looking for his ass too. Humph, well, join the crowd. He done robbed our church. Now, what kind of man would steal from the church?"

As I approached Momma, she noticed me. My distress was obvious to her and anyone in close proximity. Stepping away from the crowd, she motioned for me to come to her and gently embraced my shoulders. Looking at me with fear and concern, she asked, "Gurl, what in the world? What happened to you? You all right?"

Her succession of questions rattled out so quickly, I wasn't sure which to answer first.

"Momma," I finally said, out of breath.

"What is it, child?" Daddy asked, seemingly almost afraid to hear the answer.

"It's Aunt."

"What's Aunt, is she okay?"

I motioned for him to lean down towards me, and then I whispered, "No, Daddy, and neither is Uncle Simee." I was so nervous, I could hear my own heart fighting its way from my chest.

"Okay, Momma's here. Tell me what's going on. Where's Aunt, and where's Uncle Simee?"

Before I could open my mouth to respond, Rev. Evans motioned for Daddy to bring me inside the church. As we all stepped away from everyone, I heard Deacon Thee attempt to settle the growing uneasiness weaving through the crowd. His efforts were in vain.

Momma held my shoulders as we walked up the steps to enter the church. Once inside, I realized that something else had happened and this stabbing was probably the outcome. Without any hesitation, I began to share with them what I just seen and what Aunt told me to do.

"Oh Lawd, not again," Momma blurted out to the surprise of all in the room.

"Huh?" I said, with the curiosity of a cat. Only saying what the others were sholl thinking.

"Oh. Nothing. Never mind," she said, shaking her head as if that would erase what had just left her mouth.

After her retort, the others in earshot of her voice noticed the comment, but had no time to inquire, shed a tear or rejoice, for that matter. And if they did, I didn't see it. Before I could catch my breath, I was on my way out of Columbus without a suitcase, a toothbrush and most importantly, any of my books.

32

Louise

Me and Edga made sho Pearline was safely off with Thee. Then me and a few others from the church made our way over to Honey's. Before we could get halfway up the road, just about every other person associated with The Quarters was trailing behind us. That odd-acting Mrs. Cromwell and her sons wedged in the crowd right along with everyone else. I guess she speculated that the crowd must be going somewhere of importance, if not to Simee, then probably close.

I called out to Honey several times as I entered the home. It was dark, cold and much too quiet for me, immediately bringing on a terrible feeling.

"Honey, where you at? It's us, sweetie," I said as I walked from the front to the rear of the house.

"Crazy, I mean Honey. Gurl, where you at?"

"Edga, don't call her crazy."

"Sorry. Well, she can't be too far in this li'l house."

"You don't think she left, do you?" I asked Rev. Evans.

"Where in the hell um gone go, Louise?" Honey said as the back screen door snapped behind her.

"Didn't you hear us calling you? Where you been?"

"Louise, I was sitting in the back tending to my garden. Might be a while for I'm able to grow some mo collards back there."

"Stop talking like that. You okay?"

"Ah, no. Far from it. What kind of question is that? "

"Calm down, Honey, no need for spitting fire my way. Just nervous is all. We gone figure it out. Just try and calm down."

"Calm down? And why, pray tell, did you have to bring the entire church with you?" she asked as she walked over to the front window and peeped out.

"I didn't. They kinda just invited theyself. Once they saw where we were going, they just followed. Honey, everybody and I mean everybody, been looking for Simee."

"Well, look no further." She pointed to her bedroom door.

"Oh, Lawd. Not again. You didn't, did you?" escaped from my lips when I saw his feet protruding from the door of the bedroom I once shared with my husband.

"Not again? What you say?" Edga asked, probably thanking back on my comment earlier from the church.

"Never you mind that," I quickly snapped back. "Is that him?"

"Louise, if you ask me one mo crazy question, I'm going to lose it," Honey said.

"Look like you done already did that," Rufus said.

"Where is Pearline?" Honey asked, ignoring Rufus.

"Thee took her over to his folks up in Rome," Edga said.

"Lawd, I probably done scarred that child for life. I'm so sorry she saw this."

"She fine. A little shaken, of course, but she be fine."

"RaShay, what is you doing?" Turnerd asked as everyone observed him begin to rearrange Honey's furniture.

"I'm making for certain his duppy won't stay."

"Duppy?" the group asked collectively.

"Yeah, the Duppy. Gotta confuse de Man's spirit so it'll go away."

"Oooo, Lawd, my nerves already bad, RaShay. Now you talking spirits hanging around my house."

"You been smoking them funny cigarettes again?" Turnerd said. "Talking that Jamaican hocus-pocus stuff."

"Whatever, Bobo."

"Who he calling Bobo? I done told that curry-eating fool my name, it's Turn-nerd."

Miss Gloell motioned for me to lean in and whispered, "Gurl, he know Turnerd name, but where he from, Bobo mean fool."

"Oh."

"You thank me later, Honey. Gotta get the duppy out."

"Humph, I doubt that," she mumbled.

"Just so you know, Buster gone to get Mr. McLand," Edga said.

"Mr. McLand?" Honey asked.

"Yes. We gone need his help with that damn Cletus."

"What happened, Honey?" I asked with raised eyebrows. Communicating as quietly with her as possible. I couldn't help but wonder if this was *another one of her accidents.*

"Don't look at me like that. Can I have a drink of water and a blanket? All of a sudden, I'm freezing, it's cold in here."

"May Alice, go and get her a quilt, please. She should have one in that chest at the foot of her bed."

"I gotta go in there?" May Alice said, uneasy.

"Yes. Girl, just close your eyes and scoot by him."

"How in the hell am I supposed to do that, Louise?"

"I'll get the blanket," Prudence said as she primped herself and made sho her wig was straight. Lawd Jesus, I believe she even dabbed on some lipstick or were my eyes playing tricks on me. That woman stepped in that room as if to greet a suitor, then closed the door behind her.

"Here you go," she said as she returned and handed me the blanket. I was almost afraid to take it from her.

I wrapped the quilt around Honey's shoulders and handed her the cold glass of water. Fortunately, she was mo calm now than earlier.

"Go on now, Honey. We don't have long fore we have to call the sheriff out here." Rufus said.

"Look, Buster and Mr. McLand ain't here yet and I don't tend on telling this story but one time."

"Give em a minute, Rufus. They should be here shortly," Bernice said.

"I hope so. Dead man can't stay out too long before, well, you know—"

"Just a minute, Rufus," Prudence interrupted him. "Just depends. I know about these thangs."

In another few minutes Buster and Mr. McLand drove up behind a large crowd of people gathered in Honey's front yard. The crowd became so large, it spilled into the street. From the looks of it, every single person that lived in The Quarters and some outside it had made their way to Shepherd Drive. As they waded through, they were greeted with a horde of support. However, in order to keep Honey out of jail, they needed more than that.

"Evening, everyone." Mr. McLand said as he and Buster entered the home.

"Evening."

Silence fell over the room. Even Turnerd managed to hold his tongue.

"Where is he?"

"Goodness, Buster, he right over there. Don't you see his feet peeping from behind the door?" Honey said.

Turnerd looked at Spudnick and said quietly, "Did she say peeping? I don't think he likely to eva look, peep or wink again."

"Shut up, ol' fool," Spudnick said.

"I'm sorry. Is it me or is this furniture turned around?" Mr. McLand asked.

"It's not you. RaShay is keeping his Duppy out of here," I said.

"The what?" Mr. Buster asked.

"The Duppy. I'll explain later."

"He tried to rape me," Honey all of a sudden blurted out. "He actually tried to rape me."

Her comment redirected the conversation and the attention to her.

"Rape you?" Edga said.

"That's what I said."

"Now, why would a good-looking man like him have to rape anybody? Wilhelmina asked with an air of suspicion.

"What you saying, Wilhelmina, I'm lying? Is that what you thank? I'm lying?" Honey said as she approached her.

"I'm just saying, why would someone like him need to take something most women is willing to give freely?"

"Like you, Wilhelmina?" Turnerd asked.

"Well, I ain't most women," Honey sneered. "You ain't figured that out yet?"

"Humph," Wilhelmina mumbled.

"Humph, yo damn self."

"Oh, my goodness, Wilhelmina. Just stop it. And shut up, Turnerd!" Miss May Alice said. "Let her finish."

"He came here this morning, talking crazy 'bout me leaving with him. Then he tried to force his-self on me, I tell you."

"Did he?"

"Does it look like he did, Mr. Mcland?" she said, pointing over where Simee lay.

"Just tell us 'xactly what happened, Honey," Buster asked.

"I told ya'll," Honey replied, annoyed. , "He done come here looking for something he was not gone get. That's when he decided to take it." She related what had happened that terrifying afternoon. "The bastard ran after me, fell over Shakespeare and kilt his-self. That's that." Then her face showed the first signs of regret. "The problem is," she added, "I looked up and Pearline is standing there at his feet terrified. Po child." She looked around at all the stunned faces. "Ain't nobody gone believe a story like this. Ya'll even looking at me funny. But it's the truth."

And we were. All of us remained silent as we tried to absorb what she had told us.

"We believe you, Honey. You ain't neva meant to kill nobody," I said.

"What? What you mean, she ain't neva meant to kill?" Turnerd said, as everyone in the room looked my way.

"What I trying to say is that she ain't neva killed nobody. Just nervous is all, words getting tangled, Turnerd."

"Look, we don't have no time to go back and forth. We got to figure out what we gone do," Edga said. "She could easily be sent up to Milledgeville for twenty years if we don't do something."

"Wait a minute, I have an idea," Buster said,

"Yeah, we listening," Rufus said.

"We don't have to tell Cletus how Simee died. He just needs to know he died. Right? After all, when's the last time Cletus Beauregard the Second cared anything about anything that happened down here in The Quarters?"

"So what are you suggesting, Buster?" Mr. McLand asked.

"Simple. We just tell him Simee had a heart attack and fell dead. Yep, he fell dead right in Honey's kitchen."

"But he's laying in her bedroom." Bernice said

"A small bother," Buster said. "Turnerd, Spudnick, Bill, RaShay, and Rufus, come help me move him."

"Move him?" Turnerd said. "I don't touch no dead people."

"And neither do I," Spudnick said.

"Today ya do," Rufus said. "Grab his damn legs."

"Be gentle with him now," Prudence said.

They carefully drug Simee out from Honey's room and repositioned him on the floor. Being the big man he was, it took all of them to get him from one room to the other. Not to mention lay him out just quite right. Prudence even took the liberty to place both of his arms over his chest.

"Don't do that. It don't look natural," Bernice said as she unfolded his arms.

They all stood over him, peering down at him, and Buster said, Will somebody close his eyes, please?"

"Well, I can tell you this, it won't be me.," Turnerd said.

"Me either," Spudnick said.

"Move, I'll do it," Rufus said.

Once he had moved Simee's body this way and that, Edga asked, "Does he look like a man that's just fallen after a heart attack?

"Can't rightly say since I've never seen someone who died from a heart attack," Cutie Pie said.

"Why yes, you have. Remember Noxy? She died of one. Right in her sleep?" Wilhelmina said.

"If she died in her sleep, how you know it was a heart attack that did it?" Turnerd asked.

"I just do," Wilhelmina said, dabbing her tears.

"Uh, could we get back to the matter at hand?" Rufus said.

"Is ya'll blind or am I the only one who sees that big slice in his jacket? Not to mention that blood on his chest and everywhere else. I know I'm a just a regular girl and all, with no schooling, although I did sign up for and I might proudly say got accepted to Madame C.J. Walker's School of Beauty, but it look like he been stabbed, if you ask me," Spudnick said.

Everyone in the room looked down at Simee and nodded in agreement with Spudnick's assessment.

"Honey, you still doing washing and ironing for the Macys?" Cutie Pie asked.

"Yeah. Why?"

"Louise, go and get one of Mr. Macy's shirts and a pair of his pants. We gone switch Simee's shirt with one of his. If I remember correctly, he a big man like Simee and his shirt should work fine." As I hurried to get one, Cutie Pie went on. "Spudnick, put some soap and water in that bucket. We got to clean up this here blood on him and the floors."

"This mean we got to touch him again?" Turnerd asked.

"Yes, we do," Mr. McLand said. "Now, come on and help me get his shirt and pants off and these other ones on. That Cletus will be here before you know it."

As everyone bustled about the house, scrubbing floors and walls, rearranging the furniture RaShay had turned backward and cleaning up Simee, an expected knock came from the front door.

"He here already?" Buster asked. "I didn't hear that loud siren of his."

"Spudnick, go out and stall him for a minute," May Alice said.

Spudnick made his way over to the front window, glanced out, then said, "It ain't Cletus, it's that woman I saw ova at the church."

"Well, stall her then," I said as she and the rest of the crew struggled to disrobe the dead body.

"May I help you?" Spudnick asked as he stood in the door, blocking the view into the house.

"Yes, you may," she said, trying to peer over his shoulder while he countered her every move. "Sorry to be a bother. My name is Lucinda."

"Yeah, I remember you from the church."

"I'm an acquaintance of Mr. Simee Scott. I heard he might be here. Is he available?"

"Ummm, I can't say he is," Spudnick said.

"Look like he won't be available for some time now," Turnerd said as he barged in the conversation. "But listen, you might catch him over at Bernice and Rufus's place tomorrow."

"And where might they live?" she asked.

"Can't miss it. Pretty easy to get there from here. Just go on down to the church and then go where Mr. James used to plant cabbages on the side of the road near them two big rocks. Then look for where the old seed store used to be. Once you find that, turn to the left, walk to the corner by the stop sign, make a right and you should bump right into Brown's Funeral Home."

She narrowed her eyes and asked, "Is he . . . ?"

"As a doorknob," Turnerd said.

Lucy started crying, and she motioned for her sons to support her.

"Whatcha crying for, Momma? Ain't never seen you cry over no man or woman, for that matter. We'll find him for sho," one of her sons said.

"And you still ain't. I ain't crying over no man, my money mo like it. He gone with my money and my jewelry."

"Gone? Did they tell you where he went?"

"Naw, but hell would be my best guess."

33

Like a murder of crows, the crowd continued to bubble. It was never a good thing when someone died, but a suspicious death could be disastrous for not only Honey but the entire community. Basically, it would require the law, also known as Deputy Cletus, to enter the tightly woven community of The Quarters. He'd have to investigate the scene, interview bystanders and make the final determination of Honey's fate. Due to his ineptitude, anything Cletus was involved in could swing the wrong way.

Cletus pulled up with his sirens blasting, and that rotating red light on the top of his car was spinning and blinking. He loved to make an entrance, hoping to display some level of authority and importance.

"Hey there suh, how you today?" One of the ladies from the church yelled from across the yard as he exited his car. Another managed to say, "Glad to see you today, Deputy."

Cletus, being Cletus, passed the crowd without acknowledging them. There was no disappointment on their end;

they really didn't want to speak to him anyway. It was customary and expected when white authority was present.

After making his way to the front door he reluctantly banged on it. "Got mo important thangs to do than fool with these kinds," he mumbled. As he entered the home, he was surprised to see that one of the first persons he encountered was Mr. McLand. A surprise that was hard to conceal.

"Huh, huh, afternoon, Mr. McLand," Cletus said as he walked in, failing to greet the others in the room.

"Good afternoon, Cletus," Mr. McLand said. "Thank you for coming by so quickly, we do appreciate it."

"We?"

"Yes, we."

"For *you*, suh, that ain't no problem." On his slack face I could see him wondering why Mr. McLand gave a damn about these Niggers, being that he and them other white folks couldn't care less. "These here folks lucky you've taking a liking to them, alls I can say. Just plain lucky."

Mr. McLand looked away, embarrassed by Cletus's comment.

"Now, 'xactly what done happened here? I get this call that a Nigger is dead up here. No details, just dead."

"Cletus, we would appreciate if you would not use that word here," Mr. McLand said.

"Word? Talkin bout Nigger? Well, ain't that what they is?" he said.

"Yes, that word, Cletus, and no, that's not what they are. Goodness," McLand said with irritation. "See, that word is a sign of limited intelligence, and unfortunately, Cletus, it appears your limitations are limitless. Now, this gentleman, Simee Scott, has passed. It looks like a heart attack. We need you to do your investigation so we can get him on out of here for a proper burial."

It was clear Cletus had not absorbed the insult slung his way or even recognized it as one. He looked suspicious of what was just said, but shrugged his shoulders and proceeded.

"Umm-humm." He walked over to Simee, squatted and observed his body. After standing and slightly kicking his leg, he said, "Yeah, he gone, all right."

"Good grief, Cletus, we've already concluded that."

"Now, I got a few questions to ask," he said as he scanned the room.

"Okay, go right ahead," Rev. Evans said.

"Now, which one of ya'll Negra's live here?"

"The lady that lives her is Miss Betty Jean. She's sitting right over there," Rufus said.

"Uh-huh, now, and when did this occur, Betty?"

"I believe bout thirty minutes or so ago."

"Thirty minutes you say. Okay."

"Bout that. Yes suh."

"And what was he doing when he fell?"

"Uh, uh, uh, I guess standing." She stuttered a bit, and I could tell she was not prepared for that question. "I was in the other room when I heard a loud bang. When I came back in to see what had happened, he was on the floor."

"The floor, you say, huh?"

"Yes, the floor. Right where he laying."

"Scuse me, but it's hotter than hell on a hot day in here. Get me"— Cletus asked as he caught a glimpse from Mr. McLand—"I means, may I have a glass of yo water, please?"

"Yes suh," I said as I nervously grabbed a random pitcher and poured him a glass.

Cletus wiped his brow with a dingy cloth and proceeded to drink. After several big gulps, he began choking, coughing, turning red, and wheezing. He stumbled and grabbed a chair to sit.

"Woman, what on earth did you just give me? This ain't damn water," he said as he continued to cough uncontrollably.

"Oh, my. I'm so sorry, suh. I must have grabbed the wrong pitcher. Here you go. I'm so sorry." By that time I had realized that the random pitcher that I poured from was shine instead of water. With trembling hands, I handed him a glass of real water this time.

After taking it and smelling it, he began to drink. "Awww, that's better."

My nerves were so bad, I turned away from everyone and privately poured myself a small glass of shine, drinking it quickly. Deputy Cletus took out this little writing pad from his shirt pocket, then his pencil. After licking the pencil to take a few notes, it occurred to him that his right arm was still gone and the left one had no intention on cooperating.

"Now, you was saying," he said.

Honey sounded more confident this time. "He was on the floor. That's it. Can't say what he was doing. Remember, I was in the other room. I came in and there he was hugging the floor."

Cletus took a seat and began thumbing on the table with his remaining hand. He began looking up as if he was in deep thought. After getting up and walking over to Simee one more time, he finally said, "Well, looks like that's all I need. I tell you, you Negras dropping like flies round here. I just investigated old Job a few months back. Just dropping, I tell you."

"Cletus, being that Mr. Job was well over a hundred, I suspect there wasn't much to investigate," Mr. McLand said.

Looking annoyed, Cletus looked away and said, "I don't anticipate no problem with this. Anyway, I got more important crime matters to take care of. Duty calls."

"Good. Is that all you need, Cletus?" Mr. McLand asked.

"Looks like that's all I need. Open and shut case." He brightened up as that came out of his mouth. "That's what them detectives says on the Hollywood movie screen. I always wanted to say that. You know, I probably could be a Hollywood movie star detective like Perry Mason or something."

"Or something," Bernice muttered.

Sheriff Cletus extended a firm handshake to Mr. McLand and then slapped him on his back. Finally, he was leaving. A collective sigh of relief flowed through the room. It was almost over. This nightmare was coming to an end.

As the deputy walked toward the front door, he stopped suddenly. Then he slowly turned around with a look of confusion on his face.

"Oh, wait a minute, one more thing. How could I forget to ask this?"

Everyone in the room stood with bated breath, not knowing if this next question could change everything. Honey held her stomach, I held my hands together and Rev. Evans clutched his Bible so tight his fingers locked up.

"Yes, what is it?" Mr. McLand asked just as nervous as the rest of them.

"Can I have a glass of that other water to go, please, ma'am?"

"Huh? What other water?" I asked, trying to grasp his question. I finally understood him and said, "Oh, that other water. Oh, yes, you sho can." I poured an extra large jelly jar to the rim with peach shine and pulled out another one for him too, filling it with white shine. I even sliced up some banana nut bread for him to take with him.

"Why, thank you kindly, miss," he said as I handed him everything. After concluding he could not carry everything with that one arm, I motioned for Spudnick to accompany him to the car.

"Me? Why me?" Spudnick mouthed.

"Yes, you. 'Cause I said so."

Slightly drunk from the first glass of liquor he unknowingly gulped, Cletus spoke to Simee and tipped his Stetson as he was departing the house. "Why, 'scuse me, suh. You have have a good day now."

To the relief of everyone, the so-called interrogation lasted all but a few minutes. After all, the dead man was Colored. Not much concern in the death of us around here. The honorable Deputy Cletus was known to say, "One less Nigger, one less headache."

34

My chile got back in Columbus just in time for her uncle's funeral. It wasn't much of one, though. The mourners consisted of Rev. Evans, Edga, Prudence, Pearline and me. Wilhelmina was still too mad. It would have been just the four of us, but Prudence insisted on coming. Told me it was her duty. Pearline wanted to go too. We decided to let her. Still not sure if that was the best decision. The funeral was short but far from sweet. Not one tear found its way from anybody's eye, including Prudence.

After Rev. Evans prayed over Simee and threw some dirt on that wooden coffin, we all walked away without looking back. I can't speak for nobody but myself, but I felt like looking back might turn me into stone. It did surprise me when Edga and the church agreed to bury Simee in the church's cemetery instead of the Colored grave yard, Porterdale. That grave yard so old slaves buried out there. I hear Ma Rainey at rest there too.

Heavenly Rest Funeral Home prepared his body and the deacons built his coffin. Bernice told me they nailed it down real good to make sure that demon stayed inside.

"Even dead, when it comes to Simee, it's best to know where he is than where he ain't."

After we buried him, I believe is when Pearline's mind started to go bad. It took a minute for me to notice the change in her, 'cause she act so much like a grown-up, that child spirit older than mine. I noticed that every day she started looking more and more tired, like she ain't slept in days. Then she started keeping track of how long it had been since she found Simee dead.

"Momma, it's been two weeks, two days and five hours since Uncle Simee died." Not too long after that would come, "When I woke up this morning, I made sure to write it down in my journal that it's one month, one day, and about ten hours now."

"Pearline, why you doing that?" I asked. "No need to keep thinking on him. That man dead and buried, baby. He can't hurt nobody else. Now, that's God's will and you need to stop that."

"I know, Momma, but I-I just can't stop thinking about it. Maybe if I'd gotten there a litter sooner, things would have turned out different."

"That ain't no way true. A hard death was gone find that man sooner than later."

Even beyond the grave, Simee Scott was still causing problems. My child was having bad dreams that were full of him. She said it was the same dream, night after night. That knife, his bloody chest, and that look he had on his face looking up at her. Right when night took over and we was all in the bed, she'd get to screaming, scaring everybody in the house. I stopped sleeping too. I'd just lay there and wait 'cause I knowed them screams was coming.

The child is too young to have gone through all of this. I feel guilty that I even sent her over there. I tried to be patient and I done told everybody in this house they better be too. Shoot, can't imagine seeing all this as a youngun.

I make sure each night to pray with my child and over her too. Sistah Stewart, the strongest praying woman I know, told me to keep praying and that she would too. She surprised me one Sunday evening and came by the house with all the church mothers. They walked through the house singing, "Pass Me Not, O Gentle Savior," praying, and even speaking in tongues. Then she had Pearline stand in the middle of them and they all put they hands on her and prayed, and prayed, and prayed. We all got to jumping up and down in the house that day. The spirit was sho-nuff in my house on that day. I believe Edga shed a tear or two. Next thang I know, my child fainted. We got her over to the bed and laid her down. After dabbing some oil on her forehead, Sistah Stewart nodded and said the healing done started. The peace and relief I felt when the mothers left is hard to put into words. I knew then she was gone be all right.

I'll never forget the day we all overslept 'cause that was the day Pearline didn't wake up screaming. It was a Tuesday early morning. I got up in a panic, looking for her. Then I realized I was in my bed and not hers. I tiptoed in her room and she was still fast asleep. This was the first time in weeks that we all slept through the night.

It's Saturday morning and the men done gathered again. All of them outside standing shoulder to shoulder with their backs against the world. They reminded me of a wall protecting what's inside and blocking what's out. It was pretty normal for them to do this once a week. And since Simee's death, they sometimes got together twice that.

Every since Mr. McLand left that woman, he was a regular with the men and in The Quarters. He moved in with Buster for a while, then got his own place downtown. It ain't half as fancy as what he left, but I guess peace of mind outweigh some fancy living any day. Rumor is, he lost some of his longtime customers. He told Buster, they weren't worth his time no how, said he lost more money with them than he made. The ones most important like the Mayor, some of them preachers, and the Governor was gone stay put. He had been lawyering for them for years, and I'm sure had more dirt on them than they'd care to have to repeat.

I sit at our kitchen table listening to them drinking, lying and laughing. Watching them almost made me feel like things round here were back to normal, though I know they wasn't. We still didn't have that deed.

"You gone pass the peace or keep it all to yourself," Thee asked Edga as he watched him sling back that brown liquor they tried to hide in a paper bag.

"Thank you kindly," Thee said as received the bottle. "I been thanking."

"You know that ain't a safe thang for you to do. Thinking is too much activity for that brain of yours."

"Shut up, Turnerd. I'm serious. Maybe it was her hormones to make her do something like that."

"Who and what you talking about, Thee? Edga asked

"I'm talking 'bout Honey and her killing Simee."

"And what in the world is a harmon?" Buster asked.

"They's called hormones." He repeated. "I can't think of no other reason she'd stab Simee like that. No reason at all."

"She said he fell on it, remember?" Edga said.

"You believe that? Well, if you do, I work for the United States gov-ment and I was sent here by LeeAnn's son for ya'll. And I also just met Santa Claus this morning. He landed on my porch. Him and his three tiny reindeers."

"Now, hold on there, Turnerd. That ain't right. We believed Simee. Not right for you to say things like that. Not right at all," Rev. Evans said.

"Please explain what in the hell is homones?" Edga asked, interrupting.

"I heard MinLee say that all women's have these what they call hormones and they can make them a little crazy sometimes. It was something she read in one of them ladies magazines. She say they make women get riled up, ornery, just mean as hell at least once a month."

"Yep, you may have a point there, Thee. That could explain a lot," Mr. Buster said.

"At least once a month, ya'll know during that time, my wife just get pure evil, like she done grown horns or something. Sometimes I just catch her staring at me. Like a crazy woman. Ya'll ain't gone believe this and I should be too shamed to tell ya'll, but one time after an all nighter at the juke joint, I came home real late in the night. I call myself tiptoeing in the house, made sure not to wake her or them chilluns up. Crawled in the bed and fell right off to sleep. When I wake up the next morning, I had to pee, so you know, I tried to hop out the bed."

"Tried?" Rev. Evans asked.

"Yeah, I could not move a thang. Not my arm, leg, nothing. That woman had sewed me down to the bed."

All the men stopped what they were doing and looked at him. They even leaned in just to be clear they heard correctly.

"She what?" Rufus asked.

"That's right, sewed me straight to the bed with her needle and thread. At first I thought I had woke up dead, maybe I was in heaven. Then I saw her standing over me smiling. I said to myself, can't be no heaven if she here. Then I got scared I was in hell."

"She did what?" Rev said again, confused.

"You heards me right; her crazy ass sewed me to the bed. Told me the next time I stayed out late like that, drinkin and all, fooling with them womens, she'd sew down something else if I didn't watch it. It was at least two hours for she let me up. I just laid there magining if I was gone kill her in her sleep or just shoot her on the spot."

Rufus nudged Edga and whispered, "See, I told you her ass was crazy as hell and she bout to drive him right there with her, believe me now."

"Yeah, Rufus, you got a point there."

The men were silent, thinking on their own near misses with their wives and with their other womens.

All of sudden that fool Turnerd said, "Well, I don't know nothing 'bout no hormones, but I have been known to make a ho or two moan."

The men stopped, looked at Turnerd and burst into laughter. I even chuckled at that.

Once the laughing settled, the gathering turned serious again. The men knew they had to locate that deed and until they did, the church no longer had proof that they owned that land.

"Where is that damn deed? We've looked high and low in all of his stuff. It's nowhere to be found," Edga said.

"It wasn't on him when we buried him," Rufus said. "I checked his pant pockets, socks, even shoes, everything, even that sliced-up shirt he had on."

"Yeah, I hate to add more bad news on top of this," Mr. McLand said.

"How can this get any worse?"

"Well, Rev, it can and it has. I'm sure you all know Jeb Snyder, who owns Synder Processing Plant."

"We know who he is. He one of the meanest crackers I know. Even the dogs cross the street when he coming," Turnerd said.

"Yeah, that's him," Mr. McLand said. "Well, good, then you also know he owns most of the land in this county."

"Yeah, he do, but what that got to do with us?" Edga asked.

"There's a lady that works in his office that I helped out a while back. Her boy got into a lot of trouble. Judge Harland was gone send him to reformatory school, but I got him to change his mind and allowed her to send him over to Alabama to live with her daddy. She was so grateful that she brings me cakes, cookies, and sometimes dinner to my office at least once a week. Well, last night she stopped by my office and told me that she knew I was friendly with ya'll and thought this information might be helpful."

"What information?" Edga asked.

"Snyder plan on buying that land," Mr. McLand said. "She said, he heard that the deed was missing and without proof of ownership, it was as good as his."

35

Pearline

"If it ain't one thing, it's another. Honey feel like this her fault. Like she the one that caused all this trouble," Momma told Daddy.

"Ain't her fault. It's that damn Simee. You think putting his ass six feet under would have solved all these problems. I bet he somewhere just laughing away at us looking for that deed."

Momma and Daddy sat in the kitchen talking and drinking coffee. This morning we were greeted with some heavy rain. It pounded on the roof like it wanted to come in.

"Shoot, Edga, we done looked high and low. Went through his bags of clothes, even went back over to the place he rented from Buster and cleaned it from top to bottom. Nothing. Can't find nothing. Maybe we got a li'l hope, though."

"How?"

"Rufus told Rev go down to the courthouse filing room where they keeps all the titles and deeds. Said he might find a copy there. It's got to be one somewhere."

"I guess Rufus ain't talked to McLand."

"Why you say that?"

"McLand told Buster that Mr. Snyder done already went down there and cleared out whatever copies he could find. From my understanding that land more valuable than any of us ever thought."

"Excuse me, Momma?" I said as I entered the kitchen. I'd been hanging out in the bathroom reading, something I'd not done for a while. The bathroom was the only peaceful place in the house, but walls were very thin.

"Yes, Pearline."

"I have something to share that I think is really important about Uncle Simee."

"Girl, what I tell you 'bout tending to grown folks' business? Gone somewhere and sit down."

"But, Momma, I think this is one time you won't mind."

"Let her talk, Louise. Right 'bout now, we need all the help we can get," Daddy said. "What is it?"

"Well, the day after Mr. Thee brought me back from Culbert, Miss Cutie Pie came by to talk to you."

"Yeah, she did."

"I remember because she had a bag with her stuff under her coat. When she came in the house, she took it out, whispered something to you and you two went out back."

"Yeah, Pearline. We did."

"I thought it odd that you two were starting a fire, but then I saw what you were doing."

"You saw all of that? No wonder you was having them bad dreams."

"What did she see?" Daddy asked.

"She saw me and Cutie Pie burning Simee's bloody clothes. And they was bloody."

"Oh."

"Yes, Momma, I did. But I also saw you dump everything on the ground before you threw it all into the fire, including the bag."

"Uh-huh. We needed to get rid of it. The last thing any of us needed was for Cletus to find some bloody clothes with knife slices through them. So, we burned everything we took off of him."

"Momma, you didn't burn everything."

"Yes, we did."

"No, what about his coat jacket?"

"His jacket?"

"Yes, his jacket. When I ran out to get you from the church that night, he was wearing a jacket. It was the same plaid black and white jacket I complimented him on once at church. He told me he got it from a fine department store in Chicago and that one day he'd take me shopping there. He also gave me a whole dollar that day. I remember, Momma."

Momma pushed back from the table and paced back and forth. I knew she was trying desperately to recall exactly what was burned. Then it hit her.

"She's right. We burned his pants, his shirt, underwear, and undershirt. Everything he was wearing, we took off 'cause it was blood everywhere. We even put him on clean socks. There was no jacket."

"Where is the damn jacket, Simee? Daddy asked, as if he'd get an answer.

"Aunt Honey should know."

"Honey?" Momma asked.

"Yes. When I left them in that room, he had that jacket on."

"Pearline, grab your coat and run tell Rev and Buster to meet me and your daddy over to Honey's. You need to do that right now. Tell them it's an emergency. And make sure you tell them ain't nobody dead, but they need to get over there quick."

"Yes ma'am."

⅏

I walked as fast as I could to Rev. Evans' house, then to Mr. Buster's. Although the rain slowed me down, I got to them pretty quick. I shared exactly what Momma told me to tell them. They both looked relieved when I added no one was dead. When we arrived at Aunt Honey's, Momma and Daddy had just made it to her front door. Daddy knocked.

"Yes?" Aunt Honey said as she came out, surprised to see us all on her porch. "What ya'll doing out in this here weather?"

"Honey, where is that jacket of Simee's?" Momma asked.

"What jacket?" She said as she adjusted her sweater.

"The black and white jacket you took off of Simee the night he died with yo crazy ass," Mr. Buster said.

"Buster!" Rev. Evans said.

She cut her eyes at him and said, "I don't know what ya'll talking about."

"Gurl, stop playing these here games. Do you still have it?"

Aunt Honey was beginning to realize that something serious had come up. "I just might, Louise."

"You might?" Rev. Evans asked.

"Okay, goodness. When Pearline left, I stood over him and for some reason decided to take his stupid jacket off and keep it. I know it sounds crazy, but since he tried to take something from me, I was gone take something from him."

"So, his life wasn't enough, Honey?" Daddy asked.

A fire appeared in her eyes. "I didn't take his life. All that was an accident, just like I said."

"Where is it?"

"Outside, Louise."

"Outside?"

"Yes, I didn't want it in my house, so I-I planted it, I mean, put it outside."

"Where, Honey?" Daddy asked.

"Meet me in the back. Ya'll ain't coming through my house with all them dirty wet shoes," she said as she closed the door on us. "Dirtied up my house the last time ya'll was here."

Once they met up in the back, she walked over to her garden and said, "It's over there."

"Over where, Honey? Mr. Buster asked.

"Right by the tomato plants."

Mr. Buster grabbed the shovel leaning on the fence and started digging where she pointed.

They all stood and watched as he began to dig. The rain and the wet ground made it a challenging task, but finally he hit a hard surface which made a hollow thumping sound.

"Hold this," he said, handing the shovel to Daddy. After pushing away a pile of mud, he pulled up a metal container.

"Well, open it," Momma said.

Mr. Buster opened the lid and removed a plastic bag. When he opened it, Aunt Honey quickly pulled the jacket from it and handed it to Daddy. I noticed that a couple other items fell out too, but everyone was so fixated on the jacket they didn't notice. Daddy started to feel the jacket inside and out but felt nothing. Disappointed, he handed the jacket to Momma.

"Let me see it," she said as she fumbled with the jacket. After what felt like an eternity, she said, "Wait a minute, feel here. Why is this collar so stiff? I can't even get them this hard. Anybody gotta knife or blade?"

Aunt Honey said, "I'll get one."

Like clockwork, they all said, "Naw, that's okay."

Aunt Honey just sneered at them.

"Here you go," Daddy said as he handed Momma his pocket knife.

"Well, I'll be. Here it is. That brother of yours done sewed the deed in the collar of this jacket."

Life has pretty much returned to normal in The Quarters since that deed has been located. Rev. Evans quickly took it over to Mr. McLand's office and established that the deed was indeed legitimate and with its rightful owner—him. The news wasn't received well by Mr. Snyder. He protested, tried everything in his power to discredit the church's right to that land, but legally, it was over. All of the excitement prompted the church to move quickly with building the school on it and extending the church.

The sistahs resumed running their enterprise, and Daddy and his friends continued to gather, tell tall tales and enjoy the twin's labor of love. Miss Wilhelmina's place still thrived and she was still in charge of Sunday school. I was doing well in school and even became fluent in French. Fortunately, nothing ever happened to Miss Agatha. Right after the McLands separated, Mrs. McLand and a group of her auxiliary members made the mistake of going over to Miss Agatha. She was determined to reprimand Miss Agatha for colluding with the Colored folks. That was a big mistake. Miss Mae Alice and Miss Cutie Pie saw the entire exchange from their front porch and they couldn't wait to tell it.

"I ain't never seen no white woman run as fast as them womens did the day they decided to mess with Agatha. Ain't that right, Cutie Pie?"

"Sho is. We was both standing there with our mouths wide open watching that foolishness," she said, chuckling. "About five of them went strolling up to that woman's door all bold and fancy with they hats and white gloves on. Humph. They knocked and she let them in. That door wasn't closed ten minutes before all of them tore out of that house hollering. Agatha was right behind them running, waving a rolling pin in one hand and a pot in the other. Lawd, she was talking that French faster than she normally do," Miss Cutie Pie said.

"Me and Cutie Pie asked her if she was okay when she walked back down the road to her house. She started talking in French again, swooped that hair out her face and nodded yes. Couldn't rightly say the same for them other womens. I know she scared them. Shoot, she scared me. I doubt if they do that ever again."

Momma and Aunt Honey finally decided to start their own business doing laundry and cleaning houses. We were all excited. These two were going to be the first business owners in our family. Once Granddaddy heard, he offered his old truck to them. It was perfect for transporting clothes and their supplies back and forth. Plus, they could get more customers with a service vehicle. That truck livened up once they had it painted pink and purple. They also put their business name, Pearl and Honey's Cleaning and Laundry Service on it. I was flattered that Momma chose my name. I suggested that she use hers instead, but she insisted. She told me that after everything that I'd been through, she wanted to do something special for me. Plus, she thought it had a nice ring to it.

Pearl and Honey's started to flourish. Business seemed to fall out of the sky. They picked up two commercial accounts. One from the hospital and one old folks' home, washing bedsheets, linens, and towels. Word spread to some soldiers stationed up at Fort Benning that they were very good with ironing. Next thing you know, she had ten soldiers wanting their uniforms washed and pressed with heavy starch every week. Not to mention the families they were cleaning for.

Eventually, they had to hire some help. The first woman, Clara Jane Moore, was fired shortly after being hired. She didn't last a week. That girl did more talking and gossiping than anything. I knew the moment I met her, her employment would be short-lived. Then they hired a young woman named Rissa Williams. She was too quiet in my opinion, but a hard worker just the same and they both liked her a lot.

Everything was going great, until one chilly October morning a stranger knocked on our front door. I was the only one available to answer the door at the time. Momma was busy cooking, Daddy wasn't home, and the boys knew not to touch that door.

"Pearline, answer it," Momma ordered.

"Yes, ma'am," I said, while at the same time reprimanding my brothers Floyd and Felton. "Would you two knuckleheads stop wrestling round here and get that paper off the floor? Momma told you two about that. Daddy said he's gone beat the both of you. And not a minute too soon, if you ask me."

"Who asked ya?" Felton said right before I pinched his arm.

Finished with that business, I twisted the knob on the front door and opened it to a handsome gentleman.

"We ain't buying nothing," Felton yelled from behind me.

"Shut up," I yelled back, then turned to the waiting gentleman.

"Well, hello young lady," he said before I could greet him. "Hello."

"Is your momma Louise Scott?"

"Yes."

"Is she home?"

"Yes sir. One moment, please." I turned to call her, but she was already behind me wiping her hands on her apron. "Momma, there's someone asking for you."

"Yes suh, can I help you?" she asked, keeping the screen door closed and latched between them.

"Why, yes ma'am. How you doing today?"

"Doing good. What can I help you with?"

"You are Louise Scott?"

"I am. Now what can I help you with?"

"I just wanted to make sure I'm talking to the right missus. My name is Harland. Detective Harland Crowder. I was given your name and your sister's name by some folks down in Preston. They said you two might be able to help me."

"Help you with what?"

"I've been assigned a missing persons case."

"Missing persons?"

"Yes ma'am, missing persons. About fifteen years ago, three teenage boys went missing down in Preston. Their names are Joe, Ned, and Bo."

45120373R00190

Made in the USA
Lexington, KY
17 September 2015